CHOP LINE

Also by Henry V. O'Neil

The Sim War Series
Glory Main
Orphan Brigade
Dire Steps

CHOP LINE

The Sim War: Book Four

HENRY V. O'NEIL

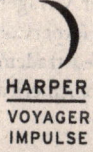

HARPER
VOYAGER
IMPULSE

An Imprint of HarperCollins*Publishers*

This is a work of fiction. Names, characters, places, and incidents are products of the author's imagination or are used fictitiously and are not to be construed as real. Any resemblance to actual events, locales, organizations, or persons, living or dead, is entirely coincidental.

CHOP LINE. Copyright © 2016 by Vincent H. O'Neil. All rights reserved. Printed in the United States of America. No part of this book may be used or reproduced in any manner whatsoever without written permission except in the case of brief quotations embodied in critical articles and reviews. For information, address HarperCollins Publishers, 195 Broadway, New York, NY 10007.

Digital Edition NOVEMBER 2016 ISBN: 9780062471673

Print Edition ISBN: 9780062471697

Harper Voyager, the Harper Voyager logo, and Harper Voyager Impulse are trademarks of HarperCollins Publishers.
HarperCollins is a registered trademark of HarperCollins Publishers in the United States of America and other countries.

FIRST EDITION

17 18 19 20 21 OPM 10 9 8 7 6 5 4 3 2 1

*This book is dedicated to the graduates
and instructors of the
Defense Language Institute in Monterey, California,
past, present, and future,
but especially my classmates in the
Mandarin Chinese course
1992–1993*

CHOP Line: Naval term derived from the phrase "change in operational control" indicating the boundary between two commands at sea. In the space war against the Sims, the CHOP Line separates the war zone from the rest of the galaxy.

CHAPTER 1

Lieutenant Jander Mortas leaned the back of his head against the wall of the personnel carrier, feeling the vibration as the vehicle fell from the sky. A stabilizer puffed twice on the outer hull, keeping the armored box upright as it coasted toward the planet's surface. All around them, other chariots of war were riding the energy tunnel that Human Defense Force ships had cut through the atmosphere all the way to the ground. Known as cofferdams, they were a relatively new invention in the decades-long war against the Sims.

The carrier lurched, sending the boots of the seated men up off the steel plates for a worrying instant before dropping them back down. Even in the low light, the boots showed a reddish discoloration earned on a planet which they'd left only two days earlier. Looking at the familiar faces seated across from him, Mortas felt no surprise to see that most of them were asleep.

Though tired himself, he couldn't summon the serenity to drop off. A year in the war zone fighting as part of the walking infantry had made him leery of its mechanized cousins. The armored personnel carrier felt like a giant coffin, trapping him, blinding him, putting him at the mercy of its driver and commander. The harness crisscrossing his torso armor didn't help; it had snugged down as the vehicle had dropped into the cofferdam, so tight that he couldn't move. Seated on the webbing of a long bench folded out from the APC's bulkhead, loaded down with grenades and ammunition, Mortas was eager for the touchdown that would release him.

Oddly enough, the torso armor had become like a second skin, and he barely noticed its presence at all.

His rucksack was jammed under his seat, and Mortas now wished he hadn't left his helmet and goggles strapped to it. An earpiece and throat mike allowed him to communicate with his troops and the APC's commander, but the goggles would have provided him with imagery for the operation to come. Though fully briefed, he wanted to review it yet again.

Twisting inside the body armor, he worked a thumb and forefinger into a cargo pocket and pulled out his handheld. Activating the device, he called up the map of their landing zone. It was too close to the enemy spacedrome for his liking, but the Sims had chosen a difficult location for their string of recently discovered settlements. The terrain was quite restrictive, with dense forest on a maze of hills, leaving only a few open spaces large enough for cofferdam touchdown. As this was a division-sized assault against three spacedromes many miles apart, the first wave in each of the cofferdams needed to hit the ground and get out of the way.

Narrowing the focus on the handheld, Mortas was studying a wooded ridge near their landing zone when a finger appeared in front of his face. Startled, Mortas looked up to see a man who looked like a bug. Darkened goggles protruded from a bulbous plastic communications helmet, and the rest of the soldier was clad in a green coverall. This was one of the personnel carrier's crewmen, a member of the riding infantry. The space inside the behemoths was too cramped for torso armor and canteens, and so the mechanized troops didn't wear them.

"Put it away, Lieutenant." The mouth beneath the goggles moved, and the voice came over his earpiece. "Messes with our communications."

The weight of the last few weeks abruptly pressed down on Mortas, and anger pushed back against it. He outranked the man giving him this order, and also knew that his handheld posed no threat to the carrier at all. His Scorpion rifle was clipped over his head, far out of reach, but it wasn't his only weapon.

His left hand took hold of the man's shirtfront, yanking him down while his right came up holding a long black dagger. The point pressed against the flesh near the soldier's windpipe, and for a moment Mortas remembered the first time he'd used the weapon.

"You know what this is?" he asked.

"Human Defense Force regulations place every passenger in this track under the command of the crew, regardless of rank," the man stammered. The mechanized unit to which Mortas's platoon had been attached was from Tratia, where quoting the rules always won the argument. "You are in violation—"

Mortas put more pressure on the knifepoint, and the words stopped.

"This is a Spartacan fighting knife. Heard of the Spartacan Scouts? Rough boys. This knife belonged to one of them. He died saving my life." Mortas drilled angry eyes into the darkened goggles. "He used it to kill an HDF major who'd gone nuts on us. You starting to get the picture?"

"I'm going to report you to my commanding officer."

"I'm a lieutenant in the Orphan Brigade. Your CO's not an Orphan, so I don't care what he thinks." A buoyant whoop sounded in his earpiece, and he saw that the confrontation had awakened his men. Expressions ranging from amusement to outrage lined the opposite wall. "This operation here is our third back-to-back mission. So why don't you fuck off?"

Another hand appeared, this one from the Orphan strapped in next to Mortas. That was Prevost, a savant with the grenade launcher known as a "chonk" because of the sound it made. Prevost took hold of the Tratian's arm, pulling him away. Mortas lowered the knife, knowing what was coming, and studied the evil blade as Prevost shoved the man across the floor plates.

"Your CO's right through that hatch. Guys, help him get there."

A dirty boot kicked the Tratian in the buttocks just as he stumbled into range, and then he was propelled down the two rows of seated Orphans, being shoved or slapped as the harnesses permitted. He ended up on his hands and knees, and disappeared into the tiny compartment containing the driver, gunner, and the company commander.

Mortas slid the knife back into its sheath, nestled among the magazines strapped to his chest. It had been a long time since he'd thought of Corporal Cranther, the knife's previous owner. The desolate planet where they'd been mysteriously marooned with two others. The conscientious objector Gorman, the best of the unlikely quartet, who'd died only a short time after Cranther. The alien that had impersonated Captain Amelia Trent, a Force psychoanalyst captured and murdered so that the shape-shifter could take her place. Though little more than a year in the past, it seemed a lifetime ago.

"That true, sir?" The words didn't come over the earpiece. Prevost had switched off his throat mike, and whispered the words from Mortas's shoulder. "About your Spartacan buddy killing a major?"

The question startled him. Mortas had never told anyone about that episode, fearful of Force discipline, and had pushed much of the event from his mind. The four maroons had encountered the major and his ragtag command purely by accident. The Sims had attacked the disorganized band shortly after that, but the major had somehow survived. Mortas recalled the man's crazed accusations, and saw again the Scorpion rifle pointed at him while enemy parachute flares lit up the night sky.

He considered telling Prevost that he'd been joking, but after fighting alongside the man for so long he simply couldn't lie to him. Mortas switched off his mike.

"It is. He'd gone insane, and was about to shoot me."

Prevost gently bounced a fist on Mortas's thigh. "Well fuck him, then."

Mortas returned to the handheld, watching the first phases of the assault. The Sims had established this colony on the previously unoccupied planet UC-2147, while the Force had been distracted by other matters. The human civil war on the planet Celestia had caused the recall of most of the Celestian units from the war zone, and operations had been chaotic since then.

Overhead imagery showed Mortas the steady bombardment from orbit, the warships pumping rocket after rocket into the enemy spacedromes and the surrounding settlements. The enemy, known as Sims because of their physical similarity to humans, had become expert in digging shelters far beneath the surface of the habitable planets which were the prize in the interstellar war. Even so, they were taking quite a pounding and Mortas saw that the spacedrome closest to his cofferdam had been virtually destroyed. Circular clouds burst into life with each rocket's impact, and numerous fires generated streaming tendrils of smoke.

Manned HDF spacecraft were now entering the fray, racing back and forth over the target area alongside drone gunships. Here and there a bright dot moved across the ground, the heat signature of a Sim vehicle trying to escape. Rocket and cannon fire quickly knocked the dots off of the settlement's unimproved roadways.

With growing concern, Mortas noted the absence of the flickering specks that would have indicated individual Sims. Whether fleeing the carnage or trying to help their fellow colonists, there should have been more evidence of enemy personnel. Going back to the cofferdam's landing zone, he studied the curved, wooded ridgeline that was simply too close for comfort. He remembered the Tratian intelligence officers assuring the Orphan leadership that the ridgeline had been under electronic surveillance for days. His battalion commander, Major Hatton, had warned Mortas and the others not to take that assessment at face value.

No heat signatures showed anywhere on the ridge, despite the presence of the cofferdam's gigantic energy column. The shaft would be visible for miles, and should have attracted any enemy who could reach it. Cofferdam descent took a considerable amount of time, and the Sims knew their only chance was to destroy the assault force as it touched down. Concerned, Mortas shifted the view to a wider resolution. The string of settlements bordered a valley surrounded by weaving escarpment and dense woods. Three open areas had been selected for the cofferdams, all of them offering relatively flat corridors for the tanks and APCs to strike the different spacedromes. There would have been more of them, allowing the force to spread out, except these were the only suitable sites anywhere nearby.

"Air assault touching down. Air assault touching down." A mechanical voice alerted the entire force that two flights of personnel shuttles had flown in and landed. The Orphan Brigade's commander, Colonel Watt, had tried to get his troops assigned to that mission, shuttling in from orbit before the armor arrived. It was a job much more suited to the Orphan infantrymen, but instead they'd been assigned to accompany the mechanized units of the Tratian division.

Mortas watched the shuttles landing at the bases of two ridges to the north and west of the colony, the black rectangles disgorging groups of swiftly moving dots. The heat signatures of the infantrymen spread out almost in a line, and then began rushing up the slopes. Their job was to establish blocking positions on the high ground that would prevent the Sims from escaping north or west once the armored units had landed to the east and south. The lead dots made good progress while tiny clusters fell behind, probably groups of men humping heavy weapons toward the crest.

Mortas flipped the view back to his own cofferdam, pleased to see that the first vehicles would be touching down in less than a minute. Coasting a half mile below him, they would drive hard as soon as they landed in order to get out from under the next arrivals. Outside, the APC's stabilizers fired simultaneously, the first of several decelerations that would hopefully bring them to the surface with no more than a hard jolt. The lights in the compartment gradually brightened, and Mortas felt the restraining bands of his harness start to ease up.

He shut off the handheld, stuffing it back into his pocket just as the harness lock released, and happily shook free of the bonds. The Orphans around him quickly pulled their rucks from under the web seats, sliding goggles over their eyes and fastening helmet chinstraps. One of the platoon's rocket teams was riding with him, and Mortas watched as they unstrapped the large-bored launchers known as boomers. Although they were supposed to ride to the mechanized company's assembly area, the Orphans had to be ready to jump out and fight if the APCs encountered enemy resistance.

His goggles came to life, and Mortas went through a series of commo checks by reflex. First check was with B Company's commander, his immediate superior. Captain Dassa's familiar voice responded through the ear pads in his helmet, speaking from a vehicle a mile overhead.

"I hear you, Jan. Be ready to bail out with all your people." Dassa had even less faith in the Tratian intelligence assessment than Major Hatton.

Mortas called his platoon sergeant next. Sergeant Dak rode on a different vehicle so that the platoon wouldn't lose its top leaders in one wreck, and the rest of the platoon was likewise cross-loaded across the Tratian infantry company.

"Got ya, Lieutenant." Dak's words grated, as if he were standing right next to Mortas. A strong NCO, Dak was one of the relatively few Tratians in the Orphan Brigade. Tratian society was highly regulated and loaded with informants, which made most of its citizens poor candidates for a unit like the Orphans.

After speaking with his three squad leaders, Mortas attempted to contact the commander of the mechanized company his platoon was supporting. Captain Ufert had already made it clear that he didn't like having the walking infantry cluttering up his command vehicle, so Mortas wasn't surprised that he had to call three times before receiving a terse acknowledgment.

Microcameras all over the APC kicked in as they approached the ground, allowing Mortas to see the vehicles in the first group touching down. The landing zone's tall grass had been flattened by the cofferdam's energy field, and the tracked vehicles churned it up as they drove out of the way. He widened the view to get a closer look at the wooded ridgeline, just in time to see it explode in smoke and fire.

One of the APCs on the ground jerked as if pulled by a towing chain, its back end sent sideways by the impact of the anti-armor round. The stubby twin cannons on its turret turned toward the ridge, but a second hit enveloped the vehicle in a bright flash as the radios all started shouting at once.

"Concealed gun! Concealed gun! Ridgeline to the west!"

"Get clear of the landing zone! Move out of the way!"

"Hit! We're hit! There's more of them—"

Communications protocols shut down the babble of voices in his helmet, allowing Mortas to speak to the platoon on the different vehicles. "Flatten on the floor! Be ready to dismount!"

The Orphans all went to the deck, hugging weapons and rucksacks, and Mortas joined them. Captain Ufert now wanted to speak to him. "Mortas, we're going to drive north and hook around the end of the ridge! Dismount your people there, and kill those gun emplacements!"

The APC slammed into the ground before he could respond. The armored, ammo-laden infantrymen bounced into the air and then crashed back down on the plates. The track's engines screamed, sending an earthquake vibration rattling through their bodies. Something exploded nearby, rippling one side of the vehicle with fragments. They sounded like incoming bullets to Mortas, but he told himself they were just rocks thrown up by a near miss. Focusing, he tried to find the end of the ridge on the map inside his goggles.

The surging behemoth stopped with a metallic bang that echoed through the troop compartment, and he didn't need imagery to know they'd slammed into another track. Enormous gears clashed, and then they were beetling backward. A hurricane seemed to have found the vehicle, rocking it violently as explosions burst all around.

"Dak! Dak!"

"Yes, Lieutenant." The firmness of the platoon sergeant's voice never failed to calm him.

"I'll mark my position when we bail out. Stay with your track long as you can—"

The command vehicle shuddered to a halt. Ufert's commands broke into the transmission.

"Get your people out, Lieutenant! We're stuck!"

The back wall was already detaching at the top, howling winds entering. Mortas flipped his goggle setting so that he could see what he was doing, marveling at the bright blue sky that appeared as the ramp lowered.

"Take the rucks!" he shouted, struggling to his knees in time to see that the troops were way ahead of him. Camouflaged bodies rushed for the exit, dart-ing left and right as soon as they were clear. The sound dampers in Mortas's helmet snugged down and stayed that way, protecting his hearing from the booming thunder of the enemy guns and the cracking explosions of incoming rounds. He yanked one strap of his ruck over his shoulder and, Scorpion in the other hand, lurched for the ramp.

As he leapt for the grass, his body twisted in midair because of the load. His face turned up toward the sky, but it was no longer blue. Dense gray smoke billowed all around, and his goggles adjusted to let him see that it was a smoke screen, the two APCs generating the clouds while they fought to disentangle themselves. Turning, Mortas raised the rifle over his ruck while getting his bearings. The Sims dug into the ridge had shifted their fires back to the landing zone, trying to cover it with wrecks.

"Marking target, enemy machine gun position," Sergeant Frankel, a squad leader who'd been riding in one of the other vehicles, announced. Mortas's goggles picked up the location, a tiny glowing dot appearing in his vision that remained on the same spot even when he turned his head. It looked like any other part of the wooded rise, but then a sputtering light erupted around the marker. Its chatter lost in the explosions, the Sim machine gun winked at them from a perfectly camouflaged position.

More roaring engines. Mortas popped his head up, looking back at the landing zone, seeing the approach of three more APCs. The grass here wasn't flattened, and he knew that half his platoon was out there somewhere.

"First Platoon, get to the high ground! Move move move!" He came to his feet, the ruck on his shoulder again, the heavy bag slowing him down. The ruck meant ammunition and batteries and water, and simply could not be left behind.

Behind him now, both of the trapped APCs started firing at the ridge. The twin cannon gave off a double-bang whump, the concussion shoving him from behind, almost knocking him flat. Other vehicles were already firing, smoke rounds throwing up fireworks before blooming into dense clouds meant to blind the enemy gunners.

Already exposed for too long, Mortas threw himself into the grass. Dry blades rasped against his cheeks as he fell, but he was already switching the goggle view. Overhead imagery showed the chaos on the landing zone, tracks driving every which way to get around the ones that had been knocked out, while more coasted down toward them. Inside the smoke shrouding the ridge, incoming and outgoing rounds erupted in flashes and flickers. Most important, small moving dots of light in the grass finally showed him the half of his platoon that had dismounted.

Mortas struggled to fit an electronic glove onto his right hand, kicking himself for not having it on already. Instantly, a hologram menu appeared in his goggle view. Tapping and swiping at the air, he drew a box around his troops that would appear on the controls of every vehicle near them. Popping his head up, he saw that the marker had had no effect on the approaching tracks.

Back down, tapping directly on the lead carrier's image, creating a link to its commander.

"Hey! You fuckin' blind? Can't you see my men in front of you?"

"I'm seeing a lot of guns trying to kill me, Orphan!" a harried voice responded. In the background Mortas heard the clang as the turret cannon reloaded. "How about you get your people out of my way and do your job? Get up there and silence those guns!"

"Kiss my ass!"

"Terminate link!"

The transmission ended. Turning back to the imagery, Mortas saw pulsing red markers on the forward slope where the Orphans had identified two anti-armor positions. The scattered pairs and trios of his men were almost at the base of the high ground, and he needed to catch up to them. Before moving, Mortas drew three lines running up the ridge that would appear in the goggles of every man in his platoon.

"Frankel!" Carrying the ruck low, Mortas rushed through the grass.

"I see your sector lines, El-tee! I've got the gun to the east!"

"I'll take the one to the west!" he shouted, the experience of numerous combat missions taking hold.

The men knew what to do without being told, and now separated into two groups. The platoon's normal squad organization had been badly scrambled by the cross-loading on different vehicles, so they were reconstituting on the fly.

His helmet dampers protected his ears from the unrelenting blasts and explosions, but microphones all over the headpiece kept him from being rendered deaf. Rocket blasts shattered several tree trunks up the slope, the gaps pointing out the two gun positions. Mortas turned his head slightly, and a vertical blue line appeared in his goggles to show the sector boundary he had just created.

Reaching the base of the high ground, he threw himself down again and let go of the ruck. Outgoing anti-armor fire boomed over his head, and the stutter of an enemy machine gun sounded from up the slope. He was just about to rush for the cover of a reasonably thick tree when a robot voice stopped him.

"Inbound missiles! Inbound missiles! You are danger close! Seek cover!" The words continued, but he was already facedown. Somewhere in orbit, sophisticated fire control systems had logged the red flashing targets while also recognizing the presence of human troops. Every Orphan at the base of the ridge had received the warning, and were pressing themselves into the grass and dirt.

Mortas flipped the image so he could watch the strike, and two drones swept into his vision a moment later. They discharged their rockets, breaking left and right as two black ovals raced for the markers. The bombs thumped into the ridge, right on target, primed to detonate a second after penetrating the ground. The explosions sent more trees crashing downward, and then he felt shovel-loads of dirt landing on his back.

"Sim machine gun! Marking!" He had no idea who'd said that, but another target appeared in his goggles. Leaving his pack, Mortas rose and dashed for the base of the nearest tree. His goggles let him see through the smoke, but there was a drawback to that capability—he had no idea if the smoke was concealing him or not. His straining breaths pulled a lungful of the acrid mist into his lungs, and he decided it was still pretty thick.

A quick peek around the bole of the tree earned him a volley of heavy slugs that kicked up dirt and bit off bark, but then a chonk sounded. The grenade sailed up the slope through the remaining branches, arcing beautifully before disappearing into the ground. Looking around the opposite side of the trunk, Mortas just made out the narrow slit where the machine gun was nestled before the grenade went off inside the position.

Had to be Prevost. Only Prevost could have made that shot.

Voices sounded in his ears, First Platoon Orphans urging each other on, and he jumped up in response. Camouflaged figures were rushing and diving all around him, exposing themselves for only a few seconds before disappearing again. Mortas reached one of the new-fallen trees, dropping behind it and raising his Scorpion. Wispy smoke rose from the blasted opening where one of the anti-armor guns had been sited, only twenty yards up the slope and fifty yards to his left. That was the gun in his sector, and the drone strike seemed to have knocked it out.

A hundred yards to his right, in the sector claimed by Sergeant Frankel, a startling boom shook the ground. The missile attack on that emplacement hadn't destroyed the gun. Looking toward it, he saw rushing figures as Frankel and the others raced uphill past the gaping hole with its felled trees and chewed-up dirt. An Orphan boomer team fired from down below, and one of their bunker busters sailed into the opening after an echoing crack. Its delayed fuse went off underground, and then Frankel and the others were back at the hole, heaving grenades into the gash from above.

"Lieutenant! Lieutenant!" Dak's voice, tense, muffled by heavy fire. Mortas slipped down behind the trunk and flipped the goggles again. The ridge was a narrow finger, and he'd sent Dak's half of the platoon around its tip. To his horror, he now saw that the tracks which had been carrying them were far to the north, moving away, and that they'd deposited Dak and the others in open ground.

"I see you!" he yelled.

"Yeah, Sam sees us, too!" Dak answered, and on the imagery Mortas picked up the flashes of enemy fire. The Sims were dug in on both sides of the ridge, and half of his people were exposed to all of the fire coming from the opposite slope.

A sack of mud landed next to him, and Mortas turned in surprise to see Prevost. The chonk gunner was covered in dirt and broken bits of wood, and he aimed the grenade launcher over the trunk. He loosed off a round at something near the top of the incline, reminding Mortas that the enemy didn't care that he was concentrating on Dak's predicament. Raising his rifle, he started swinging it back and forth to give Prevost protection.

"Dak!" he yelled. "Mark targets and call in the drones!"

"Already tried! They're a little busy!"

Looking back toward the landing zone, Mortas watched as another serial of personnel carriers slid down the cofferdam. The energy tunnel stood out like a stationary blue tornado, but its base was a junkyard. Smoking vehicles seemed to be everywhere, and even at that distance he could see that several of the new arrivals had landed on some of the earlier ones.

Enlarging the overhead imagery told a worse story. One of the two other cofferdams was likewise jammed with vehicles and under fire from numerous concealed guns. Gunships, manned and otherwise, were desperately pounding the sources of the enemy's concentrated firepower. They zipped back and forth, but Sim antiaircraft guns on the hills were making it hot for them.

"Come on!" he shouted at Prevost, slapping the chonk man's armor while trying to rise. A hand yanked him back down.

"Just a second, sir." Prevost brought the grenade launcher up, and when Mortas looked he saw a quartet of bodies struggling toward the top of the ridge. They were carrying a heavy machine gun on a tripod, free arms swinging with their exertions. He saw the flanged helmets of Sim infantry, so different from the head-hugging protection worn by the Orphans, and then the chonk round erupted from Prevost's weapon.

The grenade sailed through the gaps in the trees, landing just ahead of the group. Set to explode a yard off the deck, it blew all four of them in different directions.

"First Platoon! Up and over the top!" Mortas yelled, vaulting the wooden trunk and rushing uphill. Prevost did the same, weaving through the trees to his left. They ascended into a view of the entire battle, catching glimpses of the towering cofferdams, the pirouetting aircraft, and the blasts and smoke from the separate engagements.

"Dak, this is Dassa!" B Company's commander called to the First Platoon Orphans caught in the open. "I've got rockets for you. Mark me new targets."

The words didn't register with Mortas as he crested the long hill. Needing to see what was happening to Dak and the others, he stayed on his feet behind a tall tree. The ground ahead and below was covered in grass, but a shorter variety that wasn't as thick as what he'd passed through earlier. His goggles instantly picked up the ragged line of rucksacks several hundred yards away, tiny sticks pointing over them. The roar of the battle kept him from hearing the machine guns firing on the slope below, but he could see the fusillade chopping the grass.

Next to a low rise roughly two hundred yards beyond Dak's position, an APC spewed smoke and flame. Mortas spotted the silhouettes of other carriers beyond that, unable to reach his trapped men because of the Sim guns. The APCs fired smoke rounds at the enemy positions below him, and a gray cloud started to rise.

Prevost was already heading down, rushing from tree to tree in a crouch. If the emplacements on that side were a mirror of the ones they'd already silenced, he'd be spotted in no time. Drifting smoke covered much of the area, a less effective blanket fired by the chonk gunners pinned down in the field.

Dak hollered over the radio, answering the company commander. "I can't identify them! Marking likely targets!"

Frankel, somewhere to Mortas's right, called out to Dak. "Got one! Spot my smoke!"

Prevost had vanished, so Mortas left the tree and ran downhill. Chonks began coughing to his right, Frankel's people firing colored smoke rounds at the enemy gun they'd located. The chatter of the Sim machine guns filled his ears now, and he followed the noise. A single bullet suddenly smacked into the tree closest to him, forcing him back down.

"Orbital rockets on the way!" Dassa called, the words finally getting Mortas's attention. Warships in space were firing guided missiles that would fly directly over Dak and slam into the ridge. Right where he and Prevost and Frankel's people were searching for Sim positions. At most they had two minutes to clear out.

"First Platoon! Rockets inbound! Pull back over the ridge!"

Mortas raised his head, trying to see through the trees and the underbrush, looking for the chonk gunner who'd gone ahead. A giant's finger flicked the tree inches from his helmet, biting bark off, before the ground below and ten yards to his right erupted in a red cloud. The explosion was inside the anti-armor emplacement, and he recognized the sound of the marking munition. A chonk smoke round. Fired from well below.

"Prevost! Get back up here! They're gonna blow this whole side to pieces!"

With the rockets inbound, the waiting APCs broke from cover and headed for Dak. The concealed gun fired a round at them with a titanic roar, but it went high and sailed over them. A second chonk round burst just outside the firing aperture, more red cloud to blind the Sim gunners.

To his left, a Sim machine gun started firing, a sustained growl. Knowing who they were shooting at, Mortas pushed off from the dirt and just managed to get behind another tree before his Sim shadow pumped another slug into it.

"I'm pinned down, sir! Get outta here!" That came from Prevost, somewhere below, seeing Mortas and knowing what he was trying to do.

"Where is it?"

"Five yards to your left, ten yards down! No time, Lieutenant! Run for it!"

The grenade was in his hand, and he was skittering down, juggling the rifle while yanking the safeties out of the explosive. Rounds hitting the nearby trees gave him speed, and then he was down again, hugging the dirt and peering around for the machine gun.

"You're right on top of it!"

Squirming forward, feeling the tug as a bullet snatched at the fabric covering his torso armor, the churning roar of the machine gun filling his ears. Amazed when he found the horizontal slit below him, seeing just a sliver of the crossbeam's wood, almost invisible, camouflaged with living sod, the vibrations of the machine gun rattling his chest through his armor.

"El-tee! We killed your sniper! You're clear!" Frankel calling.

Mortas armed the grenade, surged forward, and heaved it into the darkness. His hand felt the heat and the trembling air of the slugs racing out of the concealed barrel, and then he was rolling away. His goggles strobed with red for half a second, and then the robot voice was back.

"Rocket impact imminent! Take cover! Take cover!"

Prevost was next to him, grabbing his armor, hauling him to his feet, adrenaline jetting through them both as they raced for the crest.

CHAPTER 2

In a specialized sleep tube on the research vessel *Delphi*, Ayliss Mortas dreamt. The ship hurtled through space, an unusually long Step voyage this time, while sophisticated sensors recorded the brainwaves of the craft's unconscious complement. Though heavily sedated, Ayliss knew her dreams were being monitored and, in a quiet back room of her mind, wondered if that awareness was influencing them.

Her Step dreams had always been based heavily in reality, often a reliving of especially intense events, and this one was no different. She felt the weight of the torso armor, the heat reflecting off of the black standing rocks so common to the planet known as Quad Seven, and the burning in her right cheek. The face looking up at Ayliss could have been her own at the time; the hair was cut close to the skull and the contorted features were blackened for concealment.

Lola, leader of the colony's Banshee contingent, had taken the full force of the explosion meant for Ayliss.

"I will die for you, Ayliss." Lola spoke through lips flecked with her own blood, and then subsided. The stench of high explosive stung Ayliss's nostrils in the dream as she lowered the dead warrior to the dirt.

"I will kill for you, Lola," Ayliss heard herself saying, a fragment of the Banshees' pre-battle ritual. "I will kill them *all*."

The dream diverted from reality at that point, so that Ayliss was looking down into Lola's living and disapproving eyes. The face paint was gone, and a pale Lola raised herself on an elbow.

"That's not how it goes. When I say I'll die for you, you say you'll die for me." Lola stood, now dressed in a flowing white dress that Ayliss had never seen before. The black spikes all over the plateau dissolved into nothing, and she was standing on an empty beach with the ocean crashing in. Lola was far away, abandoning her, the gown blowing in the breeze.

"Didn't I try?" she called after the figure. "I stood up in front of McRaney's ship, trying to fire a missile that didn't even *work*!"

Lola appeared directly in front of her, furious. "You aren't *supposed* to die for me, dumbass. You're supposed to live for me."

Ayliss blinked, and then she was alone. She looked around, knowing that this time Lola was gone. The wind took on an edge, chilling her, and the sun dimmed. Ayliss dragged a toe across the damp sand, drawing a line. In a child's voice she whispered, "Dying would have been easier."

The line disappeared under the incoming tide, and a wave smashed into her with a roar. She started, realizing she was back on the plateau, choking in the smoke from the battle, the useless missile tube dropping from her hands as the saucer of McRaney's ship blotted out the sky. Its ugly cannon barked, and stone chips flew up from the entrance to the tunnel under her feet where so many of the colonists had taken refuge.

Not caring about them at all, Ayliss rushed to the edge and looked across at the wrecked Zone Quest mining complex and a brilliant white house that had briefly been her home. Blocker's enormous figure was already there, holding a launcher that actually worked, while she shrieked a warning that the stricken ship would land on him.

"Get your head down, darling!" the man she knew as Big Bear shouted, and then she felt his hands shoving her to the dirt even though that was impossible. He was hundreds of yards away, firing the missile that destroyed McRaney's ship.

They both fell flat, the engines on the smugglers' craft screaming as it tried to stay aloft, and then it settled backward, destroying the white house, collapsing much of the embankment, and then exploding. She was crushed under debris, the right side of her face was on fire, but Ayliss fought madly just to turn over and see.

She was trapped under Blocker, the man who had been her childhood bodyguard. He'd survived the explosion in real life, and promised never to leave her again when she'd found him pinned under the wreckage. Both his legs broken, but alive.

The big man raised his head with effort, blood running down his cheeks from the enormous wound in the back of his head.

"I will die for you, Ayliss." The words grated as if his mouth had filled with dirt, and then he sagged against her.

"Don't leave me, Big Bear." She fought to stay calm, knowing it was a dream.

"Ayliss, this isn't going to work unless you're completely truthful with me." The woman speaking was Mira Teel, the de facto leader of the group known as Step Worshipers. The *Delphi* was their ship and, with the exception of its captain and most of its crew, the passengers were almost exclusively her followers. Since coming aboard, Ayliss had privately started referring to the Step Worshipers as Steppers and mentally referring to Mira as the High Stepper.

"Truthful? About a dream?" Ayliss leaned back into the curved sofa in Mira's quarters. While the Steppers preferred loose-fitting, colorful garments, Ayliss was wearing a set of sand-colored fatigues. Her blond hair was cut short, and an oval of tiny scars marked the right side of her face. Struck with rock fragments during the fighting on Quad Seven, Ayliss had refused to have the scars erased.

"I don't understand why you're fighting me." Mira reclined in a chair facing the couch, blowing on a mug of tea. "I thought we'd become good friends, back on Earth."

"I'm not fighting you. And we are friends. My father trusted you, and so do I."

"Your father disappeared in the Step because of that trust."

"No. He disappeared because he was trying to contact the entities that gave humanity the Step in the first place."

"I'm glad you see it that way."

"He told me all about his plan before I went to Quad Seven. Personally, I think he succeeded. I think he made contact with those entities."

"I do, too. And that's why I still hold out hope that he will eventually return. Or that, through our efforts here, we might find him."

"We were never particularly close, you know. He pushed Jander and me away from him, after our mother died."

"Olech told me all about that. But a mere blood relationship isn't why you're here. You and your father share a similar experience while in the Step, one that is not common. Very few people dream during a transit, and the dreams come in two varieties. Either they replay events that actually happened, which we call a 'memory' dream, or people from the dreamer's past interact with the dreamer in a way that they never did in real life. We call that a 'message' dream."

Ayliss remembered Lola's outlandish attire during the just-completed voyage, and the words she'd never spoken. "I already know that. We've had this discussion before."

"Apparently we need to have it again. You and your father both had dreams of the second variety, as have most of my colleagues here. We believe those dreams are attempts by the entities to communicate with humanity." Mira placed the mug on a nearby table, and swept an errant gray hair back into place. "From the moment your father disappeared, no one in our group has had a single message dream. In fact, an entire month went by before anyone in a transit reported having any dreams at all. And, despite countless voyages made since then just to regain contact, so far the ones who've started dreaming again have only experienced memory dreams."

"So your associates keep telling me."

"You can understand their frustration. They dedicated their lives to communing with a higher form of existence, and then saw that link severed by someone who is not of the group."

"They blame my father for the lost contact?"

"Fairly or unfairly, yes."

"You helped him. We both did."

"Everyone knows of my role. You may not have noticed it, but some of the hostility they're directing toward you is also coming my way."

"Good thing it doesn't bother either of us."

"It doesn't bother me because I have a higher purpose. I'm not sure why it doesn't bother you. Or why you keep telling me virtually the same dreams, over and over, regardless of how many transits we make."

"Memory is imperfect. Subconscious memory even more so."

"When I first met you, you had no difficulty remembering your Step experiences in detail."

A hand waved at the cheek scars. "I've been through a lot since then."

"We're all very impressed by your actions on Quad Seven. You risked your life, fighting off the Sims alongside your colonists. I was hoping you'd show the same loyalty to us."

Ayliss sat up. "We weren't attacked by Sims. It was a smuggler named McRaney, human as you and me, hired by a Zone Quest station manager named Rittle. As discharged veterans, my colonists were given control of Quad Seven by my father. Rittle and the rest of ZQ didn't like that."

"Your stepmother told me about this before sending you to us. Between the loss of your father and the civil war on Celestia, she felt that an accusation against one of the largest mining organizations in the war zone would have been too much."

"So you admit that Reena put me on this voyage to keep me quiet."

"Oh, I doubt she thinks anything could keep you quiet for long." Mira laughed, reaching for the tea.

The humor was genuine, and Ayliss gave her a grudging smile. "And I don't want you to be quiet. I want you to trust me, and to tell me what's happening in your psyche when you're in transit."

"I told you I dreamt of Blocker."

"Yes. A memory dream of him comforting you when your mother died."

"He's on my mind. Since we're skipping around the cosmos with no real destination, could we arrange a stopover so I could see him? It might help me to focus."

"He's convalescing at Larkin Station, yes? In the war zone?"

"Yes. From what little he's told me, it's not going well."

"I can have the captain arrange it." Mira stood, her colored smock dropping into place. Ayliss rose as well, but the older lady blocked her exit. "I have no interest in whatever it is you're planning, although it sounds like it may involve revenge against this Rittle character. Our race has been at war with the Sims for four decades, and I've never taken an interest in any of that violence at all. I have one goal here, to reestablish contact with the entities."

"I'll help you all I can."

"That's all I ever ask of anyone aboard." Mira stepped aside, her face darkening. "I'd consider it a personal favor. I'm not dreaming at all anymore, no matter what kind of transit we attempt. If this silence goes on much longer, I don't think I'll be able to stand it."

As always, Ayliss left Mira's quarters with relief. The High Stepper's link with whatever existed in her Step dreams might have been severed, but her skills as an inquisitor remained. In the time she'd spent with Mira before Olech's fateful journey, Ayliss had come to view her as a clairvoyant when it came to reading people's thoughts. She knew she wasn't the only one who considered Mira to be almost a witch in this regard.

Despite the discomfort of these post-Step interviews, there were several aspects of life on the *Delphi* that Ayliss enjoyed. Over her stepmother Reena's strident objections, no bodyguards were allowed aboard the research vessel. It was a welcome respite from a life that had become cluttered with overprotective men and women, and their presence here would have been pointless. Every human aboard the *Delphi* had to go into a Transit Tube whenever they initiated a Step, so if anyone meant her harm they'd have plenty of opportunities. Not that there was much chance of that; as a group the Steppers felt that violence was beneath them. Their resentment of her father's role in severing their dream link had so far manifested itself only in a standoffishness that Ayliss secretly appreciated.

She turned a corner, and almost collided with a tall Stepper coming the other way. Her multicolored robe hung to the deck, and a shaved head sprouted from its top. Ayliss had noticed this one before, hovering nearby, and had thought the face was familiar. The suddenness and proximity of their meeting brought the proper memory to life.

"I know you." Ayliss extended a finger. "From the party circuit at university. What's your name?"

The Stepper didn't flinch. "Margot Isles. And I left that life behind me."

"Isles. Munitions family. Made a fortune off the war. Right?"

"Sounds like the Mortas family, to me."

"Wrong. Your people sell the weapons." Ayliss leaned in, showing the cheek scars. "My people use them."

She stepped around Margot, pretending to have forgotten her but mentally recording the incident for later consideration.

The ship's engines hummed through the bulkheads as she walked, and to Ayliss it sounded as if the spacecraft was recharging. The cycle of putting everyone into the sleep tubes, generating a Threshold, completing a Step, and then awakening them occurred at roughly twenty-four hour intervals. Analysis of the dream data and post-Step interviews required substantial effort from Mira and the other interlocutors, but the rank-and-file Steppers had plenty of down time. Ayliss passed several more individuals, male and female, as well as a clutch of Step acolytes enjoying a laugh at the junction of two passageways.

The laughter died when she approached, and didn't resume once she'd passed.

The walk ended at another hatch, and Ayliss

punched in the access code. Stepping into the space, she stopped abruptly.

The tight compartment was lined with banks of communications gear, and a canted control panel ran around three of its walls at waist level. Christian Ewing was seated in the center of the room, and a female Stepper was sitting in his lap. Short and slim, very much like Ewing himself, she took her time standing up. After running spread hands through an impressive mane of red hair, the woman leaned in to kiss him farewell.

"Ayliss." She offered a noncommittal smile, and left.

The communications expert grinned up at her while she moved the compartment's other chair a little closer. Ewing was wearing a khaki flight suit, and didn't try to intercept her when Ayliss reached into one of its side pockets. Her hand came out with a folding row of individually wrapped discs which the redhead had deposited while saying her goodbyes.

"Transdermals. Your Stepper friends trying to help you stay awake?"

"They're very interested in the music I hear out there." Ewing pointed a finger at the ceiling. "I think they're living vicariously through me, now that their dreams have gone cold."

"Music that nobody but you hears." Ayliss handed the drugs back. "Those things are going to kill you, one of these days."

Ewing raised his eyebrows. "Your addiction's likely to do that sooner."

"'Touché." Ayliss raised open hands. "Give me an update."

Ewing punched a button on one of the consoles, and an eerie soundtrack filled the space. Many voices, not human, sighed and moaned in a high octave. The calls and answers drifted over each other, sometimes mixing melodically. Ayliss recognized it as the recording of whales singing in Earth's oceans, only because it was Ewing's standard defense against eavesdropping.

"Our friend never leaves the war zone. That's why he's advanced so quickly inside the company." Despite sophisticated anti-surveillance equipment embedded in the walls and the masking sound of the whales, they still talked in code about Vroma Rittle, the Zone Quest station manager from Quad Seven. "He's very well connected, inside and outside his organization. If First Sergeant Hemsley hadn't banned me from radio watch back there, I think I could have figured out that our friend was on good terms with the smugglers."

"How so?"

"The chatter is all around us. You just need the gear to grab it, and the sense to sort through it. This rig you got for me is perfect, by the way."

"It was one of my conditions for coming on this trip. Don't forget that my stepmother's people put this all together, so you can bet they're monitoring everything you do."

"They're not the only ones. Somebody on board, not the crew or the command element, has been trying to hack into my work. Not sure who it is, but it's obviously a spy of some kind. It's strange, because even if they succeeded, I doubt they could figure any of it out. So much data, and I look at it from a lot of different angles."

"You're disguising the results with disinformation."

"You really are a wily one, Minister."

"Don't call me that. I'm not in charge of a damned thing anymore."

"Neither is our friend. He hasn't been given a new station to manage, but that's not surprising. The war zone's a mess right now, Sam attacking everywhere, so many troops sent to Celestia."

"You don't suppose the Guests would send him there, do you?" Ayliss used the veterans' derogatory term for the overbearing mining company. Zone Guests. Profiteers in the war zone.

"Celestia's loaded with important minerals, and most of the production's been stopped by the fighting. Our friend would be a good candidate to get things running again, once they've pacified one of the mining areas." He paused. "They might be tempted to send him there, despite the rebellion."

"That would be wonderful." Ayliss's gaze lingered on the wall, but Ewing knew she was somewhere else. An entire world consumed by blood and fire, where humans were slaughtering each other that very moment. "In all that chaos, an accident would be easy to arrange."

"It's not my place to say anything, but that's never

stopped me before. Maybe you should let this one go. Everybody who's anybody knows the real story about Quad Seven, good guys or bad. You get rid of our friend, the Guests are going to know it was you."

"What are you saying? Just be a good sport? He poisoned me, he killed my . . . my man. He treated you and the other vets like shit, and then he paid someone to wipe us all out. He managed to kill a lot of your fellow colonists."

"You don't have to remind me. I was there a lot longer than you, being ground under that bastard's heel. If I ever run into him, I'd be tempted to do something. But I wouldn't go out of my way, is my point." Ewing turned back to the controls, pretending to play with the music mix. "The galaxy is loaded with assholes, Minister. You can't kill them all."

"I can try."

"I saw you after the battle. You like it a lot, don't you? The violence."

"Yes."

"Well with all the god-awful suffering in this war, I suppose somebody ought to be enjoying it."

"The patient still shows marked weakness in the left leg." Physician's Assistant John Scalpo spoke to the air while pressing down with both arms. His hands held Dominic Blocker's left ankle, and the big man was easily raising his leg to full extension despite the resistance. Scalpo grinned at him. "The patient's poor state of physical fitness prior to his wounds is the most likely explanation for his slow recovery."

Blocker mouthed a pair of obscene words at the PA, and Scalpo released him. Though in his sixties, Scalpo still had a full head of hair that was completely white and cut very short. An olive-colored set of medical scrubs hung from his lean frame, and thin lines ran across his forehead.

"Recommend maintaining the patient here on Larkin Station for at least another month, with additional physical therapy sessions."

He stepped over to a desk and began typing notes. Seated on the exam table, Blocker looked at a gallery of pictures slowly rotating across a screen on the wall. A new one appeared, a rising sun peering over a brown horizon made up of dirty sand dunes.

"I know that one. That was the view from the main support base on Selo Six."

"Now how would you know anything about the view from the rear area? Big bad platoon sergeant."

"Rear area? Didn't Sam overrun that base?"

Scalpo stopped typing, his expression suggesting a pleasant memory. "He did. I bagged three of those bastards that very night. And the clerks and cooks did much better than that, once they got into the spirit of the thing."

"It's a game anybody can play."

The PA finished his notes, and then shut off the console. Rolling his chair back, he gave Blocker an appraising look. "You sure you want to do this?"

"You sure we can talk here?"

"I had the auto-sterilizers scrub the room down just before your appointment. No mike known to man could survive that. And the confidentiality software is fully engaged."

"Yes. I want to do this. Rittle has to pay for what he did on Quad Seven."

"Known you a long time, Dom. Why are you getting so worked up about some Zone Quest functionary?"

"He shit on a bunch of discharged veterans, and then tried to murder them. Isn't that enough?"

"No, it's not. From what you told me, half those colonists ran away when you needed them."

"Most of 'em weren't combat vets. All things considered, they did all right."

"Still not good enough to take this kind of chance. ZQ will know what this is, and they will not take it lightly. So what's really behind this?"

Another picture appeared on the screen, the only one so far that contained people. Two men in camouflage fatigues, both covered in gray dust and sporting blood-tinged bandages, smiled up at the camera. They were sitting on the ground, backs to what looked like a wrecked aircraft, holding out water bottles in a toasting gesture. Blocker walked over for a closer look.

"You don't display that photo with other patients, right?"

"I don't show that one to anyone. Remember how thirsty we got?"

"My platoon had plenty of water when we got to the crash site. And you took every drop for the wounded."

"What did you expect to find on a wrecked medevac bird?"

"Honestly? A bunch of dead bodies."

"Sammy Sim sure tried to make that happen. Long two days."

"When the relief finally got there, one of them handed me a canteen of water. It was the best thing I ever tasted in my whole life. You used yours to wash your hands."

"Still had wounded to tend."

Blocker sat down again. "In a way, so do I. Ayliss Mortas isn't going to let Rittle get away with what he did, and she's not discreet when it comes to killing."

"So you're going to bear the backlash, instead of her."

"I abandoned her when I went to the war, Chief. Lately I've been thinking she might have turned out differently, if I'd stuck around."

"You were her bodyguard, not her father."

"She doesn't have a father anymore."

The PA gave a slight shrug. "I'll carry you as long as I can. You should have been shipped out of the war zone long before now. So you better make your move soon."

"It's probably better if you don't know any of the details."

"All right."

"Chief, there is one more thing."

"There always is."

"Yeah, we been real busy these past few months. Sam's taking advantage of things out here, and some of the ships have come in with big-time damage. A lotta new faces, too. I swear, half the civilians this side of the CHOP Line have decided to ride out the storm right here." The man was of normal height, but walking next to Blocker made him look short. His bright orange coverall bore the logo of one of the corporations that moved supplies in the war zone, and his identification badge said his name was Deek Orton.

"You're better off busy," Blocker answered Orton, turning slightly to let a civilian in a business suit slide by. Though large, the corridor was filled with people of every type. All around them were Human Defense Force members wearing different uniforms, office workers speaking cryptically into headsets, and maintenance people dangling everything from tools to oxygen tanks. "Whenever I couldn't find enough for you to do, you always got into trouble."

Orton laughed. "That's true enough. I gotta hand it to you, Sarge. You took a young knucklehead who thought he was a tough guy, and turned him into an old knucklehead who finally realized what the tough guys were all about."

"Old. What are you—thirty?"

"I'm offended. I just turned twenty-seven. You'd think my former platoon sergeant would know my age."

"So you figured out what the tough guys were all about?"

"I did."

"Good. You're gonna have to explain it to me sometime."

They slid out of the throng in the main passageway, and into an orange-colored corridor. The walls were marked in several places with warnings about personal safety and authorized access, but none of the security alarms activated when they passed through. Weaving their way through several twists, turns, and hatches, they finally ended up in a darkened cargo hold. Orton led the way through a maze of tall racks holding an eclectic array of repair parts, finally stopping in front of a dark hatch set into the back bulkhead.

"This is a good spot for stashing things. All the stuff you see around us? Outmoded. Almost nobody comes back here." Orton stopped short. "What the—"

A slim figure emerged from the shadows, a young woman dressed in black fatigues. Her dark hair was cut short, but even in the gloom it was apparent that her almond-skinned features were extremely pretty.

"Relax," Blocker growled. "I arranged for her to be here."

Orton tried to sound suave. "Oh, Sarge. You shouldn't have. I know I'm doing you a big favor, but—"

"Careful. She's an ex-Banshee. You know what they do to men who get out of line."

The technician covered his crotch with both hands and took a step back. Blocker turned to the woman.

"How's the leg, Tin?"

"You know." Without a sound, she twisted sideways and swung her right leg up so that her boot stopped an inch from Orton's face. "Continuing weakness, attributed to the patient's lousy state of physical fitness prior to getting shot on Quad Seven."

"Switch legs."

The right boot disappeared, replaced by the left one a second later. Tin stayed in that position, perfectly balanced, looking into Orton's eyes with a mischievous smirk.

"Good enough." The Banshee dropped her leg, gracefully pirouetting until she was looking up at Blocker.

"Sarge?" Orton had recovered just a bit. "How'd she get in here?"

"She spent too much time around a Spartacan Scout deserter. Picked up some bad habits." Blocker nodded toward the hatch. "Show her our little surprise."

Grinning proudly, Orton deactivated a pair of contact locks that he'd attached to the opening. After entering an access code, he extended an open palm like a magician. The black plate moved upward, and a dull light turned on in the closet-sized compartment.

Looking slightly battered but functional, one of the full-body armored suits used by the Banshees stared back at them from its support frame.

Tin stepped up to it, the glow reflecting off her eyes and her teeth. She ran light fingers down the front of the suit, and then Blocker felt her other hand doing the same on his arm.

"Oh, Dom," she cooed. "You shouldn't have."

CHAPTER 3

Though seated in a large room on Earth, Reena Mortas floated free in the universe. She'd always hated this chamber, the way her missing husband had spent so many hours alone inside it, the terrible way it had hurt him that one time. And yet now, sitting in his chair both literally and figuratively, she'd come to understand the attraction.

The room was in the center of the tallest tower of Unity Plaza, the sprawling political headquarters that had been her home for many years. All around her was pitch darkness, and Reena knew that if she just scooched forward a few inches she would plummet from the raised seat to the hard floor twenty feet below. Her right hand rested on a rectangular control panel, and she tapped the buttons from memory.

The void came to life, planets and asteroids and comets flashing by in a sophisticated light show. It was impossible not to feel a thrill, charging through space as if enclosed in an unbreakable air bubble shot out of a colossal cannon. She hurtled along for another few seconds, and then the preset voyage ended in a gentle deceleration that once again put her nowhere.

The darkness closed in again, but Reena knew this spot and waited for her eyes to adjust. Distant stars provided flecks of light, and then spectral waves of dust began their lazy circuit. Many of the spectacular sights offered in this room were merely laser-light-show representations of the charted portions of the galaxy, or simply good estimates based on long-range observation. But other spots, where machines and spacecraft were at work, showed her live feed on a modest delay.

The empty spaces at the end of each leg of her daily trip were such spots. Closely observed by probes or robot spacecraft, they were the destinations her husband Olech had intended to briefly visit when he'd disappeared. Twenty consecutive Step voyages, round trips from one point bouncing off of ten others in succession. The Step had been suspended across the galaxy—which meant it was suspended across the universe, as the Sims did not have this technology—so that Olech's there-and-back movements could attract the attention of the entities that had anonymously given mankind the Step in the first place. Asleep in his special capsule, Olech had believed he would receive some kind of communication during that circuit.

Only he hadn't reached any of the ten selected locations. He'd barely started out, his craft approaching the very first Threshold, and then the capsule had vanished. The Chairman of the Emergency Senate, the most powerful politician in humanity, had simply disappeared.

"Where are you?" Reena whispered to the space dust. "I know you're alive. I *know* it. I've got so many people looking for you, they have to find you. Won't you help me find you?"

Of course the void didn't answer.

After waiting for some time, Reena activated the room's voice controls. A technician located elsewhere in the towering building answered immediately.

"Ready, Madame Chairwoman."

"Show me Celestia."

Dim lights came up, revealing the bare gray walls and the hard floor, but then the darkness descended again. It brought with it an image she knew intimately, that of the planet where she'd been born and raised. It grew larger and larger until she felt like the pilot of a ship reluctantly coming into its orbit.

"Start the briefing."

A recorded voice began the daily update of the upheaval on the mineral-rich planet.

"Good morning. As always, the briefing will start with the status of Fortuna Aeternam." Reena's head shook once, minutely. The eternal fortune of the planet's capital had ended several months before, in an explosion of mindless violence that she'd accidentally triggered with the assassination of Horace Corlipso.

"Recovery efforts continue in all sectors of the city." The planet rotated and enveloped her, as if she were floating down on the metropolis. Its outline was the same as she remembered, and she noted the broad boulevards and curving canals as she descended. As a child she'd loved to walk along the blue waterways, the air filled with the scent of fruit trees planted on the banks. The picture below her showed a brown river choked with debris, bordered by trampled dirt. The fruit trees that hadn't been destroyed in the fighting had been chopped down for firewood long before.

"Electric power has been reestablished in sixty percent of the areas outside the Seat of Authority. Unimpeded food delivery is occurring in forty-five percent of the areas outside the Seat of Authority. Violent crime has been reduced by six percent over the last month."

"Outside the Seat of Authority," Reena muttered, and the briefing stopped. The SOA's walls loomed not far from her, encompassing a compound covering several square miles and protected by Human Defense Force troops. What remained of Celestia's upper crust was safely ensconced there, continuing their luxurious existences as if the slave revolt had never happened. While that was obscene, at least it kept them out of Reena's hair. Many of the oligarchs had fled the planet at the first sign of trouble, and she'd worked overtime to find them sanctuary somewhere other than Unity. A hardcore element of Horace loyalists had managed to secure lodging with her, largely because no one else would take them.

"Shall I continue?" the voice asked.

"Skip to the latest developments."

The presentation whirled like a silent tornado, and then stopped far from the city.

"The Dracilipine mining complex has been declared free of rebel forces after three months of nearly continuous fighting." Reena now looked down on a denuded mountain range, its brown soil covered with buildings, pipelines, roads, and rail lines. So much of those had been wrecked that for a moment Reena thought she was looking at an elongated garbage dump. Armored vehicles and assault aircraft stood in clusters or defensive rings, military convoys were freeze-framed on the roads, and dense clouds of smoke smudged several acres of the mine.

"The bulk of the rebel troops withdrew two weeks ago, leaving small groups of holdouts behind. The holdouts set fire to the richest veins in the complex, and these are currently burning underground. Command estimates that getting Dracilipine back in production will require a minimum of one year at maximum effort, after the fires have been extinguished. Command intelligence suspects that many of the rebels were former workers at the mines."

"Slaves." The term came out unbidden, and the briefing stopped again. Raised amid the luxury of the Corlipso family, Reena had been subtly indoctrinated in the wordplay of the elite when it came to their labor force. She remembered the gray-haired woman whom she'd believed to be her mother, gently explaining that the mines produced important minerals for the war against the evil Sims and that someone had to work them. That people flocked to Celestia from all the other settled planets, attracted by its greatness, and that some of those people refused to do their fair share for the war effort. That was why they weren't slaves—they were workers.

By the time Reena had been old enough to doubt that logic, she'd had bigger questions for her mother. Questions about how none of Reena's many siblings had red hair like hers, or how Mother and Father were so much older than her schoolmates' parents. It had been a difficult day when they'd explained that her eldest brother Horace was actually her father, and that her biological mother had been a worker who had died giving birth to her.

Despite this revelation, the charade had continued. Horace Corlipso had gone on to become Celestia's ruler and one of the shrewdest politicians in the alliance against the Sims. He'd instructed Reena in the subtleties and brutalities of power politics, and she'd flourished under that tutelage. Horace had dispatched her to Earth to work with the widowed Olech Mortas, in the belief that the two politicians would eventually pair up.

Though a resident of Earth for many years, she'd known that slavery had been extended into every part of Celestian society under Horace's rule. The slaves outside the mines had been called servants, and one of them, Horace's latest sex slave, had murdered him at Reena's command. Olech had planned the assassination just before his fateful voyage, having already arranged for Reena's appointment as Chairwoman if he didn't return. She'd secretly given the go-ahead shortly after taking her husband's place at the head of the Emergency Senate.

It was fitting that Horace's execution would be carried out by the latest girl forced to warm his bed, and a small revenge for Reena's true mother. The girl's name had been Emma, but she'd gotten carried away. Stabbing Horace to death on a balcony overlooking Fortuna Aeternum's crowded square, Emma had kicked off the rebellion that had taken Celestia and all its vital minerals out of the war. If anyone ever linked this debacle to Reena, she'd quickly be removed from the position that controlled the search for Olech. Rumors were already circulating, and one of the loosest of loose ends from the assassination was still untied.

"Madame Chairwoman?" It was the voice of Nathaniel Ulbridge, the security operative who was second-in-command to Hugh Leeger. Leeger directed the spy apparatus created under Olech, but he was away on a delicate mission. Having worked with both men for many years, Reena welcomed the distraction from her dismal thoughts.

"Yes, Nathaniel."

"I need to speak with you."

"Come in." The lights came up slowly, taking her away from Celestia and back into the chamber which some people had derisively called Olech Mortas's throne room. Ulbridge strode across the floor while Reena's chair descended to meet him.

"Apologies for interrupting you, Madame Chairwoman." Short and blond where Leeger was tall and dark, the powerfully built forty-year-old already knew all the secrets.

"This must be serious." Reena tried to sound unconcerned, but knew better. The throne room was one of the most secure spots in Unity Plaza for delicate conversations.

"It is, ma'am. I have a coded message from Hugh."

Reena felt her muscles relax a notch. Far too many urgent messages carried bad news these days, but Leeger's mission held extraordinary potential. She'd memorized the full range of code phrases he might send, and tried not to anticipate the one she wanted.

"What did he say?"

"It's good news, ma'am." Ulbridge softened his normally formal manner, almost smiling. "The jogger has qualified for the race."

"**R**eally, sir, you do need to eat something."

On a Force space station not far from Earth, Gerar Woomer's personal assistant looked down at an untouched tray of food. In front of him, the famous Step physicist sat at a giant console, right where he'd been for hours.

"That's all right, Jerry. Please take that away." The aged voice was tired, but calm.

"Forgive me for saying this, sir, but perhaps you need a break."

"I'll get some sleep in a bit."

"That's not what I meant. You've been studying the same data for the past six months, trying to figure out what happened to Chairman Mortas. And now, with the news about your grandson . . . you should get away from here."

Woomer tapped a single button, causing one of the console's screens to come alive. Lines jumped across the monitor for only a few seconds before Jerry shut it off. "You've been staring at those readings long enough. We're never going to identify the source of the . . . accident that claimed the Chairman."

The words echoed in his mind. Source. Accident. Claimed. As much as Woomer appreciated Jerry's concern, his assistant was wrong about what he was studying. He no longer paid any attention to the energy spikes associated with the Threshold they'd been generating when Olech disappeared. Months ago he'd discovered the blip at the bottom of the screen, the tiny Threshold that had snatched the Chairman's capsule just as it launched.

Before it could even begin the daring series of Steps that he, Gerar Woomer, had plotted. A series of Steps that should have ended with Olech's capsule crushed in what appeared to be a freak mishap. He'd plotted that, too.

"You should be with your family," Jerry went on. Despite his intellect and training, like everyone else he'd missed the blip entirely. The Threshold that was so powerful and so focused that its source could only have been the entities Olech had been trying to contact. They had snatched him, when Woomer had meant to kill him. "There's still time for you to attend your grandson's funeral."

His grandson. Roland. Rollie to the family. As he'd done countless times over the many long weeks, Woomer studied the earnest young face in a photo set into his workstation. Motionless amid the screens with their jumping data, the picture of his grandson in the HDF had provided some small respite from the guilt and fear. He'd done it for that face, betrayed a man he'd respected and admired, to save the boy. He saw another face now, his colleague Timothy Kumar, who had been Horace Corlipso's science adviser before the assassination. He heard Kumar's silky words again, vaguely commenting on the dangers of the war zone. Promising a safe posting if Woomer helped them, and darkly suggesting that refusal would seal Rollie's fate.

Woomer had cooperated, and for what? Olech's accident had never taken place, but the hand of fate had struck the boy instead. The irony seemed to know no bounds. Horace was dead and Celestia was in chaos, but Kumar was now safely ensconced at Unity Plaza, no doubt trying to win Reena's favor. Though a marginal scientist, Kumar was shifty enough to reveal Woomer's complicity while leaving himself in the clear.

"I've never been a big fan of funerals. Never saw one change anything."

Tears filled his eyes as he looked at the immobile teenager again. Woomer tried not to imagine the permanently stilled body, crushed into the mud by a runaway mover. That was what the notice had said; a terrible accident while offloading supplies. He couldn't stop comparing the forces of the man-sized tires and their enormous load with the pressure that would have murdered Olech Mortas if his pointless plan had succeeded.

"At least come away from your work for a time, then. What if we just went for a walk around the station?"

"That will be very nice." Woomer turned in his chair, raising grateful eyes to his assistant. Reaching out, he placed a small cylinder in Jerry's hand. "First, I'd like you to send this communication to my special correspondent. Use every precaution."

"Yes. I'll do that right away." Jerry looked at the cylinder, knowing it was meant for a secretive group of scientists who opposed the never-ending war with the Sims. "This is a positive step, sir. It's a good idea to busy yourself . . . in other pursuits."

"Yes, it is." Jerry started for the hatch, and Woomer

stopped him. "Leave the tray. I'm feeling a little hungry, after all."

When his assistant was gone, Gerar Woomer took out another cylinder, this one containing hundreds of small pills. Removing the lid, he filled his mouth and started chewing with his eyes fixed on the photo.

CHAPTER 4

"Here's what we know so far." Colonel Watt, the Orphan Brigade's commander, spoke into the earpieces of his officers and NCOs scattered across the battlefield on UC-2147. The Tratian division's headquarters was still in orbit, and so Watt was trapped up there, too.

"The three spacedromes and surrounding settlements were almost empty. The Sims chose this location because they could easily predict where the cofferdams would be established. Their concealed emplacements destroyed numerous APCs, blocking the original landing zones and causing the division command to postpone delivery of the follow-on waves. New cofferdams have now been established, and the rest of the division will begin deploying shortly. Enemy strength is still unknown, so our forces on the ground are directed to hold defensive positions through the night."

Mortas half-heard the update while moving in a crouch. Darkness had fallen, and First Platoon had established a strongpoint on a knob of high ground a half mile from the ridge they'd assaulted earlier. Crossing the silent perimeter, he encountered Sergeant Dak going the other way.

"I repositioned Catalano's machine gun so it covers more of the woods, interlocking with Tado's gun." Dak pointed across a shallow saddle between their position and a low finger of ground covered with trees. The other three sides of the strongpoint looked out across flat terrain scorched black by the fires that had sprung up during the battle. "Mecklinger's marked the open ground with targets, and fire support central has locked it in. Anybody comes at us, we can call artillery, bring in the gunships, or drop rockets on 'em."

"Good," Mortas whispered. "I don't want any more surprises. Everybody stays awake for now."

Dak snorted. "Like anybody's gonna fall asleep, after the day we've had."

Mortas clapped him once on the armor and continued across the perimeter. Approaching Catalano's position from behind, he duckwalked the rest of the way. Three Orphans were stretched out on their stomachs around the machine gun and its tripod, and he gave them a warning hiss before sliding in next to them.

Colonel Watt continued his update. "All things considered, we took far fewer casualties than might have been expected. I'm very proud of the way you all responded to this situation, and how well you're working with our mechanized brethren."

"El-tee." Catalano breathed the words out so that they were almost silent. "Does Colonel Watt know we're no longer with our brethren?"

"Let's hope not." He tried to match the stillness of the other three Orphans. Looking across the low saddle, Mortas studied the raised ground beyond it. The goggles showed him the individual trees and bushes in the darkness, and would have alerted him to the presence of anything—Sim, human, or otherwise—generating body heat. "Captain Ufert didn't want us along in the first place, so he probably won't say anything."

"It was a dumb idea, pairing us off with the mech guys with no time to practice. But they came through for us at the end, driving out in the open to shield Dak like that."

"Could have moved faster, you ask me." That came from Lonkott, Catalano's assistant gunner. "Any more word on Slauern, sir?"

"No updates yet, but Doc Vossel said he was stable at medevac." Ufert had used the evacuation of the wounded as an excuse to leave First Platoon behind, and Mortas had not objected. Ufert's company had lost five men and had twice that number wounded, so First Platoon had been lucky by comparison. Only one of them had been killed, a rifleman in Mecklinger's squad named Bass. Slauern, a chonk gunner also from Mecklinger's squad, had been shot through both arms while pinned down with Dak.

The gun team quieted down, and Mortas switched his goggle view to explore his surroundings. The imagery, a combination of feeds from overhead drones and the ships in orbit, presented a confused picture. Only half the Tratian division had been inserted as planned, and the battle had left them scattered around in seemingly random defensive positions. Fires still burned in numerous spots, consuming the dry grass and creating large heat blobs that a determined enemy could use to conceal their movements.

Mortas slid the lenses up inside his helmet for a moment, reaching grimy fingers under the frames where they pressed into his cheeks. Closing his eyes, he smelled the smoke from the wrecked carriers and the smoldering fires, mixed with the pungent odor of spilled fuel. Lifting his head just a bit, he looked to the west in search of the newest cofferdam. Many miles away, the shaft stood out as a blue-gray pillar against the night.

Mortas heard the puttering sound of a drone circling overhead, and lowered the goggle lenses again. Changing the view, he studied the military symbols jumbled around them. Neat ovals and circles laid out the perimeters of the scattered units, each one surrounded by target markers. He changed the view again, and the tidy symbols were replaced by the heat signatures that showed the ragged arrangements of men and machines.

Seen from above in the darkness, they reminded him of a photo of a star cluster he'd seen in school. Dotted outlines indicated the positions of separate infantry platoons like his own, while larger chains showed the locations of entire companies of personnel carriers. Not far from the nearest Sim spacedrome, a bright white circle momentarily convinced him that a gigantic fire was ablaze. He then recognized it as the location of the field headquarters of the mechanized brigade to which First Battalion was attached. Somewhere in that cluster of running engines and coughing generators was Major Hatton and the battalion staff. Hatton had bitterly opposed the dispersal of the battalion across the mechanized brigade, but to no avail. Mortas smiled at the memory, feeling the exhaustion from the day's events starting to take hold. He would have to find Dak soon, and arrange a sleep rotation for the platoon.

"Jander?" Captain Dassa spoke into his ears. B Company's commander was with the mechanized battalion's command section.

"Yes, sir."

"I need you to rejoin Captain Ufert."

Mortas came awake instantly, fueled by a combination of anger and dread. He'd just finished setting his platoon up for the night in a good defensive position, and had no desire to waste that effort. Even more worrisome, Ufert's perimeter was five miles away, across lethally open ground. The Sims were still operating in the area, but the greatest threat was the thousands of jumpy human troops hunkered down along the route. Sam's trickery had cost them dearly, and they wouldn't hesitate to call down gunships and rockets on any suspicious sightings.

"Request to stay in place." Mortas searched for a reason that Dassa might be able to sell to the mechanized battalion's commander. "My platoon is occupying a good observation point, on a likely enemy avenue of approach."

"Negative. Your platoon is needed to provide security against the possibility of dismounted enemy attack. Get your men moving." The company commander's overly military speech told Mortas that their conversation was being monitored by the Tratian command.

Dak appeared on the ground next to him, helmet and goggles rapidly shaking disagreement. Mortas nodded, and came up with a suggestion that might do the trick. If Ufert was so concerned about Sam sneaking up on his perimeter, he probably wouldn't want to leave it.

"Request personnel carriers to move my platoon. It will be faster, and we won't run the risk of being mistaken for enemy."

"Already denied. I have marked the lane you are to use, and the battalion fire support center is coordinating protection. You will be covered with every bit of ordnance available, and no missions will be cleared anywhere near you without our approval."

Next to him, Dak blew out a loud, frustrated exhale. Inside his goggles, Mortas now saw a zigzagging corridor that ran from his location to Ufert's. Most of its terrain was level, and much of it had been burned barren. Mortas was running out of ideas, and so he blurted out a half-formed argument that he regretted immediately.

"The ground we're to cross could be mined. Again, request—"

"Stop dragging your feet, and get *moving*, Lieutenant!" Dassa shouted, the words stinging because they were so out of character. Mortas squeezed the tip of his nose, hard, and then answered.

"Understood. Moving out."

Even with the aid of night vision, the soldiers looked like wraiths. Humpbacked by their rucksacks, features distorted by their helmets and armor, they moved across the open ground in broad arrowheads.

"There's no good way to do this." Dak had agreed with him when they'd been plotting the move. "Sam's out there somewhere, but he ain't moving around, not with all the surveillance we've got up. If he does attack us, it'll be mortars or artillery. We can mitigate that by spreading out over a few hundred yards—but that's its own problem. Some jumpy troop on the high ground, seeing just a few dismounts, might think we're infiltrators. So we'd be better off if they saw a recognizable movement formation."

The platoon now walked in a blend of the two, three inverted V's separated by fifty yards apiece. Individual soldiers were no closer to each other than ten yards, ready to hit the dirt at the slightest sign of danger. Katinka's squad had the lead because it was almost at full strength, Mecklinger's battered group was in the middle, and Frankel brought up the rear. Mortas shifted around in the big opening between the first two arrowheads, and Dak did the same between the last.

The terrain offered no concealment, and very little cover. As a seasoned infantryman, Mortas knew that small rises and minute folds in the ground could shield a man from direct fire, but that they'd provide scant protection from mortar rounds falling from above. The first mile they'd walked had crossed empty acres of crunchy soil blackened by the earlier fires, and only now were they beginning to see clumps of the dry grass. Periodically they'd cross the wide-toothed indentations left by a tracked vehicle, but apart from that there was nothing.

Looking ahead, Mortas recognized each of the men in Katinka's squad based on their gear or their gaits. The back-to-back missions had cost the platoon five of its members—two dead and three wounded—but it had also left most of the rest with minor injuries. All the long walking, desperate running, throwing themselves down and then jumping back up, had taken its toll.

Mortas picked out Dorillet a good seventy yards away, just based on his stride. Short and stocky, the rocket gunner carried the boomer tube across his shoulders. One arm swung gently in a short arc while the other was draped over the launcher, but the man's normally graceful step was thrown off by a badly pulled muscle in one calf. Turning, the platoon leader walked backward for a few steps so that he could survey Mecklinger's people. Ithaca, a dark silhouette on the far right, was limping as well. He'd wrenched his knee a week before, and had refused medical evacuation. He slept with it propped up on his ruck, and spent the first few minutes of every day hobbling around on the swollen joint until it loosened up. Other silhouettes bobbed along with sore feet or bruised ribs.

He checked their progress in his goggles, a stark reminder that they had a long and hazardous way to go. A mile to the east the ground sloped up into a chain of wooded hills, and those hadn't been scouted yet. Mortas turned to look at the gray band that stretched between the flatness and the sky, wondering if even then a Sim observer was calling in the coordinates of almost fifty humans inexplicably walking in the open.

Mortas flipped one lens of his goggles to an overhead image while leaving the other on night vision. Months of service in the war zone had trained his eyes to close or focus based on the need to check the map or to avoid tripping over something. He widened the scope of the image, comforted to see that there were no heat signatures of any kind on the high ground to the east. Sam might still be there, dug in and watching, but he couldn't have tunneled into every hill on the planet.

"Approaching azimuth change," Katinka whispered, from the front of the arrowheads. Mortas flipped one lens to the navigation view, seeing the lane marked out by Dassa. The other lens showed it too, but as a faint blue glow many yards to his right. Mortas turned to look west and saw the opposite boundary, a blue fog in the distant grass. A drone muttered at him as it passed overhead, one of many systems covering and guiding them. Only two more course changes, and then they'd have to stop and call ahead to Ufert's troops. As dangerous as it was to be walking around out in the flat like this, the most perilous part of the movement would be the final approach to friendly lines. Somehow, no matter how hard they tried to avoid it, somebody with his finger on a trigger always failed to get the word.

"Hey, anybody else seeing that?"

The words jolted him, but Mortas recognized the voice of Bernike, a chonk gunner in Katinka's squad. The entire platoon knelt, its weapons and eyes covering all directions.

"Whatcha got?" Mortas asked.

"Overhead view. Hills to the east. Looks like a firefly going crazy in the woods."

He didn't see it right away, but Bernike's description pointed it out. At the edge of the trees, a dot of light was flitting around at great speed. There was no explanation for what it was doing, as it turned and looped with no apparent direction.

"Got it," Dak answered from the rear of the platoon. "Has to be big, to be registering like that. Drop rucks and get ready to fight from here."

Sliding out from under his backpack, Mortas hit the emergency bypass that connected him with the orbital fire control center. Although the imagery came from numerous sources, fire control always had the last word.

"Fire control, we are seeing an unidentified heat signature to our east. I am marking the area where it's moving around." His fingers flashed in the air close to the dirt, selecting an ovular icon and sliding it over the frenetic firefly. "Do you see it?"

"We see it, Orphan," a crisp voice answered. "Patching into intelligence."

"There's another one." That came from Mecklinger. "They look like they're playing, like dogs of some kind."

"Big fuckin' dog, you ask me," one of the other troops answered, causing a flurry of whispered comments.

"You don't think it's one of those *things*, right?"

"From the intel briefing?"

"Who stayed awake for that? What you talking about?"

"They said they were like wolves."

A half-remembered fragment of the intelligence briefing they'd received aboard ship. The weary platoon gathered in a darkened room with projections beamed onto one wall and a droning voice that put half of them to sleep. A blurred image of what looked like a cross between a wolf and a stegosaurus, racing for the cover of the trees. The promise that the lupine monsters would flee any area that became a battleground between the humans and the Sims.

A low moan hummed into life from the direction of the hills, and then it broke into a full-throated howl. Another one joined in, and Mortas decided to act.

"Sergeant Dak, I want two squads facing east and one facing west. Oval perimeter. Let's get all three machine guns facing east, boomers and chonks the same. I'll coordinate with fire control."

"Understood." Dak began selecting squad assignments, and the men quickly reoriented themselves. Katinka's and Mecklinger's squads simply turned in place while Frankel's men jogged off to take up dispersed positions twenty yards behind them. On the imagery, Mortas saw more than a dozen fireflies were now zigzagging around in the distant trees.

"Fire control, I'm seeing more and more of these things popping up on the high ground. Must be cave openings where they live. Request immediate suppression."

"Just a second." An apathetic voice joined the conversation. "This is intelligence speaking. I don't think there's anything to worry about. Just a few wild dogs frisking around."

The howling was now continuous, and Mortas felt its vibration in his blood. Raucous and discordant, it still carried a clear message. The pack was forming for a hunt, its members psyching each other up, and his platoon was the only meat available.

"Intel, I don't care what you think. You're up there, we're down here. There's at least fifty of those things forming up, and I got nothing but empty air between them and my people. Fire control, I am marking a linear target across the face of the high ground. I want rockets on this target, *now*."

He saw Dak hustle by, assigning sectors of fire. Tucking the butt of his Scorpion into his shoulder, Mortas watched his goggle view take on the optics of the rifle. For the first time he was able to detect the bobbing glow of the wolves' heat signatures, prancing around just inside the tree line. It was hard to tell, but he guessed there were now more than a hundred of them.

"Fire control, what's the holdup?"

"Your request has been challenged by intelligence. Your divisional fire control center is adjudicating."

"My division? This is First Platoon, B Company, First Battalion of the Orphan Brigade! We aren't part of a division. Now give me those rockets!"

"You are temporarily assigned to the Tratian mechanized division on the planet surface. Their fire direction center had rejected your request. They are citing regulations preventing them from expending ordnance on the local fauna."

"Local fauna?" Mortas hopped to his feet, grabbed his rucksack with one hand, and ran up to a gap in the eastward-facing side of the perimeter. Dropping the backpack, he threw himself down and began sighting again. "Are you seeing this imagery? There's *hundreds* of them."

"Jan," Dassa broke in. "I see your situation. I'm working it from this end. Stay cool."

"Hey, how about sending a few of those armored boxes with the big guns our way? Might be helpful."

"Working on it."

The howling died down in only a few seconds, and through the sights Mortas watched the first glowing orbs leaving the wood line, headed their way.

"Chonk gunners, boomers, you got 'em first. Fire as soon as they reach max range," he chanted, checking the sectors Dak had assigned. "Use high explosive. Let's see if we can scare 'em off with the noise. Once they're closer, switch to anti-personnel rounds."

"Machine guns, watch your sectors. Sweep back and forth." Dak continued the commands. "Riflemen, plug the gaps. Aim for the ones who get through."

The wolves slid down the hills individually, looking like gobs of melting quicksilver in his goggles. The trickling droplets were followed by steady streams, and finally a torrent. Once they reached the flat, their glowing signatures blended together briefly until they looked like a tidal wave hurtling toward landfall. The rolling cloud of light rippled and contorted with the movement of its individual members, and as they got closer they resolved into images right out of a nightmare.

Enormous heads with triangular snouts and close-set eyes. Jaws that opened and shut to draw in air or to snap at nothing as they charged. Massive shoulders surging forward simultaneously, sending broad forelegs reaching out for the dirt with paws that extended into curved claws. The dust rose up under their pounding strides, and for the briefest moment Mortas almost laughed, thinking that he was about to be struck by one of the massed cavalry charges of ancient history.

Then the rifle's optics showed him the cruel, pointed teeth in the flashing jaws and the obsessed intelligence in the slanting eyes, and he wasn't amused anymore.

"Nice doggies. Good doggies." A tense voice came from the firing line, trying to sound funny but failing. "Go *away*, doggies!"

"Don't show weakness," Bernike responded. "It encourages them."

"Yeah," Ithaca joined in. "Whatever you do, don't let 'em see they killed you."

The jest got much of the platoon laughing, and Mortas joined in. The rippling onslaught came on with terrifying speed, and the mirth died down as the men sighted in.

"Let's toss the first grenades as a volley." Prevost

had taken informal command of the chonk gunners, his calm helping the entire platoon settle down. "On my mark. Three. Two. One."

The air exploded with the startling concussion of the grenade launchers and the platoon's three boomers. The rockets struck first, detonating on the hard-packed dirt just behind the lead wolves. Brief flashes of red and orange, followed an instant later by an echoing whump that tossed several of the beasts through the air. The horde was pressed in so close that the flying bodies took down numerous others in a cascading tangle of kicking legs and flying dirt.

The grenades struck right after that, with less force but throwing deadly fragments in all directions. Stricken wolves ran on for a few more strides, wobbling, tripping, giving the ones behind them time to swerve. The machine guns opened up next, a stuttering roar that tore tunnels through the onrushing mob. Staring through the Scorpion's optics, Mortas could now make out the thick hair on the predators, swept back as they ran. He selected one of the biggest, loping slightly ahead of the rest, and the rangefinder in the corner of his goggles flickered to let him know the target was almost close enough.

"Fire control." The words came out dry and hoarse. "How 'bout you send a little help our way? Or do we have to get eaten first?"

There was no response, and the whole subject left his mind as if it had never been important. His vision was taken up by snarling lips and jagged teeth and rippling muscles and bouncing eyes that seemed focused directly on him. Then the red dot appeared right between those eyes, indicating that his chosen target was in range, and he gently squeezed the trigger.

The charging beast bobbed at the last second, but the round struck it just above the right eye. Its entire head jerked to the side, as if slapped by an invisible hand, but it didn't fall down. Its jaws opened in pained fury, and it shook its head in a brief spasm before powering forward. Astounded, Mortas put two more rounds into the monster before it swerved to the side, tumbling over and taking two others down with it.

The troops were already calling to each other. "One shot ain't gonna do it! Three-round bursts!"

The wall of teeth and muscle came apart just then, the machine guns having piled so many bodies in three spots that the others were racing around them. The boomers stopped firing, running short of missiles, but the chonks kept up a steady rain of explosives that convinced the separated knots of wolves to break up even more. Though still visible through the goggles, the wolves peeled off into the darkness to either side of the platoon.

Mortas ejected the Scorpion's spent magazine, popping his head up to see what the animals were doing. Ducking back down to reload, a bizarre fact entered his mind. He was hugging the ground because in every other battle someone had been shooting at him or shrapnel had been chopping the air.

For the first time ever, his opponents weren't able to threaten him that way. Mortas pushed himself up, but then stood with growing confidence. He breathed in the acrid air with a sensation of unreality, marveling at the unfamiliar freedom, before remembering why he'd had to rise. Looking out over the plain showed what he'd feared. The cloud of gray hair and claws had separated into smaller groups, and several of those gangs were running off to his left and right.

"Sergeant Frankel, back your men closer to us. These fuckin' things are cuttin' around."

The rear squad adjusted quickly, moving in twos, and then Dak was shifting one of the machine guns to join them. All around him, Mortas heard the men reorganizing themselves and reloading the weapons. He was just about to renew his call for fire support when the radio started babbling with robotic warnings from a variety of weapons systems.

"Danger close! Danger close! Rockets inbound!"

"Seek cover! Artillery impact imminent!"

"Mark your platoon frontage! Gunships preparing to make a run!"

Several of the NCOs were standing when the warnings came in, and many of the other men were crouched or kneeling. They immediately pressed themselves into the dirt, but Mortas remained on his feet. Partly motivated by a perverse annoyance that the ordnance was finally arriving, he now wanted to see it land. But standing there, with the sharp smell of explosives and gunfire all around him, the truth was that he relished the freedom of being upright when he shouldn't have been. He flipped the view in one lens to confirm that his tiny perimeter was clearly marked, and that the pulsing targets all around them were locked in.

The rockets hit first, slamming into the far hills where the wolves lived. He saw the distortion in his goggles' night vision as the missiles shot down into the trees, a trembling ray of blue light followed by geysers of fire and the deep booms of enormous explosions. The artillery struck next, a doughnut of steel fragments with his troops at their center, and that finally put him on the ground. The deadly chunks of metal rent the air all around them, but his helmet microphones let him hear the exultant whoops of his troops over the concussions.

The artillery stopped, and he looked up to see long furrows being torn up out of the ground in straight rows. Gunships chewed the earth between the humans and the wolves, and somewhere in that symphony of destruction Mortas heard the keening of the animals again.

That was wrong. They should have fled this otherworldly carnage and its unnatural noises. The platoon's meager weapons had broken their first assault, but the titanic support that now fell from the heavens should have sent them running for their lives. Sliding across the dirt on his chest armor, Mortas reached his rucksack and peered up over it. Human voices now took over the fire control net, calling off the bombardment in order to assess its effectiveness. The taller grass outside the perimeter was ablaze, its short-lived heat adding to the confusion.

"You hearing that, Sergeant Dak?" he shouted.

"Yeah! Sounds like there's *more* of them!"

Mortas came up on one knee, but his goggles seemed to be malfunctioning. Out beyond the grass fires, coming from the direction of the hills, was a wall of rolling heat three times larger than the original lupine charge.

"Holy fuck! Look at 'em all!" He recognized Catalano's voice, and then Prevost's.

"Chonks! Stand up with me! Direct fire! They're comin' too fast!"

Silhouettes popped up to either side, and Mortas saw the grenade launcher men firing their weapons with the barrels level with the ground. The machine guns started up again, and he came to his feet knowing what he was about to see.

If the original assault had been a tidal wave, this was a tsunami. The rockets must have driven the entire colony from its caves, and they were charging toward the obvious source of their torment. He raised the Scorpion, and then lowered it. A cold throb started in his stomach, and for the first time he looked at his rifle as a tiny, useless thing.

"Fire control, we need a final protective fire across our eastern frontage." Mortas spoke slowly, surprised by the feeling of resignation that had taken hold. "Give us everything you got. It's our only chance."

Someone told him that the rounds were on the way, but he was already firing. The solid mass of seething rage was coming on so fast that he couldn't miss, and he ran through a magazine without really aiming. Once again the machine guns were felling the beasts by the dozen, creating a fracturing domino effect, but this time it didn't break up the attack at all. The detonations of the chonk rounds appeared in his goggles as bright sparks only, their full explosion blocked by the sheer mass of flesh.

The rockets landed just then, only a few hundred yards out, much too close, knocking the chonk men down. Mortas was thrown onto his back, gasping for air and clutching his rifle against his armor. His entire field of vision turned a blinding orange, as if he'd been thrown into a fire, and dark shapes were being hurled through the air all around. A form smashed into the dirt next to him, sounding like a bag of fertilizer dropped from a great height, but he knew it was one of the wolves and shot it just as it began to recover.

The dampers in his helmet locked out all the noise in the face of the concussive avalanche, and so the next few seconds were in dead silence. The explosive rain continued to fall, wind slapping him one way and then pulling him the other way, bubbles of fire like lava erupting to his front. Mortas saw one of the machine gun teams working the weapon back and forth, and then they disappeared under a pile of writhing, rending, biting monsters the size of horses.

He was shooting into them, so were others, and the beasts paid no heed until the shots killed them.

The entire fiery world suddenly disappeared behind a head the size of his rucksack that butted straight into his chest armor, knocking him flat. The behemoth was going so fast that it somersaulted over him, clawed paws and spined tail flailing, but then it was on him, something scraping across the top of his helmet like ice falling off a roof, the jaws descending, his arms holding the Scorpion out crosswise, and the beast yanking it out of his grip and flinging it away like a twig.

His hand was fumbling for the knife, Cranther's knife, if the rifle was useless the dagger was simply a joke, when the jaws snapped shut on his left leg. Certain he'd been caught in the workings of some gigantic machine, Mortas felt the teeth piercing the fabric and the flesh and then the pressure smashing the bone within. The massive head was swinging side to side, his whole body left the ground, and then he was thrown clear.

Mortas landed hard, but was unaware of it. He relaxed into the dirt, it was all right, he was infantry and the dirt was home. He felt warm liquid all over his left thigh and wondered if he'd peed himself, it didn't matter, none of it mattered, the stars were out in the blackness overhead and that was where he was going.

Flashes like lightning crossed the sky, but it couldn't be lightning, it was coursing straight across, very close to him, he might have been able to touch it if his arms would just respond, and then the flashes were gone and the stars were back. Somewhere in his fading consciousness he knew he should be worried about the animal that had killed him, but it seemed so terribly unimportant.

Hands were yanking his helmet off, then his goggles, liquid was flowing across his face, cold this time, and he looked up to see Dassa holding him. B Company's commander wore no helmet and no goggles, and his face was streaked with smoke.

"Stay with me, Jan! Stay with me!" he yelled, and even though their noses were practically touching, the words came to Mortas from miles away.

CHAPTER 5

"Mother. Finally."

Dreaming in the Step, Ayliss stood on a hill covered with waist-high grass. Wind whispered all around her, and the sun was warm. Unlike so many of the other dreams, she'd been alone in this one for some time. Walking in an inexplicable calm, not recognizing any of the features of the rolling grassland, aware that she was asleep in a Transit Tube.

The figure came over the rise several hundred yards distant, but Ayliss knew who it was right away. Her dream self just stood there, not understanding why she wasn't running to the woman who'd died when she was six. Tall and slim, Lydia Mortas had always moved with tremendous grace and bearing. She did that now, and the wind played with her dark hair as she seemed to glide through the green stems.

"Sorry I was gone so long, dear." Lydia spoke in a

detached voice, her face blank. Ayliss looked her up and down, startled to see her mother in a set of outdated army fatigues. The olive drab fabric was ripped in several places and blotched with dried mud, but Lydia herself was unharmed.

"I tried so hard to remember what you looked like," Ayliss answered, her words making as little sense as anything else in this unconscious hallucination. "Even with all the pictures and the videos, I forgot over time. But then I'd look at Jan, and I'd see you."

Lydia turned her eyes away, surveying their surroundings. "If you wanted to see me, you had only to look inside yourself."

"They all kept telling me I was like Father, and that Jan was like you."

"But you found out they were wrong." The dark eyes came back to her. "Didn't you?"

"Jan's a soldier now. He's had to kill a lot of the Sims, just like Father."

"And what about you, daughter? Who did you kill?"

Ayliss looked down, surprised to feel ashamed. "I only did what I had to do."

"What did Blocker tell you about me?"

"He said you were the most dangerous member of the family, not Father. And that I was just like you."

"Blocker always thought in absolutes. Friend or enemy. Right or wrong."

"Was he wrong? About us? Me and you?"

For the first time in the dream, Lydia showed emotion. Her mouth twisted into a hard smile, but she didn't reply. Her left hand went into one of the uniform's baggy pockets, and she held out a closed fist.

Ayliss reached out as well, and her mother deposited something small and hard in her waiting palm. Looking down, she saw a small piece of polished stone, dark gray but flecked with yellow that sparkled in the sun. A tiny loop of gold metal had been driven into the rock, and she recognized it at once.

"Father gave me this." Hot, angry tears blurred her vision while her speech picked up speed. "While you were still alive, he was gone so much, and when he came back he'd give me a stone from wherever he'd been. I hung them on a bracelet. I loved that bracelet."

"But you threw it away."

"How could you know that? You were already dead. He pushed me away, me and Jan, but he kept giving me more of these rotten things, like it somehow explained everything. I didn't need trinkets, I needed my *father*!" Ayliss looked up, startled to see that Lydia was now at the top of the hill. She said the next words in a voice too low to hear. "I needed my mother."

The sun was in her eyes, but she knew that Lydia had departed. Looking around, seeing nothing but grass, clutching the stone so hard that it hurt, she heard the wind speak.

"Sorry I was gone so long."

The male Stepper who opened Ayliss's Transit Tube wore the blank mask that they all aped in her presence, but Ayliss barely noticed. She knew the debriefing session with Mira was going to be difficult, because the emotions stirred up by Lydia's appearance were impossible to hide. She took her time getting some water, struggling to concoct a phony story that would explain her condition. Normally adept at deception of that sort, Ayliss found her thoughts whirling uncontrollably as she went down the passageway.

She recognized the attendant standing outside Mira's quarters, one of the few Steppers who didn't turn to stone every time Ayliss approached. The woman was obviously waiting for her.

"I'm sorry, but Mira can't speak with you right now." Ayliss studied her open face, trying to glean some indication as to why the all-important post-Step questioning of Olech's daughter would be canceled.

"That's all right. I'm not feeling particularly well." The words rose up on their own, her political upbringing kicking in. "I'll be in my quarters."

Her mind went back to the dream, and Ayliss found her hand opening and closing as if searching for the charm from her childhood. As usual, nothing in the dream made any sense, and normally she would have dismissed the whole thing. This time, however, the experience lingered in a way she didn't understand. It was like the aftermath of a heated argument that she couldn't put out of her mind, and Ayliss knew she wouldn't be able to keep it from Mira.

A trio of Steppers stood close together outside the hatch leading into the ship's mess, but they didn't notice her at first. There was something unusual about this gathering, something furtive that caught Ayliss's attention. No matter how disappointing they might have found their attempts at communion with the entities, the Steppers were a loud bunch. One of them was whispering rapidly and, even though Ayliss couldn't quite hear the words, she knew it was important news.

She stopped without meaning to, causing the trio to look in her direction. Expressions of mild surprise turned into the standard rude dismissal, and they disappeared inside the mess. Ayliss stared after them for a few moments, intrigued that they hadn't stood their ground. That was different, and she decided it meant that whatever they'd been sharing was more important than staring down their unwanted shipmate.

Ayliss was still pondering her dream, and the strange Stepper behavior, when she punched in the code to access Ewing's communications center. The hatch closed just as she realized that the figure at the console was too tall and too bald to be Ewing.

Margot Isles swung around in the chair, a winsome smile directed at the door. Fright jumped into her eyes when she recognized Ayliss, but she extinguished it. She stood up with a loud sigh, and made a show of straightening out her robes.

"You startled me, Ayliss. I was looking for Christian."

"I'm sure he's in there somewhere." Ayliss pointed at the console's main monitor, where a blizzard of data was racing by.

"Oh, that? I think that was running when I got here." Margot turned and bent over, pretending to scrutinize the blurry text. Her robes almost hid the movement when she reached for a rectangular device jutting from the machine. Ayliss had spotted it already, and snatched it from its mooring.

"This yours?" The rectangle was flat and silver. "But it couldn't be. Unless I miss my guess, this is some very sophisticated gear for cracking encrypted systems. Very expensive. And you Steppers don't own anything."

"Then it's probably Christian's."

"Sure. He'd need something like this, to break his own codes." Ayliss pocketed the instrument. "You thought I'd be speaking with Mira, right? Couldn't hack Ewing's gear remotely, so you decided to do it the old-fashioned way."

"You may not know this, being such a pariah, but your man's quite popular. That's why I'm here."

"You're not his type. He has a thing for long hair." Ayliss took a step closer. "Now why don't you save both of us some effort, and tell me who you're working for?"

"I don't work for anyone." Margot didn't budge, her eyes on a level with Ayliss's. "I'm a dedicated

Step Worshiper. But I'm also a loyal daughter—unlike you—and my father is very curious about your activities."

"Why? Did I cost him some money on Quad Seven?"

"He sits on the Zone Quest board, and you cost them an entire planet loaded with valuable ore. All while your father was busy getting himself killed messing up the Step. So you can understand his concern about what you're doing on this ship."

"I think Mira's going to be more concerned about what *you're* doing on this ship."

Ayliss saw the blow coming, and was already stepping back when the Stepper swung. Margot's arcing right fist hit only air, twisting her torso in a billow of fabric that left her solar plexus wide-open. Ayliss punched in and up, just as Blocker had trained her, concussing the woman's diaphragm. Margot grunted in pain, but then the robes billowed and a backhand swung toward Ayliss's eyes. She caught a glimpse of the short knife as it passed, missing her nose by millimeters, and then both of her hands were locked on the wrist that held the blade. Ayliss twisted around to hyperextend the Stepper's arm, all her attention focused on the weapon.

Margot clawed at her scalp from behind, but her free hand was caught in the garment and slid right off. Grunting with effort, Ayliss pushed the resisting arm toward the console. Expecting to have her wrist slammed against its hard edges, Margot planted both feet and leaned back with all her weight. Schooled in using her opponent's moves to her advantage, Ayliss suddenly reversed course while still gripping the knife arm. Driving her backside into Margot, she slammed the Stepper into the hatch with a satisfying crash.

The knife fell to the floor, and the bald woman sagged to the deck.

Picking up the weapon, Ayliss backed away until she was against the far wall. Reaching up with a trembling hand, she squeezed a small disc pinned under the collar of her fatigue shirt. Wherever he was, Ewing's version of the transmitter would start emitting a low, intermittent beep. It went on for several seconds, and then the link opened from Ewing's end. He didn't speak, but Ayliss could hear the strains of a woman moaning in pleasure.

"Ewing! Answer me."

There was a pause, and then she heard the redheaded Stepper speaking with annoyance. "Chris. I think it's your mother."

"Ewing," he mumbled, and then cleared his throat. "I'm here. What is it?"

"Get back to the commo room." Ayliss held up the device she'd taken from Margot. "I've got something I need you to look at."

"Right now?"

Ayliss grinned, shaking her head. "Go ahead and finish. But get here right after that."

Lying near the door, Margot groaned. Ayliss gave

her a frosty glance, and then hefted the woman's knife. The weight seemed to speak through her palm in a dark, seductive language. It would be so easy. The hatch was locked shut, and Margot had been trespassing before attacking her. Whatever Ayliss told the Steppers would have to be accepted as the truth, because she'd be the only one describing what happened. The thought brought a warm glow to her insides, a sensation that she sorely missed.

For once, reason overrode the compulsion. If she killed Margot, there'd be an investigation that might relieve her of the codebreaker. Ayliss needed to know what the Stepper had been after, and Ewing would need time to crack into it.

"This is your lucky day, party girl." Ayliss punched a button on the console, and she flicked the blade at the hatch when it opened. "Get out of here. You come near me or Ewing again, I'll tell Mira you're a spy. That is, if I don't decide to carve you up myself."

"I'm sorry for the late notice about your canceled interview." Mira took Ayliss by the hand and led her to the couch.

"It's all right. I needed to speak with Ewing." Ayliss's concerns about meeting with Mira had vanished, driven away by the brief fight. Feeling warm and relaxed, she settled into the cushions. "I heard bits and pieces of some happy conversations on my way here. Good news?"

"You could say that." Mira's shoulders jumped minutely, and a joyous expression blossomed across her features. "A marvelous thing has happened, Ayliss. This last Step. I'm almost certain I was contacted."

Ayliss remembered her vibrant dream encounter with Lydia, and wondered for an instant if the two experiences could somehow be linked.

"That's marvelous. What was it like?"

"I'm sorry, but I learned long ago not to share the substance of my experiences with anyone. My dreams are quite unusual, and describing them can influence others." Her excitement returned. "I know in my heart that communication has been reestablished."

Ayliss gave Mira an encouraging smile. True or not, this might provide an opportunity for her and Ewing to leave the *Delphi*. Perhaps Mira would now decide that her unproductive dreams were of no value, and the timing couldn't have been better. Margot Isles might not be the only enemy aboard, and an unidentified opponent might succeed where she had failed. The redhead who'd lured Ewing away was a possibility . . . perhaps Lee should look into that. Ayliss almost gasped.

Lee Selkirk. Her lover. Killed on Quad Seven, on a mission that she'd prompted. Absent from her dreams, and seldom in her thoughts. Never eager to ponder that, Ayliss struggled to concentrate on the conversation.

"Did any of the others have a similar experience?"

"No. Unless you did."

A ruse abruptly came to mind. "I'm not sure. I saw someone very important to me, and they seemed troubled."

"Was their problem something new, or something that happened in real life?"

"Something new," she lied. "An unexpected journey."

"That could be quite significant. Who was this loved one?"

"Dom Blocker. In the dream we were in his quarters on Larkin Station, and he was having trouble packing his belongings." Ayliss took Mira's hand. "Do you think we could schedule that side trip to visit him now, so I could check up on him?"

On Larkin Station, Dom Blocker stared at what appeared to be an enormous window. Although he knew it was just a flat bulkhead, the projections of numerous exterior cameras showed what was happening beyond the barrier. The blackness of space was broken up by a series of crane-like robot arms, veined with cables and festooned with tools for the repair of small spacecraft. One such ship, a luxury shuttle owned by a wealthy ore dealer, rested in the frame of the maintenance dock while the robots worked on its communications array.

The chores being carried out didn't interest Blocker at all, but the technician standing next to him was supervising the work with great care. His name was Jerticker, and he spoke to Blocker while punching commands into a small keyboard wrapped around his forearm.

"Rittle's shuttle will come to this bay for maintenance once it drops him off at Med Wing. His examinations don't take all that long, but then he heads off to meetings with the ZQ bigwigs. Most of the time, he spends at least forty-eight hours here."

"All the work on his shuttle is done by machines? Anybody help you manage this?"

"Come on, Sarge. You ever know me to work well with others?"

"When we made you, yes."

"What I mean is, they gave me this job because it's solitary. Me and the 'bots. No pain-in-the-ass supervisors, no good-for-nothing helpers. Your man's shuttle is all mine while it's here."

"What about the cameras? Anybody monitoring the feed?"

"Station security, supposedly." Jerticker snorted. "But I can show them old footage whenever I want. I do that sometimes, when I need to break a rule to get the job done."

"Sounds familiar."

"Doesn't it, though?" More commands, and the arms raised the shuttle before going back to work. "I never got the chance to thank you for getting me out of that mess. I might have been in real trouble, if that went to court-martial."

"Might? They were going to find you guilty—which you were—and then they were gonna polymer-glue your ass to a deep-space probe and launch it. But you'd kept all our stuff working, under tough conditions. I owed you one."

"I could have beat that rap."

"Don't see how. Your partner confessed, and they'd even tracked down some of the guns you sold."

"Parts. Gun parts. All damaged. They were going to turn most of them in for scrap."

"Shh." Blocker pointed at the dock, where a tiny black rectangle had just opened on one of the stanchions. A dark insect seemed to emerge from the hatch, pushing off and gliding toward the shuttle. Floating free, it elongated into the arms, legs, and torso of a human being.

"What's she wearing? Special ops infiltration suit?"

"No," Blocker answered, concentrating on Tin as she somersaulted over one of the moving robots. "Banshee scout suit. Lighter, and more maneuverable than the combat armor. Perfect for this."

Gliding forward, Tin reached out and caught one of the handholds on a passing repair arm. She used it to slingshot her body in a different direction, and then went into an acrobatic tuck that seemed to send her spinning out of control. She slowly unwound from the ball, legs extended and pressed together, bringing her upper body around just in time to catch hold of the shuttle's aft emergency hatch.

"She's good."

"She's the best. But she's also been practicing." Blocker watched Tin go hand-over-hand up the side of the craft. She stopped at the outlet for one of the shuttle's maneuvering thrusters, and detached a small box from her belt. Pressing it to her chest with her elbow, she flipped two switches before sliding the device into the outlet.

"Nobody inspects the work, once it's done?"

"Like I told you, Sarge. I'm all alone out here. Nobody's gonna see a thing."

"Reena! May I speak with you?"

Reena Mortas cringed at the voice. She should have known that Timothy Kumar was nearby; the busy grounds of Unity Plaza turned into ghost towns when the Celestian refugee was out and about. Like Olech before her, Reena enjoyed walking around the manicured lawns and exchanging small talk with members of the enormous staff. Unfortunately, Kumar spent so much time complaining about everything, from the food to the lodgings, that Unity's personnel had learned to avoid him.

"Timothy."

The tall man wore the dark tunic that had been the mark of Horace Corlipso's personal advisers. His insistence on wearing that outfit, and on calling Reena by her first name, was all calculated to remind everyone that he had once been somebody—and would be again.

"I was horrified to hear about Gerar. What a tragedy."

"He blamed himself for Olech's disappearance. And I understand he recently lost a grandson serving in the war." Reena glanced up at the sun, wondering what Kumar wanted. As Step physicists, he and Woomer had been colleagues for many years, but she knew they'd never been close.

"I know. He mentioned the boy at least once every time we talked. Was it in combat?"

"No." Why was he lying about his relationship to Woomer? What was he after? "He was in a quartermaster assignment, on a planet far from the fighting. Apparently there was an accident."

"That must have pushed poor Gerar over the edge." They continued walking, and Renna didn't respond. "I heard he took poison."

"That's what the report said." Kumar was usually smoother than this, and Reena decided to push him. "I'm a little busy today, Timothy. Is there anything else?"

"No. No." The Step scientist refused to meet her gaze, but then recovered. "I suppose there is. I don't want to sound like some kind of ghoul, but if you're in need of someone to assume Gerar's duties, I'd be honored to help."

"That's very considerate of you. I'll keep it in mind."

"All right." The eyes flashed around some more, and then Kumar took a step backward. "I'll let you go now. Do keep me in mind."

She watched as he strode off down the walkway.

Quickly at first, but then making himself slow down. Even managing to wave at a passing staffer, a young man who frowned and then stared at Kumar's back as if having seen something inexplicable.

"Don't look so worried, Timothy." Reena spoke to the air. "I will keep you in mind."

CHAPTER 6

"His name? He's a new guy. Doesn't have a name."

The gruff answer satisfied the soldier at the gate, and he waved at someone to raise the barrier. Rolling through the opening, Hugh Leeger studied the squat blockhouse through the passenger side window. The perimeter fence was dotted with them, and they reminded him of the turrets he'd seen in paintings of ancient castles.

Leeger turned in his seat to look out through the hardened windshield. Although it was late at night, the vehicle's night vision showed him the rutted road that twisted away into the darkness. He shifted around, already itchy from the paint that had been sprayed on the Human Defense Force fatigues. This part of Celestia was home to numerous mines, and the fighting had spewed an orange dust up from the planet's insides that now clung to its surface for many miles. Camouflage uniforms were in short supply, so the troops in the region had taken to spraying their uniforms with stripes of orange paint.

Not that he was with actual soldiers. The armored mover belonged to one of the many mercenary outfits attracted by the civil war, and the man driving it looked the part. Black-and-orange camouflage adorned his uniform, armor, and rifle. A dark beard jutted out from his jaw, and a black bandanna covered his head. The latest development in combat goggles hung from his neck, atop a throat mike that looked brand-new.

"The rest of my troop is waiting for us in a laager a few miles short of the target area." The man's name was Worthel, and Leeger had sent him to Celestia weeks before. "I was a little surprised to hear you were going to pay us a visit. I thought you were trying to keep our connection secret."

"I am. That's why I'm disguised as a replacement. Nobody's supposed to know I'm here." Leeger caught the microscopic twitch at the corner of Worthel's mouth, but pretended not to have seen it. "Your last report said you'd picked up a trail."

"You could say that." The mover's six big wheels bounced slightly when they rolled over debris in the road. All around them the ground was torn up and barren. "Your boy's not very subtle. He's been working with the rebels for the last four months, openly calling himself the Misty Man. Same as the code name you told me."

They crested a small rise, and Leeger tensed up when he saw sudden motion. Four legs, steel-wool fur, short tusks, and long tails. He recognized them as a family of the local scavengers before they scattered. The parents were the size of large dogs, and several smaller ones scrambled across the road with them. One of the adults was carrying something in its mouth and, just before they disappeared into the darkness, Leeger thought he saw what was left of a human arm.

"Misty Man wasn't his code name." A face appeared in Leeger's memory, a beautiful girl he'd never met, who'd murdered the head of the Celestian government. "One of our contacts called him that, because of the way he'd appear and disappear."

"That contact wouldn't have been the bitch who started this whole thing, would it?"

"Emma. Her name was Emma." In his mind Leeger watched the slave girl die again, waving the bloody knife the Misty Man had given her. Standing on Horace Corlipso's balcony, screaming into cameras that broadcast the assassination all over the galaxy. Flying off the high perch, riddled with bullets. "And no, we had nothing to do with her."

"Doesn't matter now, does it? Anyway, our Misty Man is one of the smartest of the rebel commanders. Everybody else is busy killing and burning, but ol' Misty understands that this fight hinges on food."

"The Celestians never produced enough to feed themselves, even in the good times."

"You got that right. Mining planet, not a farming planet. And now, with this chaos, food's the top commodity. All the stocks got looted or destroyed months ago, but Misty knows the army has to feed its troops. First he got good at wrecking their supply convoys and blowing up their warehouses—even on the big bases—and then he waited until they overreacted. Brought in three times the food they'd ever need, all of it combat rations. That's when Misty and his people switched up on them. Hijacking the convoys instead of ambushing them. Cleaning out the supply dumps because there just ain't enough troops to guard it all."

"Any truth to the rumors that he's been playing Robin Hood?"

Worthel gave him a long look. "Already knew he was focusing on the food supply, huh? You got some good spies working for you."

"I did."

"Yes, Misty's not greedy. He sells some of the rations—gotta pay for the bang-bang and the boom-boom and the what-have-you-seen—but he sneaks a lot of it into the refugee camps. And every time they slip in, they leave with a fresh batch of recruits."

"What about the camps? They as bad as they say?"

"Depends on your point of view." Another look, this time a broad grin inside the beard. "Desperate people, caught in a hopeless situation. You'd be surprised what the women are willing to do for a meal."

"No. I wouldn't."

The desolation slowly took on a littered look. Burned-out vehicle frames started appearing off to the side of the track, surrounded by smashed containers and broken machinery. Here and there the shell of a small building popped up, and soon after that they entered the grounds of what had once been a thriving mine. The complex itself was underground, but the surface was still covered with miles of big-bore piping designed to move miners, raw ore, and supplies. Though broken in numerous places, the forest of dirty metal ran off in all directions.

The mover slowed to take a turn at a particularly broad pipe, this one rising vertically from the ground. Someone had taken the time to scratch a symbol of the slave revolt onto it, and Leeger studied the image as they passed. Made up of different-sized triangles so that just about anyone could replicate it, the etching formed the silhouette of Emma the slave girl, brandishing the knife she'd used on Horace Corlipso. Someone had fired several slugs at it, scoring the stout pipe and marking the girl's body.

"Ironic," Leeger muttered.

"We're here," Worthel announced, topping another rise before driving into a bowl-shaped depression. Three other movers were parked there, and several armed men in fatigues and body armor were lounging near them.

"Not much of a perimeter," Leeger observed while sliding out onto the orange dirt.

"It's a laager, like I said. We'll be heading into the danger area from here."

They crunched across the ground toward the others, who stood up in a loose group. Ten in total, after three more climbed out of the vehicles. Lots of bandannas and expensive gear, and no two weapons the same. Leeger was about to comment on the value of interchangeable ammunition when he noticed the mercenaries' too-relaxed posture. Even if they were foolish enough to believe in such a thing as a safe place, the imminent mission should have had them at least a little keyed up. Scanning the sky just above the surrounding berm, he noted the skeletal frames of broken mining platforms not far away.

Leeger braced himself for what was about to happen, but even so it felt like he'd been struck by lightning. Fire raced across his entire nervous system, and a flash exploded in his eyes. Though temporarily blinded, he felt his limp muscles giving way and dropping him to the dirt. He didn't stay there long.

"Get his weapon, search him, and then put the ties on him." Worthel gave the commands in a bored fashion, as if this was a standard practice for the group.

Several hands turned him onto his back, a lifeless arm flopping across to smack him in his nose. Leeger barely felt it, or the rough tugging as they yanked off his helmet and goggles, removed his torso armor, and went through his pockets. The stun weapon they'd used had been on a low setting, and feeling was coming back to his limbs when they tied his arms to the grill of one of the movers.

"Thought this guy was supposed to be smart." His vision finally returned, and Leeger saw Worthel and two others standing in front of him. The rest of the mercs were back a way, grinning.

"I'm sure he used to be," Worthel answered. "But this is what happens when you become a house cat. You lose all your instincts. Ain't that right, Leeger?"

Strong fingers clamped down on his jaw, lifting his head. Worthel's face was close to his own, goggles off.

"I know you're wondering what we're doing, so I'll tell you. It'll make this whole thing move faster. Ya see, we couldn't help wondering why Reena Corlipso's spy chief would pay us so much to hunt down one raggedy rebel leader like the Misty Man.

"So we contacted some of the Celestian honchos and asked if they knew anything about Misty. And boy did they ever. It seems he ran a spy ring here, before the place went to shit, and he left just before Horace took the Big Step."

The bearded face came even closer, the eyes wide in mock astonishment. "Imagine that. Misty set up the assassination, and here we are, being paid to kill him. We're just a bunch of stupid hired guns, but we do figure things out every now and then. You and Reena pulled Misty out of here, but then he got away from you. So now you *really* need him dead.

"Don't look that way, Leeger! This is actually funny. Ya see, what's left of the Celestian government already knows you did it. They just need proof." The fist swung in out of nowhere, striking Leeger in the left side of his face, stunning him again. "And what better proof than a confession? You're gonna tell us everything about the assassination, and we're gonna send that video to the high-and-mighties behind that big wall in Fortuna Aeternum.

"They're gonna pay us a fortune after seeing that video, and then we're gonna hand you over to them."

Leeger shook his head to clear it. "You need to get away from here right now."

"What? You gonna try and tell me you're not alone? That there's a rescue force circling over our heads, ready to swoop down?" The entire group laughed. "Don't even try it. We've got the latest sensing gear on these trucks, and there's nothing anywhere near us."

"That gear tell you what's under the ground?"

"Nothing down there but the rebels. *They* coming to save you?"

"No. But they are homing in on the transmitter in my boot heel. They'll want to know why it's been sending the Misty Man's recall code ever since you picked me up."

Goggles on the figures arrayed behind Worthel started swinging around uncertainly. Their leader frowned for a moment, and then gave a short laugh.

"He's bluffing. Good try, Leeger. Ace, you got the camera ready?"

"I trained the Misty Man myself. And you've been in one place for far too long. By now his people have had a good look at you from all those busted platforms. They've identified me like he told them to, and called it in. You bug out now, you might make it."

"And what are they gonna do with you? Take you and your transmitter to their hiding place?"

"If he's their leader, they'll have plenty of hiding places. And the transmitter's going to be worthless once I'm far enough underground." Leeger sighed. "It's too late, anyway."

"Watch this." Worthel spread his arms and turned in a circle. "See that? Nothing happened. Watch, I'll do it again."

He was in mid-turn when a bullet smashed into his forehead. Blood and brain matter erupted from the back of the bandanna, but he stood there for an instant longer with a look of idiotic astonishment. Leeger fought to get as close to the ground as his bonds allowed while an angry ripping sound boomed across the depression. The gunfire flashed from different points in the night, rising until it sounded like one long burst. When it stopped, all of the mercs were dead.

Orange figures raced out of the night, weaving past the vehicles. They wore no body armor and no goggles, and two of them ran straight for Leeger. The muzzle of a Scorpion rifle was inches from his cheek, its owner pressing up against the mover to limit his exposure. The other one took hold of Leeger's wrist before snipping the tie that held him on that side. A different restraint was slipped over his hand, and then his free arm was twisted up against his shoulder blades. Leeger turned as directed, the remaining tie was cut, and then his hands were firmly secured behind him.

The other figures were quickly stripping the dead of goggles, armor, weapons, and ammunition. Figures moved inside the vehicles, looting them as well, and then tongues of fire appeared as they hopped out. In moments the trucks were ablaze, but Leeger had been blindfolded by then. Stout muscles gripped his arms, and he half-ran, half-floated with them as they trotted off.

The Misty Man had turned orange. And lost an arm.

When the sack was yanked from his head, Leeger was sitting on the floor of a small underground room. Not far from the spot of his capture, the rebels had passed him down a hole that smelled of a recent explosion. He guessed they'd used a breaching charge to create the new tunnel exit, muffling the noise somehow. They'd jog-trotted him several hundred yards along a horizontal mine shaft and then lowered him through another hole, a process that had been repeated several times.

Leeger squinted, despite the low light. "Hello, Misty."

"Hugh." The former assassin leaned against the

wall, facing him. What was left of his hair was shaved almost bald. His clothes were worn, but his boots were new. "How long do we have?"

Before Leeger could respond, a voice spoke behind him. "We smashed his locator."

"He's got another one, believe me."

"We're too far down for anyone up there to get a signal."

"Exactly." The Misty Man stepped closer, wincing when he squatted. "How long do we have, Hugh?"

"Two hours. They don't pick up my signal again inside of two hours, they'll collapse this whole complex from orbit."

"The whole place?" An orange hand grabbed Leeger's shoulder, pulling him half-around. Shorn head and young eyes, but a face that was aged. "This complex goes for *miles*."

"He knows that. And he knows how far we could move him in two hours. So it's more like an hour, if that." The one-armed man looked past Leeger. "Get ready to leave."

Boots scraped against dirt, scattering rock flakes, as several figures exited through a rectangular doorway reinforced with heavy metal.

"So what is this? Some kind of cave-in shelter?"

"Yes."

"Not very well stocked."

"It never was." Misty stood, his remaining arm swinging to balance him. "And no, you haven't found our HQ."

"I doubt you have one."

"Right again. So why are you here? Why broadcast my recall code, knowing it would draw the sharks?"

"The shitheads I hired weren't getting the job done."

"And what if they had? What if they'd managed to kill me?"

"I would have paid them off. A deal's a deal."

"They were about to sell you to people who were going to torture you half to death."

"That's why I'm not crying over them."

"You knew you wouldn't get to kill me, so why come?"

"The Celestians are going to capture you eventually."

"Not likely." A head tilt toward his empty left sleeve. "And even if they did, who would believe my confession? I was never anything but a worker bee."

"And what are you now? A king?"

"You have any idea how many of these bands are running around on this planet? Thousands. I'm just a guy who came late to the party."

Adjusting to the gloom, Leeger's eyes picked out an etching on the wall, more veneration of the martyred Emma. "Do they know you got their slave saint killed?"

A heavy blow struck the back of his head, knocking him to the dirt. Apparently not all of the rebels had departed.

"Stop it," the Misty Man grunted at the shadows,

before helping Leeger back into a sitting position. "They know everything I did to that girl. And they know that's why I had to come back. Why I had to join them."

"Funny, you told me you wanted to save what was left of your network."

"Not the first time I lied to you, Hugh. Besides, I knew they were already dead." He narrowed his eyes, inspecting his captive's face. "You all right?"

"Up until this very moment, I figured you'd kill me. But now I think you won't. You want to tell me something?"

"So that's why you're here. All your eyes and ears are gone. You need your old spy to tell you who's winning."

"Yes."

"Tell Reena that the rebels will eventually triumph. They outnumbered the citizens three to one before the assassination, and now it's even worse."

"You counting all the Force soldiers that have come here to fight you?"

"Of course. Half the Celestian units mutinied as soon as they got home. They've been training the rebels ever since."

"You haven't got any of the technology Command's got. They're in orbit and in the skies, which means you're stuck underground."

"You know what all that tech, and this war with the Sims, has done for the Force? It's made them lazy. They've been fighting an enemy who can't understand a word they say for so long that they don't know how to fight someone who can. You should hear how Force units use the radios; no codes, no encryption, and we monitor every bit of it."

"They're fielding scramblers, along with other precautions."

"So what? We know their tactics, their formations, their supply systems. When we put the deserters back in their old uniforms, we can travel anywhere we like. We're not stuck underground, even though it's our biggest advantage. Their systems can't track us down here, and the few times they've come below they got massacred."

"So why aren't you winning yet?"

"That's easy. Not enough food, not even with what we've stolen."

"Is that what you want me to take back? Ask the Chairwoman to send you rations?"

"No." The Misty Man leaned forward. "Did you see any of the scavengers running loose on the surface? Look like they're half rat, half hog?"

"Yes."

"They were hunted almost to extinction during the peace, but they're starting to come back. They're incredibly hardy, and they can eat almost anything. If somebody started shipping more of them here, dropping them off in the middle of nowhere, they'd multiply quickly. They're good eating."

"Shipping them from where? Some other part of the planet?"

"They're not from here—they're native to Dalat." A crooked smile cracked the orange. "I'm sure Reena could arrange it. If she decided to make friends with the side that's going to win."

"I'll take it back to her."

"Good." He waved his one hand, and Leeger was pulled to his feet. "They'll put you back on the surface. Rest assured this part of the mine will be empty long before that. Just in case you're tempted to collapse it anyway."

The bag came down over his head, and Leeger was being led to the door when he heard Misty's voice again. "Hugh? I'm surprised Reena let you off of Earth. If she's so worried about me getting caught, that must go double for you."

"She doesn't know about this part of my trip."

"The rest of that trip must have been *really* important."

"It was. It is."

"Don't let it get in the way of our deal."

CHAPTER 7

A guttural roar filled his ears, and teeth like giant nails bit into his leg. Matted, stinking fur was in his nose, and he was off the ground again, his body twisting impossibly, being yanked to and fro, hearing only the echoing growls of the predator that was killing him.

Jander Mortas came out of this torpor slowly, the drugs releasing him with reluctance. His vision was blurred, and the room's dim light wasn't helping. His throat felt roughened, and he needed water, but first he had to know. Sliding his hands around, he felt crisp, clean sheets and then the retractable bars of a hospital bed. Remembering the jaws that had clamped down on his left leg, crushing the bone and tearing the flesh, he stopped moving. After a time he shifted his right leg, relief flooding over him when he felt his bare foot against the fabric.

His eyes had adjusted by then, and he raised his head to examine the other limb. A dark hump took shape where the leg should be, a foot tall and seeming to have no end. He tried to wriggle his toes, but felt nothing. Struggling up onto his elbows, he saw that the hump was a medical casing with a fuzzy digital readout on one side. Reaching for the bed's support bars, he found a control device and began clicking buttons on and off.

The entire bed rose, so he tried different commands. The segment under his back shifted him into a sitting position, and he saw that the blankets only covered his right leg. Mortas brought the control stick up to his eyes, and identified the icon for the light switch. Ceiling panels flickered at him, gradually illuminating the room and showing him that the hump was more like a white tunnel completely covering his left leg. He dropped back against the pillows, still not certain, but reassured nonetheless. There would be no need for an instrument that size if all he had left was a stump.

After a time he sat up again, trying to identify his surroundings. The room was small, with a sealed hatch in the bulkhead to his right. He was aboard ship somewhere. That meant he'd been evacuated, but Mortas didn't recognize the sick bay's configuration. Having visited enough wounded Orphans on various warships, the size of the compartment left him baffled. There was only one other bed, in shadow to his left, and so he raised the lighting on his side to maximum. A figure occupied the other bunk, shocking Mortas into full consciousness.

Emile Dassa was stretched out on top of the blankets, clad in an olive flight suit. He was utterly motionless, his face pale, and Mortas couldn't tell if he was breathing. The light reflected off of the inch-long scar over his right eyebrow, accenting his deathly pallor. A dreadful thought came to Mortas then, something he'd heard about during his first few days in the war zone. A small compartment near a warship's sick bay, referred to as the Waiting Room, where the most severely wounded troops were quietly tucked away to die. Orphan officers always made a point of visiting the gatekeepers of the death rooms, a particularly reviled form of shipboard life known as the Triage Techs, before a mission. Led by the senior-most officer present, they would violently impress upon the techs that no one—Orphan or not—evacuated from the coming battle went to the Waiting Room.

But in the rush of the last few missions, and the confusion that had brought the brigade to this one, there had been no time to send that message.

"Sir?" Mortas tried to call out, but his vocal cords were too strained. Swallowing hard, he tried again. "Sir? Captain Dassa? *Emile!*"

The figure on the bed jerked into a sitting position, hands gripping the support bars. Dassa's eyes blinked rapidly in the light, and then he saw Mortas. "Oh come on, Jan. That was the first real sleep I've had in a week."

Dassa twisted on the covers and slid to the deck. "How's the leg feeling?"

"Where are we?"

"On the flagship. This is the admiral's personal sick bay room." Dassa smirked. "Like anything bad would ever happen to a ship jock."

Memories flooded back. The charge of the wolves, the rockets slamming down, the beasts swarming over his platoon.

"Where are my guys, sir?"

"The whole brigade's been taken back up from the surface. Sam put just enough troops down there to make it interesting, so the mech guys are mopping up now. Several of your people got chewed like you did, but we were lucky—nobody died. You should see Sergeant Mecklinger's hands; they're three times their normal size. One of the wolves got him by the body armor, and he was punching it when we shot it off of him. Catalano and his machine gun team got pretty beat up too, but nothing permanent."

Dassa let out a short grunt of amusement. "Your man Prevost got hit in the head with a flying rock during the final bombardment, split his helmet in half. You should have heard him. 'Don't take me to the sick bay! I was one of those triage assholes! They'll *kill* me up there!'"

Relieved by the light casualty figures, Mortas started to laugh. He remembered meeting Prevost in a receiving bay flooded with the wounded from the disastrous battle on Fractus. Hating the job of categorizing the stricken soldiers, Prevost had volunteered for the Orphans despite having seen their heavy losses.

"Anybody else hurt, sir?"

"A few bites here and there, but nothing to take them off duty status. I've seen a lot of strange things out here, Jan, but an army of giant wolves beats 'em all."

"You were there at the end. How'd you get to us so fast?"

Dassa gave him an embarrassed grin. "You really do owe me for this one, Jan. The mech battalion commander wouldn't give me even one APC to come help you, but I'd made friends with their scout platoon leader. He doesn't like all that rules 'n' regulations nonsense the Tratians pull, and he'd already asked me about becoming an Orphan.

"While I was trying to get the rockets cleared for you, the scouts rolled up to the field HQ. I ran out there and told their lieutenant that he was supposed to help me rescue you. I said his colonel ordered it." Dassa stopped, his lips pressing together. "He could have called to confirm that, but he just told me to hop in. Those scouts saved your platoon."

"I remember seeing the gunfire, but not knowing what it was."

"Yeah, well you had your hands full . . . or that wolf had its mouth full, I guess. Anyway, one of the scouts' machine guns took that beast off of you."

Dassa gently placed a hand on the white tunnel covering Mortas's leg. "God you were a mess. Blood everywhere, meat torn to the bone. We almost couldn't get a tourniquet on you."

They both went silent, giving Mortas time to wonder just why Dassa had been asleep in the sick bay instead of with B Company. "You in trouble, Emile?"

"Not really. Colonel Watt had to relieve me of my command, but that's just for show. We're transferring that scout lieutenant to the brigade, so somebody had to take the hit. It's not a permanent demotion, especially where we're going."

"Celestia?"

"Can't keep dodging it. Besides, anything's better than being thrown into these last-minute jobs."

Mortas pressed his palms against the sheets, trying to shift his body around. The left leg didn't budge at all.

"Oh, cut that out, will you? You won't be able to walk for days, and then you'll need a brace. So forget humping a ruck, or running under a load. You're not goin' with us."

"I'm an Orphan. I go with the brigade."

"Well that's where you're wrong, Jan. Even if you weren't wounded, you wouldn't be going. Colonel Watt's coming by to brief you himself—he wouldn't tell me what it's about. Apparently you're being sent on some kind of secret mission. Top priority orders, straight from the Chairwoman's office."

"Fuck orders, and fuck the Chairwoman."

"Odd choice of words, considering she was married to your father."

"My father's dead, and even when he was running this show I didn't let him jerk me around."

"Don't get it, do you? I've seen these kinds of orders before. You're going." Dassa walked past the bed, headed for the hatch. He stopped before opening it, regarding Mortas with affection. "You're the best platoon leader I've got, Jan. Go take care of whatever they want you to do, and then come back to us. Okay?"

"That scout lieutenant who saved my people? How about you give him my platoon until I get back?"

"Way ahead of you."

"I had the honor of meeting your father once." The admiral's personal physician had gray hair and a kindly manner. "An extraordinary mind. I know it's been some time, but I still hold out some hope that he'll be found alive."

"Thank you, sir." Jander was sitting up, his leg still encased in the tunnel, but feeling much better after a full meal. "I was in the zone when he disappeared, so I've only heard what's been officially released."

"Well that's just wrong. Command goes a little overboard, with their secrecy fetish." They exchanged conspiratorial grins, and the doctor gently rapped on the leg casing. "Continuing in that vein, I'm being told you won't be my patient much longer—and nothing else. Not that it matters; you're already on the way to recovery. Hopefully you'll get some home leave, and maybe even some hot chow."

"Sir?"

"Just a little joke. When you were coming out of anesthesia, you kept asking us where the hot chow was."

"Oh."

The hatch opened, and the stocky figure of Colonel Watt entered. His dark skin seemed to have pulled tighter across his face during the Orphans' nonstop deployments, but he was smiling just the same. A tall captain followed him through the hatch, and Mortas recognized the insignia of the Banshees on her fatigues.

"I wanted to thank you for taking care of Lieutenant Mortas, Doctor." Watt shook the older man's hand. "I kept telling him not to play with the local animals, but he just wouldn't listen."

"He's going to be just fine, Colonel. I'll let you talk." The hatch sealed behind him.

"Hello, Jan." The words and the hand were warm. "You did a fine job out there. Wolves. Talk about a surprise."

"The men performed very well, sir. They all stayed cool. That's why we were able to hold out."

Watt squeezed his shoulder, and turned to the captain. "I understand the two of you have met."

The Banshee wore no nametag, so Mortas looked her over. Tall, fit, strawberry blond hair cut short, brown eyes, and a thumb-sized burn scar on her right cheek. Though the skin there formed a shallow depression, the vertical mark stood out.

"I don't think I've had the pleasure, sir."

"Sure you have." The Banshee stepped up. "He doesn't want to admit this, but he was stark naked and I was wearing a mask."

The voice was familiar, and it clicked into place alongside the doctor's comment about hot chow. Images rose up with the memories. Arriving at Glory Main on the stolen Sim shuttle, starving, injured, amazed to be alive. Greeted by a section of Banshees, anonymous inside the armored fighting suits, all commanded by a tough captain. Mortas squinted in wonder. "Captain Varick?"

"Alive and kicking." Her eyes dropped to his leg casing. "You, on the other hand, only seem to be alive."

"I'm doing better than the thing that tried to bite my leg off."

"You should have seen him when he got to Glory Main, sir." Varick smiled at Watt. "Looked like he'd been on a month-long survival trek. Bruises, burn marks, dressed in rags. Quite a sight."

"I've seen him in worse condition. Fractus was his first battle."

"I heard about that, sir." Varick turned to Mortas. "I almost forgot to ask—did you get that knife I sent you? The one you refused to give up at Glory Main?"

"Yes, ma'am. Been carrying it ever since, although I'm not sure where it is now."

"We've got all your stuff, Jan." Watt spoke. "It'll be going with you."

"Where *am* I going, sir?"

"I don't know—but Captain Varick does." Although Watt tried to hide it, Mortas sensed his annoyance. "In fact, this is the last time we'll talk until you're done with . . . whatever this is."

"Captain Dassa said the brigade's going to Celestia."

"It was bound to happen. Don't worry about us."

"Is Emile in trouble, sir? For rescuing us?"

"The day I let an Orphan get punished for coming to the aid of another Orphan, I'm turning in my boots. Don't worry about us at all, Jan. Take care of that leg."

"Yes, sir."

"Captain?" Watt's tone took on an edge.

"Yes, sir."

"I'm holding you personally responsible for whatever happens to this man. That's the price of not telling me where he's going."

"Understood, sir. For the record, I was sworn to secrecy."

"I know that." Watt squeezed Jander's shoulder one more time. "This is one fine officer. I expect to get him back."

"**S**o, Captain. Where are you taking me?"

"I'm not *taking* you anywhere, Lieutenant. And since you and I are the sum total of this expedition, how about we drop the ranks? My name's Erica."

"My name's Jander. People call me Jan."

"Jan, you and I are under orders to travel to Roanum."

"The place where I did that survival trek."

"Yes."

"Why? There was nothing there but rocks and sand and giant snake-things in the water."

"Your father named the planet after that mapmaker who was with you."

"Gorman. Roan Gorman. He was a pacifist. Holy Whisper."

"Yes. The Whisper established a small station there, shortly after our people destroyed the Sim colony."

"So we're on some kind of goodwill mission?"

"Not really. A couple of weeks ago, a stranger walked right out of the wilderness and into the Whisper camp. The visitor appeared to be a female human, but she told them straightaway that she isn't human at all. She asked to speak to you."

A high-octane cocktail of anger, resentment, and fear surged through Mortas. "No."

"I'm afraid so."

Varick took out a large handheld that Mortas knew was highly encrypted. She punched a long sequence of code into it while he shifted around, unable to control the torrent of emotions. When the device let her in, Varick held the screen so he could see it.

"Take a good look. The image will be completely deleted in ten seconds."

The woman in the photo had short brown hair, and even in the familiar flight suit she was obviously athletic. She stood with her back to a pale wall, looking into the camera with blue eyes and a blank expression.

"Recognize her?" Varick asked. "I sure do."

"It's Amelia Trent's face, but it's not her." He remembered watching that visage dissolving under powerful chemicals, just before it exploded into thousands of fluttering specks. "It's the alien."

CHAPTER 8

"I'm surprised that your young man Lee hasn't appeared in any of your dreams, Ayliss." Mira Teel settled deeper into her chair. Steam rose from a mug on the table next to her, and she had a multicolored shawl around her shoulders. "He was taken from you so suddenly, and under such trying circumstances."

Ayliss pretended to consider the question. They were approaching Larkin Station after coming out of their most recent Step voyage, and she didn't want to reveal anything that she hadn't already shared. "I've wondered about that myself. But these communications are rather unpredictable, aren't they?"

"That's one way of putting it." Mira gave her a pleasant smile. Her latest Step experiences had restored the High Stepper's calm, and Ayliss found she liked the woman much better this way. "So difficult to know what's merely a drug-induced hallucination, and what's a communication."

"How *do* you know?"

"It's like anything of value, dear. Like choosing a lover, or a home. You simply know. Not being able to explain it is one of its surest signs."

"Is the opposite true? I've never felt anything special about my dreams, in or out of the Step. It's why I've always doubted I was sensitive in the way you and your people are."

"Oh, that's just not true." Mira shook her head while reaching for the mug. "Back at Unity, while we were shaping Olech's plan, you shared a couple of marvelously vivid encounters with us. Your father is highly sensitive, and you are too."

Ayliss felt blood rising in her face. This was exactly the kind of slip she'd meant to avoid. Mira didn't sound irked by the inconsistency, but that might be an act.

"You always speak of my father in the present. Have you detected anything that suggests he may still be alive somewhere?"

"I don't want to prejudice your experiences, so I'm not going to share too many specifics about my own dreams. No, I haven't felt anything that suggested his influence or his presence. But it's the timing that intrigues me. The entities broke contact with us completely, all across the void, when your father disappeared. I can't believe they would have done that if he'd simply died in a mechanical mishap. It wouldn't make any sense."

"It's been months. Even if he was somehow kept in stasis, I can't see how he might still be alive."

"Keep your mind—and your heart—open, Ayliss. Anything sophisticated enough to create the Step, pass it to humanity, and then use it to commune with our psyches can't be understood in normal terms. In giving us the Step, they made it possible for us to do something we simply could not. I choose to believe they did something similar for your father."

"I hope so." She let that linger before moving on. "I'd like to stay overnight at Larkin once we get there. Dom Blocker is one of my oldest friends, and his recurring presence in my dreams has disturbed me."

"Of course you can stay over. Many of our people have asked to leave the ship for a bit. Stretch their legs, pick up some personal items, get a meal not prepared in a ship galley. As for your friend Blocker, don't be surprised if he's just fine. The entities sometimes use the form of a non-threatening agent to communicate. He'll probably scoff at your concern."

"Again, I hope so."

"Tell me more about this last dream. You encountered your brother, Jander."

"Yes, but we didn't converse much that I can recall. We were children again, very young, playing on a beach where the family used to vacation. No one else was there, and it was a beautiful summer day. He ran up and handed me a shell, or a stone."

"Really?" The word was almost inaudible, and Ayliss felt she'd tripped over something important. "Which was it?"

"A shell." She lied. In reality, or the dream's reality, it had been another one of the bracelet stones given to her by Olech. "Small, pink, curled around its center."

"Oh."

The ship's intercom beeped once, and then an automated voice entered the room. "Docking at Larkin Station. All personnel authorized to leave the ship, please report to Briefing Room Three."

Ayliss stood up, trying to hide her eagerness. "I believe that applies to me."

"It does indeed. You've been extremely helpful, whether you believe it or not. Go on—have some fun."

"Thank you." She walked toward the hatch.

"Ayliss."

"Yes?"

"How did your dream end? What happened after your brother gave you the shell?"

"The strangest thing," she replied, no longer lying. "This giant dog appeared, obviously rabid, and it attacked him."

"That's highly unusual, for your dreams."

"Jan's been in the war zone for over a year now, one dangerous job after another. I'm much more concerned about what might happen to him in reality."

"I see. What did the dog do to him?"

"It knocked him down, and was biting one of his legs when the dream ended."

"Oh my." Tin lightly clapped her hands. "Steak and eggs? If I'd known you served this kind of food, I would have come by your room sooner."

Blocker set one of the plates in front of her. The dining surface and its bench seats retracted into the wall when not in use, as did the compartment's bed. He'd turned up the music so they could talk in private.

"Special meal for a special occasion."

"Sergeant Blocker. Are you seducing me?"

"Fueling you, actually. Rittle arrived an hour ago. He's not far from here, in the Zone Quest part of Med Wing. His shuttle will be at the repair dock in two hours."

"Good." Tin breathed out the word like a prayer, and then started cutting the steak. "I've been waiting a long time for this."

"We both have."

"You weren't on Quad Seven while that Tratian brigade was still there. Rittle took every opportunity to dump on us while that gang was backing him up." She began to chew, and her eyes closed in pleasure. "When the Tratians started pulling out, we stole half of everything they had, just out of spite."

"Rittle mentioned that to Ayliss. Part of the long list of crimes you and the other vets allegedly committed."

"Crimes." Tin shook her head. "He murdered half my squad from the war. Lola and the girls. I'm going to be thinking of them while I'm stuffing the bomb into that port."

"Concentrate on the job." Blocker let an edge enter his voice. "We'll drink a toast to everyone who died on Quad Seven, once we get the news that Rittle's shuttle blew up."

"You know I'm rock solid during the action." Tin gave him a playful smile. "But when it's done, when that bastard is dead, you and me are gonna party."

Blocker's eyes widened, and he slowly lowered his fork.

Tin waved a hand, giggling. "Hey, I just meant we were going to close down the bar, is all. You're under no obligation beyond that, Sarge."

"Looks like the party's canceled." Blocker pointed behind her, and Tin turned to look at the wall monitor. "In fact, our whole operation's blown."

The large screen hung near the ceiling, and it showed the passageway right outside. Two figures were walking straight for the entrance to Blocker's cabin, and Tin recognized them both.

"You gotta be shitting me!" she hissed, tossing her fork onto the table and shoving her plate away. Blocker was already up, and he opened the hatch before the guests could announce their presence.

"Big Bear." Ayliss looked at him with her head tilted in mock anger. "See what happens when you don't write?"

"Get in here. Now." Blocker pulled her through

the entrance, and a bewildered Ewing followed. He closed the hatch, securing it for good measure.

"Tin!" Ayliss called out, striding across the small room to embrace the Banshee. The smaller woman was standing by then, but her icy glare stopped Ayliss in her tracks. She turned to look at Blocker, confusion turning to annoyance. "What's going on?"

"What's going on, is you just wrecked something we've been working on for months. Why are you here?"

"I dunno, maybe I wanted to visit a lifelong friend who's recuperating from a scrape we all fought in." Ayliss turned resentful eyes toward Tin, and then back to Blocker. "And since he kept telling me he wasn't getting any better, I had to convince the High Stepper to swing by here."

"That's nice, but you have to leave. Right now."

Ewing put a hand on Blocker's arm. "Hey, lighten up a little there, Sarge. We've got some news. ZQ had a spy on the *Delphi*, and she tried to break into my databank."

"Imagine that."

Ayliss stepped directly in front of Blocker. "Tell me what's going on, Bear."

"Right now, in this very wing, our good friend Rittle is getting the mandatory six-month physical required of every ZQ deep-space station manager."

"Here? No. They're required to leave the war zone for that."

"Yeah, well Rittle's been out here so long that he earned a dispensation. Almost nobody knows about it, but my friends here tipped me off. Tin and I had it all arranged, a bomb that would go off once his shuttle hit cruising speed."

"So what's the problem? We can help. You have to let us help."

"Help? You're not supposed to be anywhere near here! Zone Quest knows what Rittle tried to do to us on Quad Seven. If he has an accident at a station you just happened to be visiting, it's not gonna take them long to put it all together."

"Oh, like they wouldn't find out two of the survivors have been here for months?"

"No," Tin barked. "No they wouldn't. And you know why? Because Blocker and me, we're just little people to these corporate types. They lost track of us as soon as the shooting stopped. But you . . . why do you think we were keeping this from you?"

"You can still do it." Ayliss spoke quickly now. "Ewing and I will get back to the ship. It'll be like we were never here. You said the bomb wouldn't go off until Rittle was well clear of this place."

"You're already on record as being here." Blocker's voice softened. "I'm sorry, Ayliss. We'll get him some other time."

"When? You said it yourself, he never leaves the war zone. Ewing's been tracking the Guests' communications for months, and he says it's impossible to figure out where that rat is going to be ahead of time. We do it now."

"It's all right. You have to know when to cancel a mission."

"After what he did?" Her voice rose, and her cheeks began to tremble. "He hired a pirate to kill us all. He poisoned me. *He killed Lee!*"

Blocker wrapped his arms around her, pressing his chin against the top of her head while she struggled. "You're right, Little Bear. He tried to kill us all, and he succeeded with too many of us. He is not going to get a pass for that. I promise."

Ayliss pushed free, but didn't step away. "Promise you'll let me in on it."

Blocker inhaled as if to continue the argument, but Tin saved him. "Dom, we have to get these two back to their ship. Rittle's security people are going to find out they're here."

"Right. We'll take the morgue route, less chance of running into anybody." Ayliss was still staring up at him, waiting, so Blocker relented. "I'll try. That's the best I can do."

Tin passed into the corridor. A moment later she waved at them from the monitor, and Blocker motioned Ayliss and Ewing to walk ahead of him. The passageway was almost empty, and after a couple of turns they arrived at an unmarked hatch. Tin pressed a transparent disc to the card reader, and the door slid inward with a loud metallic clack.

The unadorned passageway beyond the entrance was tube-shaped and narrow, with exposed cables running down its length.

"What is this?" Ewing asked as they approached a T-shaped intersection.

"It's the tunnel they use for taking bodies to the morgue," Tin answered without looking back. "Not a lot of fatalities here, but—"

She didn't get to finish, because a different quartet appeared in front of them. The new group was also moving fast, and came to a staggered halt just yards away. Two uniformed Zone Quest security men were in front, and a surprised Vroma Rittle and a seething Margot Isles walked behind them. Rittle wore the one-piece suit that he'd favored on Quad Seven, and Margot had exchanged her robes for a dark coverall.

The two groups stood frozen until Rittle spoke to Margot. "You were right. She is trying to kill me."

The security men were both large, but Ayliss's eyes were fastened on the pistols hanging from their belts. Rittle's words sent their hands drifting toward the weapons.

"No need for that." Blocker's tone was calm, conciliatory. He stepped up next to Tin, who had already turned sideways and bent her knees in preparation for a fight. "This is just a misunderstanding. We're going to go back the way we came. How about you do likewise?"

Rittle locked eyes with Ayliss, and she watched as his earlier surprise slipped away. Slightly overweight and accustomed to being in charge, he gave her a knowing grin. "It's all right, boys. Let 'em go. They're nothing."

"You *mother*fucker!" The syllables exploded from Ayliss as she charged, her hands reaching out. She was past the guards before they had a chance to react, and then it was all swirling action. Rittle swung just as Ayliss came in range, a beefy punch that crashed into her left ear. The blow carried her into the metal to her right, stunning her.

Grabbing the loose cables for support, Ayliss almost collapsed. She turned in place, her tilted field of vision taking it all in. Blocker wrapping up a security man's gun arm, his huge hand grabbing his opponent's face and slamming his head against the wall. Tin throwing a series of knife hands at the other guard's eyes, causing him to raise his arms, and then kicking him in the crotch.

Hands locked onto Ayliss's throat, and she expected to see Rittle again, but it was Margot, her face stamped with insane fury. She felt her breath instantly choked off, marveling at the other woman's strength, but then her own anger returned. Releasing the cables, she shot her arms up between Margot's, thumbs extended, digging straight for the eyes. She didn't connect, but the move broke the hold as Margot jumped back.

Howling, Ayliss lowered her shoulder and barreled into the other woman, driving her across the tube. Just before they reached the far bulkhead, Ayliss tried to straighten up while gripping Margot's torso. The motion lifted the spy off the deck, and Ayliss's driving legs whipped the bald head toward the waiting metal. The Stepper smashed into the wall with a crash that echoed, and her body went limp.

Ayliss spun, desperate to see where Rittle had gone. Both security men were down, and Tin and Blocker had their weapons, but the station manager was nowhere in sight. A choked cry came from behind her, and she rushed out into the connecting passageway.

"You son of a bitch! You rotten, smug son of a bitch." Ewing was breathing heavily, barely able to get the words out. Rittle was stretched out on the plating, with the smaller man straddling him. "What you did to us out there. Fuck you, man. *Fuck* you."

Blood flowed over the decking, where the knife no one knew Ewing carried had cut Rittle's throat.

"**G**et in here. Quick." Chief Scalpo was waiting at the exam room door when the four emergency cases ran in. Blocker, Tin, and Ayliss were grouped tightly around Ewing, to hide the red stains across the front of his flight suit. The physician's assistant shut and bolted the hatch behind them. "Is anyone hurt?"

"I told you that when I called. The injuries were all on their side."

"Okay, get the bloody clothes off of him, and put them down the burn chute." Scalpo activated one of the room's cabinets, and brought out a hospital gown in a sealed package. He handed several sterile wipes to Tin. "Clean him up, and get him into that johnny."

"I'm not in a coma, Chief." Ewing's tone was low, almost apologetic. "You can talk to me."

"No time, son." Scalpo sat, and began punching buttons on the console. "I already called Charon. He'll be here in a few."

"Charon?" Ayliss asked, helping Ewing out of his clothes. "Isn't that the boatman on the River Styx?"

"None other. It's just his nickname, but it's appropriate. He's the Force recruiter here." Chief turned in his seat. "It's very nice to meet you, Miss Mortas. Wish it was under different circumstances. Dom speaks very highly of you."

The console beeped once, and Chief returned to the screen. His fingers danced over the keys. "Blocker, Dominic. Physically cleared for active service."

"What's he doing?" Ayliss gave Blocker a look of reproach. "You're signing up again?"

"It was just a precaution, in case the bomb got tracked back to us. We're on the war side of the CHOP Line—if you reach the recruiter before the cops get you, there's nothing they can do."

Another beep prompted more typing, and Chief looked up at Tin. "You want me to do this?"

"Not a lot of choice. We just killed at least three people."

"I didn't hear that." Chief finished the entry. "Physically cleared for active service."

Ewing's bare chest and neck were now clean, and Ayliss helped him into the medical drapery. Wearing shorts, boots, and socks, he looked ridiculous in the medical garment. Ayliss finished tying the back shut while Chief began the examination.

"Raise your hands over your head. Excellent. Bend over and touch the floor. Wonderful."

"He was already in, Chief. He's the commo guy I mentioned," Blocker intoned.

"Oh, him." Chief reached out, prying one of Ewing's eyes open. "Ongoing substance abuse indicated. Not serious enough for disqualification."

He went back to his seat, and a low buzzing sound entered the exam room. Blocker moved to the hatch and activated the viewer. A tall, thin man in a Human Defense Force uniform waved at him, and he unlocked the hatch.

"Hello, everyone." The recruiter seemed pleased. "I understand we're all feeling patriotic today."

"Charon, we need to do this quickly." Chief finished updating Ewing's record, and then called up a blank medical form. "These four are about to be unjustly accused of having murdered Vroma Rittle and two others."

"Maybe three," Ayliss interjected. "I don't think I killed her, but there was no time to check."

"Rittle? Good riddance." Charon looked them over. "As soon as I swear them in, they belong to the Force. Medicals all up to date?"

"Sergeant Blocker, Corporal Tin, and Specialist Ewing are all recently discharged veterans. They're all cleared for active service. Sergeant Blocker has served two consecutive tours in the war zone, and Corporal Tin is a Banshee with extensive combat experience." Chief's fingers flew over the keyboard. "The last one is Ayliss Mortas."

"I recognized her. It's a selfless thing you're doing here, Miss Mortas."

"What *am* I doing here?"

"You're enlisting in the Human Defense Force. Just like your father."

Chief finished the entry. "She's healthy as an ox; qualified for all levels of service. Dom, you're getting a little old for this stuff. Want me to put you on limited duty of some kind, get you a staff job somewhere?"

Ayliss turned pained eyes in his direction, and Blocker winked at her. "Get us all to Special Operations Command, and my pals will take it from there. Ewing's a commo ace, so he and I will get assigned to Banshee support."

"I'm re-upping?" Ewing fingered the johnny. "Dressed like this?"

"That's nothing. I've sworn in recruits who were wearing handcuffs, and even one in a straitjacket." Charon chuckled. "They gave him back."

Blocker continued. "Tin's obviously going back to the Banshees."

"And me as well?" Ayliss tried to keep the hope out of her voice.

"A direct enlistment to the Banshees requires a sponsor," Charon intoned. "A Banshee veteran who can speak for the applicant."

Ayliss stepped in front of Tin, her eyes bright with the memory of fighting beside her on Quad Seven. "How about it? Speak for me?"

"Glad to." The words were leaden, as was the fist that Tin drove straight into Ayliss's abdomen. The blonde woman dropped to the floor, gasping for the breath that refused to come.

Tin squatted, growling. "You join the Banshees, you're not in charge of *anything* anymore. Not even your life. Back in the tunnel, you broke ranks. Dom was calling the play, and you decided to do your own thing. You will not do that again. Right?"

Ayliss grunted in pain, her arms wrapped around her midsection.

"Good. You're going to do everything you're told, and nothing you're not told. As your sponsor, I'll hear about everything you do, good and bad. You step out of line at any point, I will come to wherever you are, and beat your bony ass bloody. We have a deal?"

Ayliss's diaphragm finally loosened, the pain ebbing. "Yes."

Tin helped her up, and then hugged her. "Welcome, Ayliss."

Strength slowly came back to her arms, and Ayliss returned the embrace. Remembering the Banshee pre-battle ritual, she whispered, "I will die for you, Tin."

"Not for me. You're going to die for your squad." The Banshee held her at arm's length, smiling. "Private Mortas."

CHAPTER 9

"Hugh." Jander Mortas looked up from a couch in what had once been his father's traveling office. "You look tired."

Leeger pointed at Mortas's left leg, propped up on the cushions. "At least I can still walk."

"I can walk fine, with the brace. Just takes me a long time to get anywhere. Who gave you the bruises?"

"Don't ask." Leeger's right hand unconsciously touched the fading welts on his cheek as he walked toward Erica. "Captain Varick, I'm Hugh Leeger."

"It's a pleasure to meet you." Both Varick and Mortas wore the gray fatigues that were the traveling uniforms of Force officers, matching the gray tunic of Mortas family security now worn by Leeger. "We were beginning to wonder what the holdup was."

"It's not a holdup." Leeger moved over the gold

carpet, careful not to tread on the seal of the Chairman of the Emergency Senate. Olech Mortas's desk stood at the end of the small, tubular compartment. Leeger sat down and activated the monitors on the curved walls. "The alien left the Whisper settlement shortly after our agent finished interviewing her. She provided a radio frequency you'll use to notify her once you're in place. We don't know where she went out there, or how long it might take for her to come back. So we've got time to plan this out."

The screens brightened into the photo taken by the Holy Whisper colonists on Roanum. Jander scowled at the face that he knew was an imitation of Captain Amelia Trent.

"We code-named her 'jogger' because Trent was a long-distance runner. Our visitor appeared at the settlement out of nowhere, and immediately identified herself as a non-human. As pacifists and explorers, the HWs didn't hesitate to invite her inside. Of course they already knew about your experience with the first shape-shifter, so they asked her a few questions. She consented to having her picture taken, after explaining why she dropped by."

"Why'd she pick a Whisper colony?" Varick asked. "Why not go straight to a Force unit?"

"Apparently this version of Amelia Trent knows what happened to the last version. According to the HWs, she refers to the immolation of the original alien as if it happened to her personally. She consented to a manual scan, just to prove she is what she says she is, and then asked to speak to Jan."

"It's not a she, Hugh. Or a her. It's an *it*." Mortas spoke slowly. "It tortured the real Amelia Trent to death, just to pry open her psyche so it could impersonate her. Then it pretended to be one of us while we walked and starved and got hunted by giant snakes and then the Sims. You can't trust it."

"All right." Leeger studied Jander for a long moment, as if seeing him for the first time. "You've brought me to my next point. We already know that it has some capacity for entering the human mind. Perhaps it can read minds, and maybe even control them."

"That thing downloaded its thoughts and experiences into my head while it was being scorched in its decon tube." Mortas kept his eyes on the monitor facing him. "But until that moment, I never had the feeling that it was controlling my actions or even understanding what I was thinking. Truth to tell, I didn't like her—it—at all when we first met. I should have listened to my instincts."

"The Chairwoman decided to send a third party to conduct an initial interview. Because we don't know its capabilities, it couldn't be anyone privy to top-level secrets." Leeger continued. "Fortunately, we have good connections with the Brodan Analytics Guild. Under certain circumstances they will provide a certified practitioner to do this kind of job.

The analyst conducts the requested research—in this case, the requested interview—and then remains incommunicado for a specified time. Handsomely rewarded, of course."

"I thought the Guild was sworn to secrecy anyway," Mortas offered. The Brodans were the gold standard for the collection and analysis of information.

"That's true, but a lot of powerful organizations are on the lookout for the alien's reappearance—as you well know. If the wrong corporation, or the wrong government, gained control of a shapeshifting alien that can communicate with the Sims, who knows what might happen? We haven't been taking any chances with this."

"So how are you keeping the analyst under wraps—did you make him join the Force?" Varick chuckled at her own joke.

"He's having the time of his life on a resort vessel in Earth space. Supervised by our people, of course, but apparently he's mixing well with the other vacationers."

"You sent him on a singles cruise."

"From what I'm being told, he really needed it. When we release him, he's probably going straight to a hospital for exhaustion."

Even Mortas joined in the laughter. When it subsided, Leeger resumed the briefing.

"Despite all that, we have to assume that the news

will get out. The colonists were required to send word to Pacifica, notifying the Holy Whisper Elders of their visitor. The HWs are good at keeping secrets, but every outfit's got its spies." Leeger stopped, and looked at Jander. "I'm assuming you've heard the latest news about Ayliss."

"How could we not? It's been all over the Bounce. In a million years I never would have thought she'd enlist."

"There's a little more to it than that."

"**L**ook at it this way." Erica spoke once Leeger had departed. "At least your sister didn't actually kill anybody. That Step Worshiper is going to make a full recovery."

"Margot Isles. I remember her from a couple of state functions before I went to university. Family of climbers." Mortas almost mumbled the words, lost in thought. "I knew Ayliss fought on Quad Seven, and that she'd done well. I didn't know she'd developed a taste for it."

"It's been my experience that you don't develop that. You've got it, or you don't."

"She always had this deep core of anger. Growing up, she hated my father."

"If it's any consolation, she had good reason to hate this Rittle character. I've had my own brushes with the Guests, and they're a bunch of real assholes.

It's not clear who started that fight, so if she survives her hitch with the Banshees, she's likely to come out free and clear."

"You know something? One reason I came to the war was to get away from all the family political bullshit. And I did it, too. Out there, with my troops, it didn't matter who my father was. God I wish I was with my platoon right now." Mortas absently rubbed the brace that ran the length of his leg. "How about you? Missing your company?"

"My company? I haven't led troops since I first met you. I did command a Banshee company once—best job I ever had—but that ended two years ago. I got pulled up into high-level staff work right after Twelfth Corps abandoned Glory Main, and I haven't been on an operation since."

"What were you doing there, anyway? Seemed like a waste of good combat vets, pulling guard duty at a corps HQ."

"The Banshees you saw were a reinforced platoon that I'd been leading for a few months. Bit of an emergency reaction force. They were some really good fighters, so we kept getting mission after mission."

"I know how that feels."

"We got an offer to stop off at a nice cushy headquarters to rest, refit, get some real chow, and like an idiot I said yes. Those Glory Corps staff pukes turned us into their little palace guard."

"I'm sorry to hear that." Mortas remembered the words of his first platoon sergeant, as the man lay dying at the end of the disaster on Fractus. He'd asked Mortas to get the surviving members of the platoon safe jobs protecting his father, and it had sounded like a good idea at the time. "But you did the right thing, trying to get your people a break."

"I suppose that's true. I'd been in the war for five years by then. Sometimes I wonder if I was trying to get myself a rest." Varick gave a short laugh. "But you know Command; give 'em a chance, and they'll do you in. I hated that staff job, but they wouldn't let me transfer. That's one of the reasons I'm here. They said they had a mission for me, and without hearing one word more I said yes."

"I thought you'd like to see this." Hugh Leeger waved Mortas over to one of the shuttle's viewing portholes. The vessel had passed into Roanum's atmosphere, and was cruising far above its orange-and-red surface.

Jander looked down, shocked at the mix of emotions the vista evoked. It had been nighttime when he'd escaped the planet with the dying Gorman and the alien impersonating Trent. He'd never seen it from the sky, but he remembered the cruel miles they'd walked and crawled. Rocky mountain ranges, brown against the orange, twisted their way across the plains. Fine traceries appeared here and there in the open, reminding him of the deep ravines they'd used to travel unseen. The sides of one ridgeline showed the yellow grass that had led them to water, and just beyond the escarpment he saw a meandering river.

"You should have seen it, the first time one of the snakes tried to eat us." Mortas placed a palm against the bulkhead and leaned out over the porthole, shifting the weight off his injured leg. "Cranther, the Spartacan Scout, had warned us that predators stake out the water sources. He was sticking a long pole out into the flow, filling this plastic box, when the thing jumped right at us. All teeth and muscle, it was the size of your leg—and that was one of the small ones."

"The HWs say those things are in all the waterways. They don't like to mess with the local ecology any more than they have to, so they've built barriers into the rivers closest to their settlement."

"They'd be crazy to trust those. Once they sensed food in the area, more and more of them converged on the spot. Some of them were twenty feet long." Mortas felt his jaw clenching, and looked for a distraction. An unnatural outline on the planet surface caught his eye. "No. Is that the spacedrome?"

A long, thin rectangle stood out from the surrounding plain. The main airstrip, it was pocked by hundreds of brown craters. Smaller rectangles appeared in a cluster at one end, also riddled with blast holes. These were the outlines of the burned-out warehouses and hangars of the spacedrome that had supported the Sim colony. One of the wrecked structures, close to the runway, appeared to have suffered almost no rocket strikes when the HDF had destroyed the place.

"See that there? I blew that entire warehouse apart with a tank round. It must have been loaded with explosives. I was just trying to create a diversion, and I turned the whole place into splinters." The combat veteran inside him laughed at the memory of the destruction, but then stopped. "That blast was probably what killed Gorman. He'd been badly injured earlier, but he and the alien were slipping across the runway when I fired the cannon. A flying piece of wood nailed the alien, too. I thought I'd killed them both, but it pulled that javelin out and told me it was only a scratch."

Leeger didn't respond, so Mortas ended the tale. "What a fucker."

"Jan, I know how you feel about that thing, but you need to set that aside."

"Why? Just because it asked for me by name?"

"Yes. The shape-shifter you met was the only one of its kind ever encountered by a human. And until now, we haven't seen another. We've spent that entire time worried that one might slip through our screening, and dreading what it might be able to do. The one you bumped into was working with the Sims, but this one wants to talk peace."

"And you trust it? After everything the first one did?"

"At the very least it wants to talk." Leeger grimaced at Jander's hard stare. "Look at it this way. It knows we're wary of its abilities, and it seems to have taken that into account. I believe one of the reasons it asked for you is that you've already been, for lack of a better term, exposed to it. If it can read minds, it's already read yours. There's no new information it can get from you."

"Been a few places since then, you know? Let it read my mind about Fractus." Mortas stopped himself. "Wait a minute. That's why you picked Erica for this mission. Apart from a couple of techs who walked in after we'd been sealed in the decon tubes, she's the only living human who was in close proximity to the alien."

"Yes. Not counting the Guild analyst."

"I'm surprised you didn't send him with us."

"A deal's a deal. He earned his vacation."

"So how do you expect me to react to this thing, Hugh? Pretend to be some kind of happy-ass ambassador? Put on a trusting face when I know better?"

"I'm not asking you to trust that thing—just keep an open mind. It wanted to contact us, and it wants to speak with you. It told the Brodan that it's ready to act as a translator, and that there are plenty more like it who can do the same. Just think about it, Jan—four decades of war with the Sims, and we've never been able to communicate with them."

"The ones I've met didn't seem to want to talk."

"That's not true. Right down there, on Roanum, you infiltrated a Sim column and almost walked right onto their base with them. In your report you said it was hard to remember they weren't human. Their mannerisms, their responses, heck, one of them helped you up an incline just like a human soldier would."

"Sam's got another mannerism, you know. He mutilates our dead. I stopped comparing him to us once I saw that a few times."

"But don't you see what we could gain here? If we could just talk to them, we might find out why they do things like that. Why they fight us wherever we meet them. And maybe, just maybe, we might find out what's making them."

"Somehow I doubt they're gonna want to tell us that."

"Well then we'll have to capture a few of them, and *make* them." Leeger looked down at the planet. "For the first time in the war, we might be able to actually interrogate a prisoner or two. They'll tell us what we need to know if we get rough enough."

"What's going on, Hugh?" He didn't look at the man who had practically raised him. "You didn't used to be like this."

"We're in big trouble, Jan. For years we weren't winning or losing the war, so most people just plain forgot about it. Now Celestia's gone to pieces, and we're doing the one thing we cannot do. We're fighting each other. The Celestians are out of the war, and the Tratians are really putting pressure on the Chairwoman. If we don't come up with something big, very soon, Tratia is going to end up calling the shots in the alliance."

Mortas looked down again, recognizing the terrain that had punished him and the others with such cruelty. So much pain, so much deprivation on that ground, and yet their suffering had forged the four maroons into a unit. Drawing on the hidden strengths of each member, meeting and overcoming obstacle after obstacle, and then finally escaping. And then to discover that the only one he'd brought out alive had been playing them the whole way.

Remembering an even darker revelation only a few months earlier, on a jungle planet named Verdur where the Orphans had fought a force of fanatical Sim holdouts. The nauseating discovery that a human research station on that planet had been torturing Sim prisoners—not for information, but to learn if they could serve as a labor force. The site had belonged to an enormous corporation called Victory Provisions, and its demented personnel had possessed a videotape of the alien being immolated on Glory Main. It hadn't taken a genius to understand that they saw the shape-shifter as a means of communicating orders to their prospective slaves.

"The Whisperers told their elders about the alien before they told you. No matter how insular they are, it's only a matter of time before the news gets out."

"We were rushing to get you here, but then we learned the alien had walked off. Unfortunately, we're following its schedule." Leeger had been fully briefed on what the Orphans had discovered on Verdur. "But you're right. We have to expect Victory Pro, and others, to hear about this if it drags on."

"If it's just Varick and me and a colony of pacifists, there's not much we can do if a determined party tries to snatch that thing."

"Oh, I wouldn't say that."

"Now *this* is the way to do it." Mortas spoke to Varick as they watched the shuttle vanish in the sky. "Last time I was here, we had absolutely nothing. You should have seen us, traipsing across all this empty ground. We might as well have been cavemen."

"If we have to be here, we might as well be comfortable." Varick turned and looked at their temporary home. A one-story cylindrical drum rose out of the orange dirt, surmounted with antennae and the launching sling for surveillance drones. The cream-colored cylinder extended another story beneath the surface, and a four-wheeled mover was parked next to it.

They'd inspected the shelter with Leeger before his departure, making sure that everything worked. Communications were already established with the *Ajax*, a Force cruiser crewed entirely by Mortas family loyalists that had routinely accompanied the Chairman. The *Ajax* would remain in orbit for the entire mission, and was busily launching satellites designed to provide increased security in case unwanted guests attempted to arrive or depart.

"Let's test the perimeter," Mortas suggested. "One of us should try and walk on in. See how long it takes for a warning."

"That sounds like good, healthy paranoia, Lieutenant." Varick cracked a grin at him.

"Yeah, this know-it-all captain once told me to nurture that." Mortas raised a finger. "Wait. I forgot to show you this."

Varick waited while Mortas laboriously bent over. His left leg was held rigid by the brace, and he pulled up the tan fabric of his right pant leg. The handle of a short dagger stood up from the boot, and Varick reached down and drew the weapon.

"Hmm. Seems I've seen this before. It went missing right after all the alarms stopped ringing at Glory Main. How'd you get it back?"

"Leeger took it from the guy who interrogated me. Musta stolen it as a souvenir." Mortas frowned. "You didn't meet that prick, did you?"

"What was his name?"

"Leeger wouldn't say. He was the chief interrogator for the Glory Corps. Kept at me for days, but I never saw his face. God I wish I could have got my hands on that guy."

"I didn't hang around with anybody like that. Never have. Interrogators, internal security, just a gang of backstabbers getting in the way."

"Amen to that. Of course, I can't forget that you've been spending a lot of time with the upper-level staff types recently." Jander winked at her. "Vote's still out on you."

"I won't hold my breath waiting for the final tally." Erica walked over to the mover, her khaki fatigues standing out against the orange ground. Although the Holy Whisper settlement was five miles away, they'd requested that their Human Defense Force visitors not wear uniforms. The tan fatigues had no insignia, and were as close to civilian expedition gear as the two soldiers had been willing to go. Varick unclipped one of the Scorpion rifles from the mover's rack, and checked to make sure it was ready to fire. "I'll do the walk, while you monitor."

Holding the rifle with familiarity, the tall Banshee strode off across the flat. Watching her easy movement, Mortas looked down at his leg brace with disappointment. Fine grit had formed in his mouth, reminding him of the dust and dirt of this desolate place, and he spat it out before heading for the mover. Sitting in the driver's seat, he activated the control panel and waited for it to sync up with the shelter's defense systems.

A diagram appeared on the monitor, indicating their home as a small circle at the center of a much larger one. The outer circle was a series of hidden ground sensors, and they were already picking up Varick's movements. She was walking quickly, and was almost outside the invisible perimeter. Mortas considered launching one of the surveillance drones, which would change the display to the real-time imagery he'd grown used to in combat, but decided it wasn't necessary. Instead, he selected a narrow tube from a compartment in the vehicle's door and raised it to his lips.

Leaning his head back, he blew into the tube and watched as a slim dart shot upward and then extended gossamer wings. The wings fluttered briefly, and then disappeared as they achieved their full motion. Known as a dragonfly, the tiny surveillance drone began flying in a circle above him while its electronics linked up with the shelter's system. The monitor went white for a moment, and then shifted to an overhead image that expanded to show the surrounding terrain.

The shelter was in the middle of a level expanse dotted with rocks, and Mortas confirmed that none of the planet's serpent-filled waterways was anywhere near. The orbiting dragonfly connected with the perimeter sensors, and even though Varick was still walking away it pointed her out with a flashing red arrow.

Mortas changed the settings to pick up heat as well as movement, and a second arrow indicated where he sat in the mover. Pulling out his handheld, he spoke into it. "Okay, I see you. The sensors are picking both of us up. Start walking back."

The image jumped abruptly, and then started to go fuzzy as the dragonfly ran out of power. A moment later the diagram reappeared, and Mortas flinched when the dying aerobot hit the mover's roof. The sensors still indicated Erica's position, and when she was a hundred yards away they both got a signal. Mortas's handheld strobed a series of red and yellow lines, and then a text appeared on the screen informing him that a human life form was approaching the perimeter.

Out in the open, Varick's handheld called out a warning that Mortas was able to hear. "Attention! You are approaching a secure area, with an armed defensive perimeter. Stop where you are, and enter the proper passcode. If you do not know the passcode, leave the area immediately. If you remain, or come any closer, you will receive one warning shot and one warning shot only. If you remain, or come any closer after that, you will be killed."

He watched the tan figure tapping the sequence into the handheld, and then his own device informed him that one Varick, Erica, had been cleared to approach. Although Varick was also receiving that message, he called her anyway. "You're all clear. System's only set to electrical shock right now, anyway."

"You ever been zapped? It's no fun." Erica continued speaking as she walked in. "One mission, I ran straight into three rolls of reactive wire near this one Sim blockhouse. The voltage isn't supposed to penetrate a powered suit, but I guess all that wire multiplied it."

"That must have hurt. Did it latch onto you?"

"Of course. Designed that way. I was lucky, in that

most of it was staked down, but Sam likes to leave a few strands loose so they can reach out and grab on. My suit electronics started flashing all sorts of alarms, it hurt like hell, so I had to get out of there right away. I squatted down and kicked hard. The suit did the rest, and I went up in the air like a rocket. Broke the wire that had me, but then gravity took over."

She got close enough to be heard, and put the device away. "I landed on the roof of the blockhouse. Looked like a total idiot, but I wasn't there long. So much junk was being shot at that bunker that a concussion wave blew me right off it."

"And you landed in another patch of wire. Right?"

"Worse than that. They had an open-air latrine back there. I'll spare you the details."

"Thanks. I do have one question. Sounds like you were fighting on solid ground on a Hab. I thought the Banshees were reserved for places where there's no atmosphere, or the terrain's really bad."

"Ideally, yes. But every now and then you infantry types can't get the job done and they throw in a Banshee outfit if one's available." She fixed him with a challenging leer. "The grunts who were supposed to force a breakthrough had gotten pinned down, so Command figured a few powered suits would do the trick."

"Did it?"

"Lucky for me, yes. You see, I landed hard in that slit trench, and was basically wedged. Couldn't get my legs under me, and no amount of arm pressure from the suit was going to move those walls."

"You're kidding. You mean you were still there when they broke through?"

"Oh, it's not as embarrassing as all that. Landing in that hole probably saved my life. The rocket teams finally blew that emplacement to pieces, and the blast went right over me. I got buried under the chunks, and had to be rescued."

"I bet your troops thought that was pretty funny. Mine would have."

"Sure they did. You shoulda heard the jokes when they pulled me out. But I didn't care—I was literally in deep shit."

The two soldiers laughed together, and Mortas heaved himself out from behind the steering wheel. "Want to go visit the neighbors?"

"No reason to stand on ceremony." Erica looked down at his leg brace. "I'll drive."

"**W**e always set up next to a major water source, but we try not to disturb the local habitats." The Holy Whisperer named Dru explained the tall fencing in the slow-moving river. He and a female Whisperer named Felicity had come out to meet Mortas and Varick when they'd approached the settlement's buried perimeter. They were waiting for instructions to bring their guests into the colony, and had decided to show them the apparatus for dealing with the snakes.

"That holds them off?" Mortas had stopped a good ten yards from the sloping bank. A high black fence made of crisscrossing mesh stood in the middle of the river, gently curving up onto the ground on two sides. The waterway was still open around the obstacle, and water flowed straight through it. The yellow grass of Jander's memory had been cleared from the riverbank in the enclosed area, but it grew freely elsewhere.

"We haven't had a problem so far." Dru reminded Mortas of Gorman. Young, healthy, sandy hair, and a cheerful disposition. Felicity was a dark-haired version of Dru, and they'd both seemed pleased by the social call. "We've got sensors in the fencing, and in the water upstream and down for warning. The snakes were very interested in us for a while, but they've returned to their normal patterns."

"When I was here, their normal pattern was to sneak up on anything they could eat."

Varick turned to look at the low domes of the small colony. "How does this barrier fit into the general scheme of things here?"

"We've got pipes running under the ground that come out here. There's an identical site on the other side of the settlement. The intakes are heavily screened, of course."

"So why fence off such a large area?"

"It gets pretty hot here, in case you didn't notice."

Felicity exchanged a smile with Dru. "After a hard day's work, there's nothing like a dip in some cold water."

"You're kidding me." Mortas almost didn't get the words out. The memory of the snapping jaws and the churning water made his mouth dry. "Doesn't that attract them by the dozens?"

"Certainly. You should see the footage. But they can't come out on the banks and they can't get through the fence, so there's really nothing to worry about. They're fascinating creatures."

Erica had shifted so the two Whisperers couldn't see her face. She gave Jander a hard expression, and he stifled his more natural response. "Fascinating. I always found them so."

A radio clipped to Dru's collar beeped, and he listened as they were cleared to enter the colony. "All right. They found Elder Paul, and he's eager to meet you."

Dru and Felicity headed for their mover, and Varick fell in next to Mortas as he stiff-legged toward their own vehicle.

"Jan, I know this place is full of bad memories, but could you lighten up a little? We need these people."

"I'm trying to help them. They think those monsters are interesting. And that you can go skinny-dipping with them." He hauled himself into the passenger seat. "Imagine what they think of the alien."

"That's what I'm trying to say." Varick made no

move toward the driver's side. "If we're going to assess this scene, it would help to have the HWs speaking freely. That seems to be their natural inclination, but I suspect they're like anybody else. They'll shut up around a grousing stranger who obviously thinks they're fools."

"Okay." Mortas considered the wisdom of the words. "You sound like my dad. He was always looking for an angle to play."

"It's not an angle. We have a job to do, and if the alien is trying to fool us like you expect, we're gonna need all of the honesty we can find."

"Something tells me this Elder Paul is going to be overflowing with that." Mortas looked through the windshield while Erica crossed in front. The colony only had fifty members, and so it took up a relatively small footprint. Three sand-colored domes sat flush with the orange earth, the top floors of underground buildings. An assortment of antennae sprouted in various places, and Mortas recognized two tall towers as water processors. The colony's spacedrome was on the other side, and he watched one of its shuttles lifting off. Varick spoke while starting the engine.

"When we meet their head man, let's turn up the deference. He probably thinks we're a pair of savages, fresh from the war, so a little civility's likely to go a long way." Dru and Felicity were waving at them, so Varick waved back. "I'll bet you he looks like an Old Testament prophet."

Elder Paul was thirty years old, and looked younger. His dark skin showed only a few trace wrinkles, and his energy was magnetic.

"I think you'll find this particularly interesting." He uttered the words while leading them into a large room with harsh lighting. They'd already passed through the settlement's communal hall—Elder Paul had told them that every Whisperer station had one—and several connecting tunnels, being greeted by every colonist they passed. The oldest Whisperer was no more than forty, while a few were teenagers. The settlement was a busy place, and just about everyone they met wore coarse work clothing and boots.

Elder Paul had started out at a brisk pace, but he'd slowed down after noting Mortas's struggles in keeping up. He stopped now, standing over a waist-high table filled with brown dirt. Rows of similar stands filled the room, and a trio of colonists were inspecting one of them a few yards away. Based on the dirt and the lighting, Mortas decided the place was some kind of botanical laboratory.

"See this soil? Doesn't resemble anything you see outside, but it's native. Amazing, right?"

Varick leaned over, inspecting the dirt. "Looks pretty moist. How's that possible?"

"First, there's a surprising amount of water under the ground. Not just near the rivers, either. The plant life adapted to the more arid areas, with interconnected root systems that in some cases stretch for thousands of yards.

"But this sample here has been modified. I understand that you observed the results of the Sims' so-called 'mud munitions' when you were here, Lieutenant?"

"The aftereffects, Elder. The Sim ordnance was fired into the dirt, and turned it into deep mud in a matter of minutes. It hardened up shortly after that, but by then it had trapped most of the vehicles that tried to assault the Sim compound."

"We heard about that, and examined the site. The Sims have quite the green thumb, and have succeeded in growing food crops in some surprising environments. We took samples from the battlefield you mentioned, and also scoured the remains of the Sim settlement for clues regarding that ammunition."

"What did you find?" asked Varick.

"The HDF units that destroyed the settlement removed all of the mud munition rounds that were left, but we did find some damaged soil samples in a ruined laboratory. We weren't able to reverse-engineer their process, but we succeeded in identifying some of its properties." Elder Paul brought his eyes level with the dirt, and pointed at a single green needle that had broken through. "See that? That shoot comes from a non-native seed, planted in the augmented soil. We're very excited."

"You should be careful with that," Mortas offered. "I was also on Fractus, and saw what happened when the mud munitions got out of control. The effect basically ran away with itself."

Elder Paul straightened up, looking pained. "I've read everything about that tragedy that's been made available. What a disaster."

For a moment Mortas thought he was referring to the enormous loss of life in the chaotic battle, but then he saw that the man was speaking in an environmental sense. Varick gave him an expectant look, and he responded. "I was close to the impact area, and observed the progress of the mud field and the resulting cyclone. I'd be happy to tell you what I saw."

"That would be splendid. Thank you so much. We try very hard not to destabilize the ecology where we land, and Fractus demonstrated that even the authors of this technique didn't fully understand it." He stopped, appearing to consider a new notion. "Would you consider speaking to the settlement as a whole? This concerns everyone."

"I'm not sure everyone would find it interesting. I have no special training in this field, and from the look of things you've got a few experts."

"We've certainly got our share of specialists in different sciences, but as you may have noticed, the median age here is pretty young. They're all bright, but they won't pick up any advanced degrees until they've done a complete tour with a colony."

"Why is that?" Erica asked.

"Off-planet service is very important to our community as a whole, so we instituted a few rules like that one. We don't really need to motivate our young people to go out, but after a certain age you'd be surprised by how many of our members get a little too fond of life at Pacifica."

"Wouldn't surprise me at all. You just described the difference between field soldiers and headquarters types in the HDF."

"Now that is an unexpected comparison." Elder Paul looked at Jander. "Getting back to our original topic, I was already going to ask you to address our members if you wouldn't mind. We named this colony Gorman Station, in memory of Roan Gorman, and you knew him well. We would really like to know more about him and his sacrifice."

"I can't say I knew him all that well, Elder."

"Please. Call me Paul."

"In that case, I'm Jander and this is Erica."

"Jander. Erica. Welcome." Elder Paul regarded them as if seeing them for the first time. "And I think you're being modest about knowing Roan. He died in your arms."

"He died saving my life."

"And Amelia's."

"Excuse me?" The words leapt from his mouth, but Mortas stopped himself. "Oh, you're referring to the alien that impersonated Amelia Trent."

"Actually, our visitor asked us to call her Amelia as well. She's been exceedingly forthcoming, about her non-human nature as well as her role in assisting the Sims. While she was staying with us, she addressed the entire community and told us a great deal about Roan."

"The creature we met on this planet was incinerated soon after Gorman died. The alien who visited you did not know him."

"I wouldn't be so sure about that. She was very familiar with your travails on this planet, which we initially found hard to understand. When we asked for an explanation, she said her species shares an almost psychic link that allows every member to experience everything that happens to every other member." Elder Paul considered his next words, and then went ahead. "She spoke very highly of you."

"I'm sure *it* did." Jander ignored Erica's light kick to his brace. "It deceived me, along with Chartist Gorman and a Spartacan Scout named Cranther. Gorman and Cranther both died saving me and that thing, and the whole time it was lying to us."

"I know who Tel Cranther was, and who he was to Roan. When we landed here, we asked the HDF to provide us with their best estimate of where you buried him."

"I piled rocks on him. I didn't have the tools, or the strength, to dig a grave."

"Excuse me, Paul," Varick cut in. "Why were you interested in Cranther's resting place?"

"They didn't tell you?" Elder Paul was sincerely flummoxed. "Roan's people asked to have him interred here, once we established the colony. We thought it was only fitting that his friend rest beside him. We found the cairn you built, Jander, and moved his remains. Tel Cranther and Roan Gorman are buried side by side, on a small hill not far from here."

Later that night, Mortas and Varick sat outside their shelter in folding chairs. They'd just finished dinner, and a companionable silence had settled over them. One of their radios had been set to periodically broadcast the signal notifying the alien of their arrival, but so far there had been no response. The stars were bright overhead, and the perimeter sensors were active.

"I'm feeling a little guilty." Jander broke the stillness.

"You're thinking about your platoon."

"They're headed to Celestia, and I'm not with them. I'm here, camping out."

"Your leg's coming along, but you wouldn't have been able to join them even if you weren't on this mission."

"I suppose that's true, but it doesn't make me feel any better. The fighting on Celestia's supposed to be a real goat screw. Humans fighting humans, half of the rebels are Force deserters, and half of the loyal Force units don't like the mission. Putting down a slave revolt, and propping up a rotten government, just because we need those minerals for the war."

"I've heard the stories. The whole thing sucks. But that's another reason for us to do this job right. If the alien really can broker a peace, or just a cease-fire, it would completely change the equation on Celestia."

"The alien is full of shit. This is all some kind of trick, just like last time. We have to figure out what it's really up to, while we're still the only ones talking to it."

"You know what I'd like to know?" Varick continued. "What it was up to the first time around, when it met you. All that effort, all that deceit, just to trick its way into a corps HQ? The scan said that thing was carrying a plague virus, and Command decided it was acting as some kind of vector. They concluded it was trying to expose us.

"But what would that have accomplished? Even if it killed every human on Glory Main? This is a space war, everybody's spread out, separated by an unlivable void. No matter how communicable that virus was, it wouldn't have gone far. I never accepted that explanation as the whole story."

"Want to know the sad truth?" Jander asked. "I've been so busy learning how to be a good platoon leader, and going on missions, that I haven't given it any thought. There's been no sightings of other aliens, and the one we did see got burned up. After a while, it was like it never happened."

Varick stood, taking both of their mess tins and waving him back down when he attempted to help. "You'll clean the dishes tomorrow night. Right now, you should try and remember everything the alien said or did while you were here. You spent a lot of time together, with all that walking. I'm betting there was a clue somewhere along the way."

She went through the hatch, leaving him to look out across the flat ground. It was so familiar, and yet so foreign. So much had happened since then, so many newer memories, some of them burned into him. Varick was right; it was important to reconnect with that experience, to recall what it felt like and how the alien had behaved.

Mortas stood, flexing his leg inside its brace, feeling the muscles slowly coming back. They'd walked and walked, the hunger growing even as their hopes faded with each empty mile. Before learning that the Sims had established themselves nearby, they'd had no idea what predators might call the barren planet home. They'd used the ravines to hide their movement, and crawled across the surface whenever the latest canyon took a wrong turn.

"Now there's a thought," he said to the night air, and slowly dropped to the ground. The sensation of the grainy soil came right back as soon as he rolled onto his stomach and extended his arms. His fingers brushed against the flat yellow creepers that blended in so well with the orange dirt, and he moved his hands across them. The memories started to emerge.

Careful not to get too much of the orange dirt inside the brace, he started slithering across the familiar ground.

CHAPTER 10

On Larkin Station, Deek Orton approached Med Wing like a burglar. Blocker's abrupt departure was only a few days in the past, and of course the Bounce had been trumpeting Ayliss Mortas's selfless enlistment in the Banshees ever since. That was all well and good for the rest of the galaxy, but on Larkin just about everybody knew the real story. Ayliss and her former bodyguard, assisted by two veterans from the fight on Quad Seven, had murdered Vroma Rittle in cold blood before fleeing into the arms of the HDF recruiters.

Although traffic in the passageway was minimal, Orton couldn't be sure he wasn't being followed. Zone Quest's vindictiveness was well known, and his connection to Blocker would be revealed by just a little cross-checking of military records. There was also the more tangible problem of actual evidence link-ing him to the aborted plot. Orton adjusted the heavy tool bag that hung by his side, and ducked down the corridor leading to Chief Scalpo's office.

He exhaled loudly when the hatch closed behind him, seeing Chief seated at a terminal in the waiting room. The gray-haired PA was wrapped in a white lab coat, and was typing rapidly.

"Hello, Chief." Orton looked around, surprised that there were no patients. "Where's your assistant?"

"Sent her to help out in the lab for a few days." The typing continued. "You never know who might come calling, in light of recent events."

"Probably not a bad idea." Orton unslung the canvas bag, pleased that the topic of ZQ retribution had already been broached. "I've got a little problem, Chief."

"I've heard that line before."

Orton noticed that the hatch leading into Chief's examination room was shut, but only because a muted thumping came from the other side.

"You got a customer in there? Maybe two?"

"Not for long. The auto-sterilizer's engaged."

"It's not supposed to work, when people are in there."

"I know. That's why I disconnected the safeties. I figured the Guests would send some bully boys to show me the error of my ways." He finished typing, and updated the entry. "Well that's that. I am cleared for active duty. And Blocker has already arranged my assignment to Banshee support."

"You're re-upping?"

"After this?" Chief waved a finger at the hatch, where the thumping had finally ended. "You bet. Charon's on the way, ready to paddle me across."

He winced, and reached over to press a hand against his left side. Two red spots appeared against the crisp white, and Scalpo started shrugging his way out of the lab coat. Orton lowered the bag to the floor, and reached out to help him.

"Stupid ZQ muscle. They saw the gray hair and thought it was going to be easy." Orton lifted Chief's bloodstained shirt, to reveal a thin cut across his ribs. Getting a good look, Scalpo grunted. "Okay, not as bad as I thought. Spray some suturing foam on that, and then bandage it."

Orton found the requested items, and went to work while Chief talked. "The Guests might not know about your involvement, but when Charon gets here you should ask him to do up your paperwork. You're already medically cleared."

"Not sure I want to thank you."

"You might not have to run off. Your part in this is still a secret, so you're probably in the clear."

Finishing with the bandages, Orton stood back while Chief found a clean shirt in a drawer. "Yeah, that might not be true. That problem I mentioned? I don't know quite what to do with this."

He lifted the bag onto the desk, and unzipped it far enough for Chief to get a look.

"That's the device?"

"Yes, Chief. Blocker and Tin cleared out of here so fast I think they forgot I had it."

"It would have detonated when the shuttle reached top speed?"

"That was the plan." He pointed at a readout on the side of the bomb. "It also has a timer, but they thought that was too chancy."

Chief regarded the bomb in silence, and Orton waited as long as he could.

"So . . . any ideas about how I could safely get rid of this thing?"

"Safely." Scalpo showed his teeth while shaking his head. "You kids. No imagination."

Reena Mortas was standing on a high pavilion looking over the Unity Plaza complex when Leeger returned. The architectural plateau fronted the plaza's central tower as it tapered to its top, and she'd spent many hours there with Olech. Wooden latticework supported crawling vines all around, and she'd been thinking of the formal receptions they'd hosted there over the years.

"Jander and Captain Varick are in place, Madame Chairwoman. They'll notify us as soon as the alien returns."

"I'm wondering why it left in the first place. You'd think a peace emissary would feel at home with the Whisperers."

"Jan's very suspicious, as he should be. He believes

the thing is trying to trick us, like it played him the first time."

"You think that's what it is? The thing is playing with us?"

"I don't know," Leeger answered. "I did impress on Jan that if there's any way this could produce peace talks, or even a cease-fire, that he was to set aside his personal suspicions."

"Speaking of someone who's tried to trick us in the past, guess who wants to see me? Dev Harlec."

"He wants to meet with you? He'd be crazy to leave Broda, after the stunt he pulled on Ayliss."

"His message said he has extremely sensitive information for me. Given our mutual animosity, that sounded important enough for a safe-conduct pass. Why not? I'm getting lots of callers these days. Just this morning I had a visit from a member of Zone Quest's board. They're unhappy about Rittle."

"They're mining numerous captured planets in the war zone, making a fortune, only because you're letting them."

"That was his point. They're willing to support the story that Ayliss didn't kill anyone, if I let them start mining the planets Olech gave to the veterans."

"That 'story' happens to be true. I've seen the surveillance tapes. And the Isles girl is going to be just fine."

"I always hated that family. These days I'm discovering I've always hated most of them—including my own."

"It's all going to work out, ma'am."

"Is that what the Misty Man told you?"

Leeger flinched inwardly, surprised to have been discovered. "No. He said the rebels are going to conquer Celestia."

"Not likely, with all the troops we've diverted there. And we'll keep sending more until we snuff this out. We have to get those mines back in operation."

"He suggested we could do that more quickly if we recognized the slaves as the new government."

"You sound like you believe him."

"He makes a good point. The slaves worked the mines, and they currently control most of them. Much of the alliance is learning—or pretending to learn—about the labor force on Celestia, and they're not happy about it."

"I'm aware of that."

"Even if we crush the rebellion, we'll probably destroy the mines in the process. Some of them are already wrecked. But if we pull the troops back, we might salvage the rest."

"All the reports say we've got the rebel areas contained. They can't eat the rocks, so it's a matter of time. Not surprising your turncoat would like us to back off."

Leeger looked out over the complex. Far below, tiny figures walked along a maze of sidewalks that crossed acres of green grass and passed under spreading trees. Olech had always liked the view from up there, but for an unexpected reason. The Chairman had taken great pride in the organization he'd assembled at Unity, and considered many of its younger personnel his surrogate children.

"Ma'am, while I was on Celestia I saw a species of large hog-like animals. They were running around one of the contested areas, and the Misty Man said they were proliferating again because of the fighting."

"I know what you're talking about. They're not native to Celestia. They're from Dalat, where natural predators keep them under control. We had no equivalent, so at one point they overran much of the planet. Foul creatures. Short gestation periods, with huge litters. They're extremely destructive."

"Ma'am?"

"They're voracious, and they root up just about everything they encounter. Trees, crops, even power lines buried in the ground. Culling them was a full-time job."

"Misty asked me to ship in some more of them. To use as a food source."

"So now he's asking favors? After all he's done?"

"He was acting on my orders when things went wrong there."

"He was disobeying your orders when he ran off and joined the other side." Reena leaned against the stone wall, the muscles in her arms tense. "But the assassination—that one's my fault, not yours."

"I brought the idea to you, so the fallout is my fault. Especially the leverage that's now being applied against you. Forgive me for saying this, Madame Chairwoman, but the rebels aren't your true enemies."

"You think I don't know that? I grew up right there on Celestia, surrounded by some of the people who are leaning on me right now. The slavery was confined to the mines during those years, but it was impossible not to know the newcomers were being exploited." Reena leaned out, as if something on the ground had interested her. "I keep wondering if this is somehow a punishment for all that. For pretending not to notice. For tolerating it."

"Your husband tolerated it, in the name of winning the war. And, as much as they're pretending otherwise, the rest of the alliance knew as well."

"So what are you recommending, Hugh? That I recognize a slave government on my home planet? Act like my family didn't run the place?"

"We could deflect that criticism by showing they're not really your family. Have some trusted third parties release the information about your parentage, and then reveal what happened to your birth mother."

Reena turned exasperated eyes in his direction. "And that would justify *what*? That I waited fifty years, living in luxury, so I could murder my own father in the name of avenging someone I never met? And that I used a poor slave girl to do it, in the hopes of not being discovered?"

"We would need some very good news to go along with it. Like the announcement of a cease-fire with the Sims. Arranged by the only entity in existence that can speak to both sides—an entity brought on board by your stepson."

"Just listen to us. Talking about ending this nightmare of a war, only in terms of how it can save my ass. Honestly, Hugh, I'm not sure we haven't become the worst thing in this whole awful mess."

CHAPTER 11

Mortas slept poorly. It couldn't have been the lodgings, because the shelter was superior to every other form of military housing he'd ever inhabited. It was very well appointed, with separate cubicles for him and Varick, a small kitchen, a shower, and a communications area that also served as a sitting room. A large water tank had been buried directly beneath it, and the larder was stocked with better food than he'd enjoyed in over a year.

Despite all that, he kept jolting into consciousness at odd intervals. This was perplexing, because he'd slept soundly during the trip to Roanum. Alternately dozing and waking, he finally decided that the presence of the alien had shifted him to a combat mode of sleeping. At nighttime with his platoon, he would have been pulling radio watch or rising several times to check security. Recognizing this, Jander pushed the covers from his bunk and carefully stood. He'd removed the brace for the evening, and the weakness in his leg was immediately apparent. Using the wall for support, he limped out into the communications area and checked the perimeter signals.

The sensors had picked up some minor heat signatures in the distance, a species of field mouse identified by the Holy Whisperers, and a kind of dog that Mortas had briefly seen during his last sojourn here. Neither of the sightings had been cause for alarm, and so he'd returned to bed. The sliding door leading into Varick's room had been open, and he'd stopped to regard her sleeping form for just a moment.

The light reflected off of the scar on her cheek, but he'd become familiar with that. Her face was calm in repose, and the rest of her was covered by a light blanket. An odd thought crossed his mind, the realization that Erica was the only living human link to his travails with the alien during their quest to reach Glory Main. A warm sense of connection was forming in his mind when she stirred.

He almost fell over, putting too much weight on his bad leg while hastily retreating to his room.

He was up before dawn, this time for good, strapping on the brace and donning his torso armor over the khaki fatigues. Taking a small bag and his Scorpion, Jander quietly crossed to the hatch and deactivated the alarm. Slipping outside, he stopped to inhale the night air and listen for anything unusual. With that done, he stumped a few feet away from the hatch and sat down with his back against the shelter and his rifle across his legs.

The sky began to brighten, and he watched the scenery take on a steadily increasing resolution. Small rocks and low brush sharpened with the light, and somewhere out there a bird chirped a greeting at the new day. How many times had he witnessed that, from the shallow holes and deep ravines that had hidden the four maroons?

Once the sun was peering over the horizon, Mortas set the rifle aside and started taking items out of the bag. First he removed a folding stove, which he popped open and set on the dirt beside him. Then he took out a metal cup, which he filled with water from his canteen. The stove and the cup were both battered from use and blackened by fire. Lighting a small cube of a smokeless and odorless solid fuel, Mortas placed it inside the stove and balanced the cup over it.

Selecting the packets for the morning coffee, Jander found a razor and slowly dragged it over his beard. Periodically clearing it of stubble with a small brush, he was clean-shaven right about the time the water started to boil. Mixing the coffee, he raised the cup and inhaled with deep appreciation. The first sip was always the best, and he sighed happily as he drank.

"You do understand we've got the real thing in here, right?" Varick stood in the open hatchway, holding a steaming mug. Her hair was mussed, and she wore a light T-shirt over athletic shorts. Mortas admired her legs while raising his cup in greeting.

"This is what I'm used to. Did I tell you the Orphans had been on three back-to-back missions when I got chewed?"

"More than once. It's starting to sound like whining."

"Well get used to it." He winked at her. "When the troops aren't around, I bitch a lot."

"Somehow I doubt that." She drank from the mug, glancing back inside. "No contact from our friend during the night. Think it packed up and went home?"

"No such luck. It's gone to a lot of trouble, arranging this." Mortas reflected on his own comment. "This is the second time that thing has conspired to bring me here."

"Must like you."

"Must have a new plan. And that means we won't hear from it until it's good and ready."

"It makes no sense for you to walk." Varick spoke from the driver's seat while Mortas slid out of the mover. "I can drive you right up to it. It's not like you're sneaking up on them."

Mortas gave a light laugh before adjusting his torso armor. There had been no word from the alien, and during dinner he'd announced his intention to visit the site where the Whisperers had interred Gorman and Cranther. One of the drones was flying overhead, scanning the ground, its imagery visible inside their goggles and on the mover's dashboard. In orbit, the *Ajax* was monitoring the territory outside the drone's range.

"It's a personal thing. When we were marooned here, we walked ungodly distances, mostly at night. It wouldn't feel right to just ride up to them."

"Well let me bring you a little closer. A half-mile hump isn't going to do that leg of yours any good."

"Honestly, I think this is just what I need." Jander unclipped his Scorpion rifle from the rack, checking to see that it was ready to fire. "Keep an eye on the scan. Something tells me the alien isn't far away."

"It hasn't answered our calls. Who knows where that thing might be?"

"Exactly." Mortas waved at her, and started walking. The air was warm and the stars were out, bathing the flat terrain in a bluish light. He moved slowly, hampered by the brace but in no particular hurry. He heard the mover drive off in the direction of a low finger of ground they'd spotted on the way. As soon as the hum of the motor died out, he was surrounded by memories.

The dirt underfoot was mixed with clumps of short grass and creeping weeds. Rocks broke the surface at intervals, and a light breeze played across his cheeks. He and Erica had opted not to wear helmets, and so the wind played with his short hair. Sliding the lenses of his goggles up so that he was looking out through the frames with a naked eye, Jander saw again the glowing minerals that frosted much of the open ground.

The stars provided plenty of light, and he soon picked out the small hill that was his destination. The Whisperers had selected the distant location because of the colony's expected growth, and Mortas was grateful for the solitude. A set of wings flapped lightly over his head, and he remembered that the initial absence of birds and animals had perplexed him and the other maroons in their earliest walks. They'd had no way of knowing that a disastrous battle had chased away the wildlife, or that a Sim colony had been planted on what they'd believed to be an uninhabited planet.

His injured leg started to complain as he covered the last hundred yards, and Mortas took comfort in the sensation. So many miles he'd walked on this planet, starving, footsore, uncertain, with almost no gear at all. Tonight his belly was full, his feet were toughened by many months in the walking infantry, and he could whistle up a ride whenever he wished. He was connected to amazing technology in the form of a Force cruiser in orbit, an aerobot watching over him, the goggles strapped to his head, and the ear bud and throat mike that connected him to Varick. He was also armed, and the months of fighting had made the rifle seem like a natural extension of his body.

His instincts from that time of privation returned,

and Mortas stopped without meaning to do so. He slid the goggles back down, sharpening the view of the low hill to see what had raised his suspicions. The grass on either side of the rise was taller, and it grew thicker behind it. That told him that the river was back there, and now he heard the ripples and wondered if they came from the normal current or the dreaded snakes. They couldn't leave the water for more than a few seconds, but Jander looked around warily while taking the last few steps.

A path had been cut through the grass going up, making the climb easier. The top of the hillock was flat, and he saw starlight reflected off of the twisting waterway twenty yards beyond. It reminded him of another piece of high ground, where the four of them had observed the first sign of civilization they'd encountered in their trek. A temporary bridge erected by the Sims.

For a moment he saw Cranther and Gorman again, stretched out on their stomachs and looking at the enemy span. Then they resolved into two door-sized rectangles of dark stone almost flush with the ground, side by side and a yard apart. Words had been etched in them with a fine hand, and he read the first one aloud.

"Tel Cranther. Friend of Roan Gorman." There was nothing else, no reference to Cranther's youth, his involuntary service with the Human Defense Force, his many acts of bravery, or his sacrifice.

Mortas nodded his head in approval, and then looked at the other stone.

"Roan Gorman. Friend of Tel Cranther."

Tears appeared in his eyes, and he pulled the goggles up and off. He hung them on a canteen, and then lowered himself to the dirt between the two graves. Extending the brace in front of him, he rested the rifle across his lap and turned off his throat mike.

"Hi guys. I feel a little silly, talking to you like this. I don't know if you're even here," he whispered, stopping to listen to the wind and the water. "God I *hope* you're not here."

Mortas laughed out loud, the stress of the war easing a bit, and imagined the two other men laughing with him. "Walking in, I was thinking about when we all met. Corporal, you had no use for any of us. And Gorman, I hope you didn't notice, but I had no use for either you or Trent. I mean, the thing that was pretending to be Trent. I misjudged you, and you proved me wrong on the very first night. On your own, you tracked the stars and figured out what planet this is.

"You gutted out every step we walked, with all those blisters from those ridiculous shipboard boots. And then you plotted the course that would take us to Glory Main, even though you knew you'd never get there." He wiped at an eye with the back of his sleeve. "Most important, you stayed true to yourself no matter what happened. You never harmed anyone, and you took the same risks as the rest of us. Maybe more."

The wind ruffled his hair as if in response, and Mortas reached a hand out to the stone bearing Cranther's name. "I covered you up with rocks, far enough from the creek so that those snake things couldn't get to you. You saved my life twice that night, once by pulling me out of the fight in the ravine, and then when you killed that crazy major. I fed his body to the snakes, to distract them while I gathered the rocks. I think you would have liked that."

Jander cleared his throat, studying the rifle across his legs.

"You were right about me, Tel. I pretended differently, but I really did want that platoon. I got it, too, and they're a lot like you. Tough sonsabitches, don't trust Command even a bit, crazy senses of humor. You simply cannot break them. Here's another way they're like you: without them, I would have died a long time ago."

His leg gave a twinge from inside the brace, and he shifted it around. "Bet you're wondering what happened to me. Funny story. After surviving the snakes here, I almost got eaten by a wolf the size of a horse."

"Jan," Varick hissed in his ear. "You've got something approaching. Coming from the north, looks human."

The words shook him back into awareness, and he quickly donned his goggles. The imagery showed the white dot of his own body heat, and for a moment he stopped to consider the absence of the dots to his right and left. Roughly five hundred yards out in the flat, another heat blob was coming straight for him.

"I guess we know who that is, don't we?" He glanced at the two silent slabs, remembering how much he'd once relied on the advice of the men beneath them. "So how about it? What should I do here? Gorman, I think you'd tell me to give this thing a chance. Corporal, I know you'd tell me to trap it in another decon tube and torch it."

"Want me to come out there? If this thing can actually do mind control, you don't want to be alone." He heard Varick start up the mover, and turned his mike on.

"I've been alone with it before." Mortas struggled to his feet. The visitor was three hundred yards away. "It asked for me by name, so let's give it what it wants. At least at first."

"Got it. Don't turn your mike off again."

His goggles picked out the approaching figure, and long before it resolved into a human form he knew what it would look like. Mortas recognized the athletic walk and the easy swing of its shoulders, and then it was coming up the slope through the grass.

It stopped two yards away, expressionless. Amelia Trent's reddish-brown hair hung almost to its shoulders, and even using night vision Mortas knew that her eyes were a striking blue. She was dressed in the same olive flight suit she'd worn as a maroon, although this one wasn't the bloodstained rag discarded at Glory Main. It was like looking at a memory.

"Hello, Jan." The thing gave him a crooked smile, and then extended open palms toward the plots on his left and right. "Look at us. We're all here again."

"No we're not. Cranther and Gorman are both dead. They died because of you. And I would gun you down right here, right now, if I thought it would actually kill you."

"I remember that." The alien pointed at the front of Mortas's armor, where Cranther's fighting knife was secured. They were sitting in the dirt on the plain, having left the gravesite at Jander's insistence. When Varick joined them, the alien had greeted her as a stranger.

"I've carried it ever since he died." Mortas watched the Amelia-thing for a reaction. It shouldn't know that he'd lost both blades while a Force prisoner, or that Varick had sent the longer one to him later. The lie seemed to have no effect.

"The war's changed you. You're very different."

"You're not. You're as deceitful as ever."

"I'm here to prove that I can function as an intermediary between humanity and the race you call the Sims. Ask me anything you want, and I'll answer it."

"You should know we're recording this, both audio and visual." Erica tapped her goggles. "With these."

"The Sims asked me to contact you, to negotiate a

possible truce. It's important that you believe me, so record anything you like."

"We've got quite a few questions. For example—"

"Talk bird to us," Mortas interrupted. "Let's start with proof you actually *can* communicate with them."

The alien gave him an appraising look, and then opened its mouth. Both of the veterans gave a start when the long series of warbles and chirps came forth. The Amelia-thing went on for a few seconds, pleased by their discomfort.

"Heard those sounds way too many times," Varick said to Mortas, who gave a brief nod. "You really can talk to them?"

"Of course. My people are researchers. We've been observing the Sims for years. We infiltrated them as a matter of habit, to learn more about their race. Once we felt we understood them, we revealed ourselves. That's why we were allied against you."

"Were? You're not pals anymore?"

"My experience on this planet, with Jander and the others, provided my people with a surprising revelation. According to the Sims, you humans are a violent, narrow-minded race bent on eradicating them. In the many decades of this war, my people saw nothing to suggest they were wrong." It looked at Mortas with warmth. "Until I met you and Cranther and Gorman."

"Wonderful story." Jander spoke in a monotone.

"You mentioned your people. Who are you? What are you?" Varick asked softly.

"My race has a name, and every member has a name as well. Unfortunately, you'd never be able to pronounce any of them."

"Try us."

"You know, your Command incinerated the only one of us who ever came under their control. You'll have to forgive me if I limit your knowledge of my people."

"Elder Paul said you claimed to have some kind of mental link with the other creatures like you," Mortas commented. "That true?"

"Of course. How else would I know everything that happened to the Amelia Trent you encountered?"

"Video clips of that thing getting roasted have been disseminated all over the war zone. I was interrogated many times, and those transcripts have been leaked as well. A race of researchers—" Jander gave a brief laugh "—wouldn't have much trouble piecing together what happened. Especially with the entire Sim race collecting intelligence for them.

"You know what I think? You're just another lump of clay made out to look like Amelia Trent, fed just enough information to pass itself off as an oracle of peace."

"All right. Let me offer a few items that probably aren't part of those records. When we first met, you dismissed me as a shipboard headshrinker. You found me annoying, and you were afraid I was going to give Cranther an excuse to run off on us."

"All of that's in the reports."

The alien turned to Varick. "Would it be too much to ask for you to stop recording, just for a few minutes?"

"Not at all." Erica slid her goggles up over her head, turning them off, while Jander did the same. "Go ahead."

The alien looked at Mortas. "Did you tell them about Major Shalley, Jander?"

He shifted his injured leg, and cast a doubtful glance at Varick. "No."

"I wouldn't imagine so. You tried to split us off from his little command as soon as you met him. That's desertion under Force regulations."

"He was insane. And he was going to use us as cannon fodder."

"Oh, I fully agree. But now we've established that I know something you've never told anyone. That we encountered some of the survivors from the assault on the Sim colony, shortly before the Sims finished them off. Cranther warned you not to mention that, if you got out of here alive. Seems you took his advice."

"All right." Much of the heat had dropped from Mortas's voice. "Looks like you *can* tell the truth, when you want. So finish what you were going to say, but spare me the bullshit. You were about to tell us that what happened here changed your opinion of humanity."

"Not completely. Your species' behavior in this war indicates a propensity for excessive brutality, *stupid* infighting, and blind greed. Cranther's stories about his forced conscription, the abuse he suffered in training, and his routine mistreatment by Command all reflected everything we'd come to expect. But it was the unexpected that opened my eyes.

"Our little group was never supposed to wander the way we did. We were supposed to see Sim shuttles in the air, which would cause Cranther to lead us to the spacedrome so we could steal one of them. But the assault on the colony destroyed the Sims' aircraft, making it appear that we were on a barren planet. That set us off on the search for water, which led us through a series of trials. As soon as we surmounted one obstacle, a worse one rose up. But instead of fragmenting the group, those complications brought us closer together."

It stopped speaking, and turned to Varick. "He's not accepting any of this, but it's the truth. If it weren't, why would I even be here? The one prolonged encounter between our races showed my people that you aren't as bad as the Sims believe."

The alien looked at Jander. "You earned your race the benefit of the doubt. And that is why my people want to see the fighting end."

"I come from a political family. They're experts in manipulation, and here you're trying child psychology on me."

"Just a moment," Erica broke in. "You said your people want to see the fighting end. What about the Sims? They feel the same way?"

"With some prodding from us, yes. That's one

reason why we didn't reestablish contact until now. The Sims have a loose command structure, so convincing them to discuss a truce took time."

Mortas felt a sliver of his animosity vanish, but only because the answer to a very old question appeared to be at hand. That mystery had shaped much of his life.

"What's making the Sims?"

Varick registered surprise, and then expectation. "Do you know? Where are they coming from? Where *did* they come from?"

The Amelia-thing smiled with lips that were pressed shut. "Who's making the Sims? Something. Some force, some power, some race. We haven't encountered them, so we don't know who or what they are. And neither do the Sims."

"The Sims don't know where they come from." The anger had returned to Jander's voice. "Bullshit. I knew this was a waste of time, and that proves it."

"It's the truth. They have no idea of their actual origins because they have no link to them." The alien stared him back down into a sitting position. "When a Sim becomes conscious for the first time, it's aboard ship, in a sleep tube very similar to the ones you use. The entire ship's complement is awakened at the same time, a sort of mass birth if you will, except they're all aged between eighteen and twenty. Fully formed physically, able to converse fluently, each trained for a specific job. A great deal of information has been instilled in their minds prior to this first awakening.

"They understand why they're essentially being born in space, that there are many more like them, and that they are in a desperate survival situation. All of these things were implanted, grown, or fed into their brains when they were created and while they slept. So when they awake, they're not confused at all. It all makes sense to them."

"What? What makes sense to them?"

"Whatever is creating them has given them a detailed history. It's a lie, but they have nothing else to go on. They have no connection to their true origins, no awareness of their creators. They believe they are the descendants of thousands of human beings who were sent out on multi-generational space voyages centuries ago.

"Those original ships were essentially giant factories, because of the voyage's extreme duration. They had to be able to create smaller ships, repair parts, and any equipment they would require once they reached a habitable planet. The factory ships also created the succeeding generations. Artificially, because most of the crew was kept in a form of stasis during the voyage and they would need to generate a large population quickly once they reached their destination.

"The story goes on to say that eventually they lost contact with humanity. They succeeded in establishing colonies, and over the generations they mutated to speak the way they do. They also lost the ability to physically reproduce, largely because it was no longer necessary. They essentially became a separate species of human."

"Lost tribes," Varick murmured, and Mortas nodded. Space travel in the decades before the advent of the Step had involved numerous methods for bridging the void, and multi-generational missions had been among them. The unexplained loss of most of those ships had generated many dark theories about how the entities creating the Sims might have obtained human DNA long before the war.

"See?" The alien spoke to Jander. "That whole tale is a lie, but they believe it. The time required for such extensive mutations simply doesn't fit the true chronology of mankind's exploration of deep space, but the Sims don't know the real timeline."

"What do they know?" Varick asked. "Or, what do they think they know?"

"That humanity developed the Step long after the two species had grown apart. That when their human cousins found them, they were horrified by the changes. That all of their colonies were brutally eradicated by a race that was their closest relative in the cosmos. That to survive, they created updated versions of the long-duration ships and loaded them with the latest batches of new Sims. That they broke up into large groups, traveling different routes to the same region of space, staged to arrive at dramatically different times. That they needed to start over, somewhere beyond the reach of humanity and the Step."

The alien stopped, largely because Mortas and

Varick were no longer paying attention. Lost in the significance of what they were learning, the two officers looked anywhere except at the speaker.

"That's why they attacked, the first time they actually encountered humans. They didn't think it was the first time. They thought their persecutors had caught up with them. And they were ready."

CHAPTER 12

"Mortas, you are the slowest member of this training squad. I've seen *dead people* who moved faster than you do. *After* rigor mortis set in." Sergeant Stempful, one of the training NCOs in Banshee Basic, stood looking down at Ayliss. "Rigor mortis. Rigor mortas. I like that. You just got your nickname, Private Rigor."

Ayliss tried to ignore the taunts, focusing on the sequence for transferring the battery from a broken signal beacon into its replacement. She'd already linked the two units with a communications cable, but saving the code data from the malfunctioning beacon before the new one was powered up was tricky. Her hands shook and her mind balked, but not from stress. Her arms were sore from all the push-ups, and the lost sleep of the previous nights was catching up with her.

"Come on, Private Rigor, everybody else is already done." One of the other NCOs was speaking right in her ear, but in a whisper. The training cadre almost never raised their voices, and she'd found this more disconcerting than the expected yelling. Ayliss reached for the power button on the broken beacon, almost punched it, and then hesitated. Her tired brain started going over the steps, which she'd learned late the night before.

"Take your time, Private." Stempful's voice, in her other ear. "The war can wait. Your squad can wait. That beacon's gonna call the only shuttle that can get you out, Sam's breathing down your necks, but no one's expecting you to hurry."

Ayliss watched her finger turn off the power, and then her eyes shifted to a single indicator on the side of the replacement unit. It was a tiny red bead, almost flush against the housing, and it would light up when the instrument was ready to function. Refusing to look away, she still sensed the collective will of the rest of the trainee squad, ranged to either side of her at the long table. Success for the squad depended on every member accomplishing the task, and the penalty for failure was intense physical exercise.

The light came on, and she quickly completed the final steps while the NCOs moved away. Stempful returned to her position in front of the group, her electronic right eye seeming to bore through them.

"Never thought I'd see the day. Everybody got the

job done. And this time Private Rigor actually met the time limit." A sense of release filled the room, and Ayliss glanced left and right at her squad mates. Heads shaved almost bald, and wearing heavy fatigues that looked more like prison uniforms, their faces seemed almost identical. She'd gotten to know them well in the last few days, as the cadre had tasked the veterans to bring her up to speed on everything she would have learned in Force Basic Training. They'd all lost plenty of sleep doing that.

"Sergeant, I have a question," Yerton called out from the far end of the bench, and several of the trainees groaned.

"Don't make noises like that," Sergeant Stempful commanded. "You're a team. You support each other. How is Private Mute going to learn anything if she doesn't ask all these questions?"

"Sergeant, this drill would be unnecessary if both beacons had batteries. I've been in the Force two years now, and I've never seen a battery shortage."

"As always, Private Mute has raised an interesting point. I may have to give this some thought." The line of trainees stiffened, having grown familiar with that phrase. "Yes, I will need some time to think. How about we all do that, and from the thinking position?"

Frustrated exhalations accompanied the squad as they moved to the floor. Seconds later they were all in a row, with only their elbows and the toes of their boots touching the surface. Their backs and legs were rigid, and their chins rested on the palms of their hands.

Stempful, in the same uncomfortable posture, regarded them at eye level. Unlike the trainees, she looked like she could maintain that stance for hours. "Mute, refresh my memory. What have you been doing for the two years you've been serving humanity?"

"Maintenance technician on armored vehicles, Sergeant!"

"Oh yes. That's right. You were in a motor pool most of that time?"

Ayliss struggled to control her trembling muscles. The first few days of Basic had been nearly nonstop PT, and her entire body ached. Out of the corner of her eye she saw that little Bontenough was struggling, too. A corporal in the Force who'd given up that rank to volunteer for the Banshees, she hadn't done anything to earn a cadre nickname yet.

"Yes, Sergeant!" Yerton barely got the words out.

"I'm sure that motor pool was well supplied, and that you had everything you needed. But you see, Private Mute, we're training you for missions with the Banshees. Banshee units get dropped into all sorts of unpleasant places, often for longer than expected and far from logistical support. So when you suddenly discover that your last functioning beacon has no battery, would that be a good time to start learning how to change it out? Squad?"

"No, Sergeant!" The squad answered, sounding as if they were all being strangled.

"Recover!"

The squad sagged to the floor for a moment, and then got to their feet.

"Any other questions?" Stempful asked, breaking into an expectant grin.

"Yerton, you're going to shut that stupid mouth of yours." Private Elliott started wiping down the fake Scorpion rifle, her large hands covering much of the hard plastic. She'd been the first to receive a nickname, and the NCOs called her Private Plodder. "I am sick of doing extra reps because of you."

Sitting across from Elliott in the squad bay, Yerton looked back with hard blue eyes. "Just helping you out, Plod. You could use the PT."

"I arrested lots of troops like you, Mute. Wiseasses who thought they were clever. That all stopped once we put the cuffs on them."

"That's funny. The cuffs never bothered me." Yerton's dummy rifle lay on the floor in front of her, still dusty from the day's conditioning march.

"So you're a liar, too? You've never been in restraints—they don't let discipline cases into the Banshees."

"Never said they were Force handcuffs, did I?"

"Cut it out, both of you." Bontenough was scouring her Scorpion with a small brush. "We've got a lot to do tonight."

"The ex-corporal has spoken." This came from Litely, who sat leaning against her bunk. Like Bontenough, she hadn't been nicknamed yet. Her Scorpion was already clean, laid across her lap.

Ayliss looked over in surprise. Litely was the member of the squad who should have been called Mute. Average height and dark-skinned, she'd demonstrated a quiet competence over the past difficult days. The squad knew next to nothing about her.

"Don't need to be a corporal to know we've got to clean the whole bay including the latrine, and then practice up on the new radios for the test tomorrow. You saying we don't have a lot to do?"

"Lots and lots of talk, from people who are supposed to have so many things they need to get done." Litely inspected the fake rifle's inch-deep muzzle before shifting her gaze to Bontenough. "How about we all just keep our mouths shut for the rest of the night?"

"Hey, fuck you, Litely." Elliott glared across the floor. "And while we're at it, fuck you too, Bontenough. I'm gonna straighten Yerton out, and I don't need a referee."

"Quiet is a good idea." Amery sounded like she hadn't heard the towering Elliott. "You know they're monitoring everything we do and say, right?"

"Shut up, Legacy." Yerton's face wrinkled when

she uttered the nickname. Amery was the only trainee other than Ayliss who hadn't been a Force soldier. Her mother was a Banshee killed in the war years earlier, and so the NCOs had taken to calling her Legacy. "Whatever your dead mommy told you is a little out of date."

"She didn't tell me much of anything. She was gone most of the time."

"Well that explains why we have to spend all night, every night, bringing you and Rigor up to speed. The rest of us already been through basic training, plus a few years in the zone. Why should we have to babysit you? How about it, Rigor?"

"You keep mentioning what an old hand you are in the army. Why don't you understand that rules are rules, and we didn't make any of them?" Ayliss asked, her tired brain violating the promise she'd made to Tin. The harsh lights in the bay pressed into her eyes, and the conversation on Larkin Station seemed like an event from another lifetime. She tried to focus on cleaning the dummy rifle, but her mind drifted to a happier time, when Blocker had taught her how to use a real one. She'd outshot every vet on Quad Seven her first day, and later she'd killed close to a dozen of McRaney's pirates. The thought warmed her, and momentarily drove away the fatigue.

"Just a second, *Minister*." Elliott spoke. "Forgetting we all watched you grow up on the Bounce? Your father ran the war for years, and he gave you two high-powered jobs. For all we know, you wrote up all *sorts* of stupid rules before you murdered that Zone Quest guy."

"Don't hack on her for that. The Guests are all assholes." Litely's eyes were on Ayliss. "Besides, she's not the one who killed him. She didn't even manage to finish the one she was fighting."

"Yeah, funny how that worked out," Elliott commented. "The three vets in that dustup did all the dirty work, and Rigor's hands are clean. How about it, Mortas? Did we hear the real story, or the cover story? Were you the one with the knife after all? I bet you were. You got the look."

"Uh-oh. Plodder's gonna tell us about arresting that serial killer again." Yerton almost sang the words, the sound grating on Ayliss's ears. "What did you say he did? First time you told that story he murdered prostitutes. The second time it was the staff at an R&R center."

Elliott gave Yerton a hard stare, and then leaned her rifle against a bunk. She rose easily, without touching the floor with her hands. "Stand up, Mute. You're about to start living that nickname."

"You think I'm afraid of you?" Yerton's blue eyes danced, and she stood as well. "You're nothing without a gun and other cops."

"You talk a lot." Elliott stepped toward Yerton, and Ayliss watched in dull fascination. The former military police officer was six feet tall and heavily muscled, and she could move with an ominous deliberateness. Bontenough was already between them, absurdly outsized, but Ayliss could barely hear the words telling them to break it up. Amery had joined her, which Ayliss found surprising because the motherless trainee was only slightly larger than Bontenough. Something deep under the layers of exhaustion told Ayliss she should try to help them stop the fight, but those words were lost as well and she just sat there.

Yerton made a sudden leap to her left, as if trying to get around the two shorter women, and the whole thing ended right there. The grinding lights in the bay turned off, throwing them all into pitch darkness. Right after that the entire room strobed with disorienting blue waves, and a voice hollered over the loudspeakers, "Outside in formation! You have ten seconds!"

Weariness fled as they lunged for the door, half of them turning and running back to retrieve their dummy weapons. Ayliss went down the stairs three at a time, and then she was through the door and out into the cold night air. She raced for the single line painted on the pavement, finding the crack that was her spot. The others appeared to her left and right, and then they were at attention.

Sergeant Stempful marched into view, followed by three other training NCOs. She stopped facing the squad, ramrod straight and clearly displeased.

"Understand something, trainees. You are not

Banshees. You are a long way from being Banshees. No Banshee ever lays a hand on another Banshee, except in support. We are a team, and teams do not fight each other." The icy words drifted away in the darkness. Ayliss stared straight ahead, seeing the darkened buildings of the sprawling military complex. The whole planet was controlled by the Force, and Jan had mentioned it once. MC-1932 was the latest home of the Orphan Brigade, except that was on a different continent and the Orphans hadn't been there for months.

Stempful's frosty disapproval brought her back. "No matter what happens from here on out, you will never raise a hand to each other *ever again*. Is that clear?"

"Yes, Sergeant!" they shouted in unison.

"Sergeant Nestor, escort Private Yerton into the personnel bay. Yerton, pack your stuff. Tomorrow we'll decide whether you return to your unit, or roll back to start Basic over again with the next squad. Do you know why I'm dropping you, Yerton?"

"Fighting, Sergeant?"

"That couldn't be it, because I'd have to drop Private Plodder too. No, Private Yerton, you're being dropped because you're a constant drag on this squad. Never a positive thing to say, never doing more than you're told, and never taking the lead. Think about that while you're packing. Dismissed."

Yerton stepped backward, disappearing from the

squad. They heard her boots on the pavement, then the door to the barracks, and that was it.

"Now some of you may be thinking that your lives just got a little better." Stempful's tone hadn't changed. "You'd be wrong about that. We told you right at the start that the field load for this squad was based on its initial size, and that the load will not change no matter how many of you drop.

"There is a sound reason for this. On an operation, the equipment required for a specific mission doesn't change just because you lost some people. You have to get it to where it's needed, and then put it into action regardless of how difficult that might be. I did hope that warning might make you see that you need each other, but apparently I was wrong.

"You'll find out just how painful this is going to be later in the training, but if I were you I would try very hard not to lose any more bodies. Your load was going to be tough enough with six trainees, it'll be crushing with only five, and I don't even want to think about fewer than that."

Stempful lowered herself to the tarmac, and then raised her body into the push-up position. Without being told, the trainees did the same. Looking over Stempful's rigid form, Ayliss saw a trio of soldiers walking along in the distance, obviously returning from a night out. Their carefree voices carried across the dark compound, and her mind twisted with the desire to be over there with them, to be anywhere but where she was. She shifted her eyes to the ground, and Stempful's voice took over.

"So while we're waiting for Yerton to clear out, let's use this unscheduled break to build up those muscles some more."

CHAPTER 13

Jander awoke with a start, but didn't know why. The shelter was quiet except for the hum of its various systems, and he'd fallen into an exhausted slumber when they got back. The alien had ended their discussion shortly after describing the Sims' belief about their origins, and they'd watched it walk off into the wasteland. It had promised to meet them again, the next night, at Gorman Station.

The drone and the *Ajax* had tracked its heat signature for more than a mile before it simply vanished.

Lying in his bunk, he looked out through the open hatch. The shelter's main room was gray in the dim light, and nothing seemed amiss. His leg throbbed lightly from the evening's exertions, but it was the familiar sensation of tired muscles and so he welcomed it. He heard Varick give off a single subdued snore from her cabin, and he wondered if that was what had awakened him.

The thought reminded him of the previous morning, when he'd looked in on her sleeping form. There was a lot to admire there, and Mortas lay in his bunk guessing at what Erica looked like naked. The frantic pace of the past months had left no time for romance, even though his troops always seemed able to find willing partners at home base or aboard ship. The long abstinence and nearly constant danger had substantially suppressed his libido, which was quite an accomplishment given his young age and the crude conversations of the infantry. Now he felt the natural stirrings returning.

The gray stillness shifted for an instant, a half-seen flash of orange, and he sat up in order to look into the main room. The perimeter sensors had been programmed to wake them soundlessly if anything suspicious approached, with a rapid shaking of their bunks that so far had not occurred. Mortas squinted across the space, and finally identified the strange light. A tiny orange circle was flashing on the main control panel, and he quietly climbed out of the bunk.

His left leg argued with him as he crossed the floor, but he refused to limp. The atrophied muscles strained with the effort, and Jander felt relief when he finally reached the chair. A schematic showed the perimeter sensors were all functioning, and that nothing had disturbed them all night. The orange light kept blinking, though, and he toggled the display to see what the electronic antennae were detecting.

He could launch a drone if necessary, but decided to stay with the schematic depiction of their surroundings. The shelter appeared as a white rectangle in the center of the display, surrounded by a circle of red dots representing the sensors. That array shrunk in size, and then a small blinking blob appeared to the northeast. He zoomed in on it, and watched it resolve into a pulsing, fan-shaped icon that indicated the sensors were picking up a strange sound.

Mortas glanced back at the open hatch leading into Varick's compartment, and decided to use an ear bud so as not to disturb her. Activating the feed from outside, he almost jumped when the sound entered his ear. It was warbling and high-pitched, and he instantly recognized it as the howling of several dogs. The wound in his leg gave a twinge just then, calling up the memory of a different pack of wild creatures, much larger than the ones who lived on this part of Roanum, who had come close to devouring his entire platoon.

A hand pressed his shoulder, and this time he did jump.

"Sorry." Varick was dressed in a loose T-shirt and running shorts. "What are you hearing?"

Mortas removed the earpiece, and turned up the volume so it filled the darkened room. The mournful voices surrounded them, rising and falling in a canine chorus.

"I saw a small pack of these things when I was here before. The Sims were filling in the ravines closest to their settlement because the survivors of the assault force were using them. They sent out these two big earth movers, crushing the canyons by rolling along on either side of them, and the noise spooked the dogs. Never heard them howl, though."

"That's probably not a comfortable sound for you, considering." Varick's tone was humorous, and her hand was back on his shoulder. Her other hand pointed at his wound. "I mean, a pack of their relatives almost had you for lunch."

"Those weren't dogs. They were wolves. Wolves with armor."

"Just kidding around. I keep forgetting you Orphans are sensitive." Varick squeezed his shoulder, and then released it before walking toward the kitchen. "Time to start the day. You still insisting on that shit field coffee, or you ready to start living like a civilized man again?"

After scrubbing the dishes and utensils from breakfast, Mortas planned to do an extensive workout of his recovering leg muscles. He turned from the small sink to see Varick standing there in fatigues and torso armor. Her goggles hung from one of her canteens, and she'd taken her Scorpion from the rack.

"Get your rig on. We've got a whole day to kill, and I want to do some sightseeing."

Fifteen minutes later the drone was cruising unseen above them, and they were rolling across the plain at a fast clip. Mortas had switched to a two-piece brace with locking hinges that allowed him to bend his leg, and it made the ride immensely more comfortable. The sky's purple tinge was barely noticeable, and for a moment he imagined himself on Earth, driving around in the desert somewhere. He looked at Erica, and saw a tight smile of enjoyment as she drove. Her hair was just long enough to be tied at the back of her head, and her goggles prevented him from seeing what was holding it in place. The vertical scar stood out on her right cheek, and he felt an impulse to reach out and touch it.

The sun warmed them both, and soon they hit a stretch of ground with fewer rocks. The drone was sending them imagery from above, scanning for any dangers and also providing notice of the many ravines. It had already mapped out the area around the shelter for quite a distance, and so Varick had selected this route for its speed. The mover roared along, rattling and bouncing on the uneven ground, and Mortas laughed aloud.

"What was that?" Erica asked cheerfully. "Mr. Gloom 'n' Doom enjoying himself?"

"In all my life I would never have imagined being back here, driving around for pleasure."

"It's a crazy war. You gotta grab your fun when you can."

She gave him a sly smirk, and it was hard to tell

what it meant because of the goggles. He remembered the hand that had lingered on his shoulder that morning, and was about to ask when Erica cut him off.

"You know, if the alien is telling the truth, there's a chance the war might actually end."

"I can't imagine what that would be like," Jan answered. "Not sure what I'd do."

"I know what I'd do. Go find a mountaintop on one of the new planets, build a place there, and never come back down."

"Really?"

"Been out here five years. I've seen as much of humans and Sims and everything else as I'm ever going to want. I haven't directed anything about my own life for so long that I'm not sure I remember how."

"You volunteered for the Banshees, and you made it through their training. No one told you to do that."

The goggles flashed as they turned to regard him. Despite the bouncing of the mover's tires, Mortas thought he saw Varick's head tilted slightly, as if she were studying him.

"You're thinking about your sister, aren't you? In Banshee Basic."

"I got my officer training as a university student, so I didn't do Basic. We had a modified version one summer, but it didn't sound much like what my troops went through."

"Ours is a lot different from all of that. Lots of physical stuff, of course—you need toned muscles to operate an armored suit. The activators take their cues from muscular movement, so the more defined the sinew, the more specific the action. They'll really put some definition in her."

"She's always been in excellent shape, so that shouldn't be a problem."

"It's a problem for everybody. There's only so many push-ups and sit-ups you can do, and they push you past that. But the real game is mental. The Banshee cadre know what the trainees are expecting, so their regimen is built on doing the opposite. Almost no yelling, and they go out of their way to explain every task. It's easy to tune out a situation that's completely unreasonable. But when there's just enough sanity to it, that's when it really messes with your head—you can't get a fix on what's happening, no matter how hard you try."

"Sounds like you had a good time."

The goggles came around again, the mouth open in protest, but then she identified the sarcasm.

"Oh fuck you, Lieutenant."

They both laughed as the mover jumped over a small rise in the ground.

Looks like the Glory Corps did a pretty thorough job the second time they hit this place. Although I'm not sure why they destroyed this." Jander stood on a small, grassy hill with Varick. Not far below them, a wide creek flowed through the twisted wreckage of a small bridge.

"Twelfth Corps's commander was really embarrassed when his first strike failed. I was doing my palace guard thing at the time, so I heard him railing away. He didn't believe the stories about the mud munitions."

"They put a battalion of armor and APCs down, plus a company of walking infantry. The whole thing went to pieces when the Sims turned the ground to mud. They didn't even send the follow-on waves down."

"You learned that from the crazy major?"

"Yes." Mortas was surprised not to feel alarm. Despite his successful service since then, he'd suppressed the memories of the encounter with the soldiers from the doomed assault. The words came out easily, and he felt another weight being taken from his shoulders. "He and his senior-most NCO described it in detail. It was chaos."

"You never told anyone you linked up with friendlies?"

"We were with them for a little more than an hour, counting walking time. They were set up in a bad position, and hadn't moved in days. Sam showed up while we were there, and killed them all except for Major Shalley." The confession flowed easily, and he could almost see the words blowing away in the breeze.

"He followed me and Cranther, who was badly wounded, and was getting ready to shoot me when Cranther killed him. He died of his wounds right after that. We were near a creek, and I put Shalley's body where the snakes could get it. I needed to distract them while I picked up enough rocks to cover Cranther. You can understand why I didn't share that part of the story."

"The alien wasn't with you?"

"No, or Gorman either. We got separated during the attack."

"If the alien ever brings it up again, deny killing the major. It—and the earlier version of it—wasn't there. You and your group got chased away when the Sims attacked, so you can't get charged with desertion. And whatever you do, don't ever tell a living soul you fed that guy's body to the snakes."

"Thank you. I've been carrying that around for a long time. I was questioned over and over, after they burned up the alien. I buried that story as deep as I could."

"You were right to do that. The people in the Twelfth Corps HQ were a ruthless bunch."

"So what happened to you? After the alien got roasted."

"Command went completely nuts. They'd spent so much time and money building their little hiding place, and here it was infiltrated by something they'd never seen before. For all they knew, there were more of them already on station. They locked the entire place down, which was lucky because I was with my platoon.

"That's when the loudspeaker started calling out names. One at a time, and then about twenty minutes later they'd call another. We were supposed to ditch everything and walk to the sick bay, naked, to be scanned. You couldn't help noticing that they started with the lowest ranks." Varick's face turned ashen. "I had no idea if they were killing every one of them, but after that decon tube bonfire I wasn't taking any chances. So I refused to send any of my people, when they called the first one."

"I bet they didn't like that."

"Yeah. But they had no choice; my ladies and I were suited up and armed. So they sent a medical team in with a portable scanner, and one by one we took off the armor and got cleared."

"Then what happened?"

"A mad bug out. There was no reason for it, but the general decided the station had been compromised. If the Sims didn't know there was something hidden in that rock before then, they sure figured it out while we were leaving. Place was surrounded with a cordon of warships, and then a convoy of transports came in. When I climbed out of my Transit Tube, they told me I was no longer in command of my platoon."

"*That's* what happened? They put you in a staff job because you wouldn't serve up your people?"

"That's not how they saw it."

"And you've been stuck there ever since."

"Despite the best efforts of Banshee command. That's why, when your stepmother's people approached me, I made them promise to spring me—regardless of how this turns out."

"And here I was thinking you wanted to finally meet me."

"Hey, you didn't even send me a thank you for the knife."

Jander squatted down with effort, just to stretch out his muscles, but the lower view of the bridge brought more memories. "I used that knife to kill one of the Sims sentries, right over there. First time I ever killed anything."

"Not easy, doing it up close."

"I really fucked it up, too. Lucky for me he was too startled to get a round off. He was just some poor colony militia guy, walking a post. It's always bothered me."

"When you fight in an armored suit, it goes from long-range to right-here really fast. One moment you're directing rockets and artillery while running forward, the next you're blasting away at figures you can barely make out, and then you're passing right through them. You can do a lot of damage just swinging the arms on a suit; in Basic they show you how to use it like a battering ram. It's pretty gross when you clean your armor later on."

Mortas stood up, and they both went silent. The wind played across the water, making the grass sway, and he looked down at the creek. He wondered if their presence, too far back for the snakes to get near them, had attracted the predators anyway. Dark images passed through his mind, flailing muscles and gaping mouths full of teeth.

"You think there's any chance that the alien is telling the truth?" he asked.

"Given its past behavior, no. But so far everything it's told us makes sense. It explains why the Sims act the way they do, even if that's all based on a lie their creators buried in their brains."

"I'm having a hard time with that part. The thing says its people are researchers. For a species that knows so much about the Sims, how can they know nothing about their creators?"

"I was thinking about that." Varick spoke with eagerness. "Could *that* be the alien's real motive? If it arranges a truce between us and the Sims, the things making the Sims aren't going to be happy. Maybe this is all some ploy by the aliens, to smoke out the Sims' creators."

"If that's true, it would make us every bit the pawns that the Sims are. There's a bigger game here." Jan nodded, pleased to hear a theory that supported his distrust of the Amelia-thing. "You're really good at this."

"It fits, doesn't it? From what we know so far?"

"I think it does." Jan turned away from the bridge and looked at the mover. "Maybe we should push on that a little, when we see our friend tonight."

"This is insane. *You're* insane." Mortas spoke under his breath, standing next to an Erica Varick clad in a blue swimsuit provided by the Holy Whisper. She had just emerged from the settlement, with a large white towel draped over her shoulders. A line of young men and women, also wearing swimming gear, waited near the edge of the river where the barrier prevented the snakes from approaching.

"This is how they end their workday. They invited me, and we're trying to make friends. Since your injury won't let you participate, it has to be me." Varick waved at Felicity, who beckoned from the riverbank. "Besides, it's hot as hell out here and our friend hasn't shown up yet. I'm taking a dip."

"My injury isn't keeping me out of there. My common sense is."

Elder Paul approached, also dressed to enter the water. The waiting Whisperers all turned in his direction, and he called out to them. "All clear. Go ahead."

With a series of happy whoops, the line ran straight into the river. The bank sloped down gently, and the tall barrier was very much in evidence, but Mortas simply couldn't watch them go in. He turned away, about to warn Varick to reconsider, but she was already racing after the others. Elder Paul came up next to him.

"We've been doing this almost every day since we erected the fence. I always check the sensors myself, to ensure the barrier's integrity, and I've got good people monitoring the alarms and the underwater video. Just in case, we've got concussion grenades and long shock-staves ready. She's perfectly safe."

"Some of those monsters are twenty feet long, and they go crazy when food's nearby. One of these days, a big one is going to smash right through that mesh. And his buddies will be right behind him." Jander's heart thudded loudly while he watched the swimmers thrashing around. He couldn't stop the words. "You're gonna feel like shit when that happens, Elder."

The water churned with all the bouncing, kicking, and swimming, while happy cries carried across the air. In the middle of it, Erica exchanged splashes with an unidentified Whisperer, both of them laughing. Elder Paul stepped in closer.

"You've lost people in the war, haven't you? Soldiers under your command?"

"I lost people right here. And later. So you can bet I don't take any stupid chances with their lives."

"I understand. This is the second settlement I've supervised, and so far I've been lucky. But I have had to send bodies home, so in a way I can relate to your burden."

"It's not a burden."

"That's what it turns into, if you never lay it down." Elder Paul gave him a brilliant smile as he hung his towel on Jander's shoulder. He spoke while walking backward toward the water. "Oh, and we've got a series of smaller barriers upstream and down, just to keep the big snakes from building up a head of steam."

With a high-pitched yelp, he turned and ran straight into the tumult.

"Elder Paul said you were on Fractus." A slightly overweight Whisperer named Nibbit spoke to Jander across the table. "Can you tell us what it was like?"

Mortas signaled for him to wait while he swallowed. The alien hadn't arrived yet, and so he and Varick had been invited to dinner. The food was quite good, and all around them was the sound of talking, joking, and eating. Erica was seated at a different table, and the colonists clearly found her comments entertaining. The disturbing swimming party had ended without incident, and he'd managed to set it aside.

"The disaster was already in full swing by the time my unit arrived." The hubbub subsided a bit, as heads inclined in his direction from across the different tables. "The Sims had fired the same mud-creating munitions that they used here, but in a much higher concentration. The size of the field expanded constantly for several days, consuming miles of ground.

That territory was supposed to have firmed up again within hours, but it didn't."

"What did it look like? We heard it was like a giant, never-ending tornado."

"That's how it was at first. Above the mud zone there was this enormous cloud, filled with dirt and revolving slowly. The air all around it was filled with tiny particles of dust. We already had goggles on, it's part of the gear, but they had to issue filter masks so we could breathe. Those got clogged up fast."

The entire room had gone silent, and Mortas sensed they were more interested in the environmental effect he'd witnessed than the military debacle that had almost destroyed the Orphan Brigade. Catching his eye, Erica subtly signaled that he should stand up. He rose and raised his voice.

"I'm no expert on any of this, but I'll tell you what I saw. My outfit was on one edge of the mud zone, up on rocky terrain that was unaffected. Late one night the ground started to tremble, and we thought it was an earthquake." He paused. "In a way, I guess it was. Apparently the mud had chewed down so far that it opened up a pocket of gas or water or something, and the whole thing blew sky-high."

Elder Paul had folded his hands in front of him and rested his chin on them, his eyes fixed on Mortas. Looking over the other faces, Jander saw expressions ranging from academic interest to deep concern.

"That eruption got rid of the tornado, but replaced it with a low-hanging, dirt-filled cloud that covered the whole region. Without the optics in our goggles, we wouldn't have been able to see more than a few yards. Nothing could fly anymore, and even our short-duration surveillance drones were falling out of the sky almost as fast as we could put them up."

He stopped again, but for a different reason. So many of the Whisperers were of military age that it was hard not to see the faces of his troops among them. At one table near the back, one of the colonists could easily have been mistaken for Prevost's brother. The earnest eyes of another reminded him of Ithaca. His platoon. Somewhere without him. Mortas cleared his throat.

"Anyway, a tremendous amount of explosives got tossed around in that vicinity shortly after that, which blew the cloud away. The ground was still a giant mud field around a bottomless sinkhole." The room seemed to dissolve around him, replaced by the disaster that had followed. Columns of Sim armor surging around the mud patch, stopped only by a hastily deployed minefield and volley after volley of missiles fired from orbit. The Sim infantry charging through the woods behind them, suffering and inflicting huge losses in an attempt to clear the high ground of the humans who were directing the deadly rockets.

One of the colonists smiled at Jander, encouraging him to continue, but that only reminded him of Ladaglia. Always joking, always upbeat, until the deadly darts of a flechette round had caught him. Mortas looked at the ceiling, only to see the choking dragonflies dropping from the soot cloud, landing around the fire support man Daederus and his smashed legs. His throat constricted, and the seated colonists were now a blur. He placed his hand on his chair back, and then made eye contact with Varick.

Wearing an expression of complete understanding, the Banshee captain raised a closed fist in front of her chest so that no one else saw it. It twitched minutely, clenched in support. The brown of her eyes pulled him in, and Mortas felt his throat relax just enough.

"We got evacuated shortly after that. It's my understanding that the mud field is still expanding, and that the atmosphere has been badly compromised."

Mortas wanted to sit down, but the faces seemed to be waiting for more and he was afraid to look at them. His eyes sought out Elder Paul, and the senior-most Whisperer came to his rescue. "Thank you for sharing that with us, Jan. I'm sure that wasn't easy."

He gave the man an uncertain smile, and sat back down.

"I've figured out the alien's plan." Varick came up to Jander outside, where he'd gone to get some air. The Whisperers had thrown a modest reception after dinner, and so Mortas had spent the last hour providing more detail for what he'd seen on Fractus. Retelling the story had grown tedious, and he'd slowly drifted away from the crowd. One side of the dome had been retracted, and so he'd walked out onto a stone patio that ended in the planet's dirt.

"And what would that be?" he asked in amusement. A small amount of alcohol had been provided at the reception, and it had clearly affected his partner.

"It's genius." Erica stepped up next to him, looking back inside where the Whisperers were still mingling. "She's going to keep asking us to meet her here, night after night, and never show up. She's going to make us hang around with these people until we're pacifists."

"Just think of how great a swimmer you'd become."

"Become? I'm already a great swimmer." Varick leaned in, pressing her arm up against his. "Just a warning. I heard Elder Paul talking with Dru about having you tell the group about Gorman."

"I didn't realize I was the evening's featured speaker."

"You promised you would. Besides, you're a good talker."

"It's a family trait."

"Hey, you never know when it might come in handy. Let's be optimistic for a moment, and say that this does end in a cease-fire. You'll be out of a job, so you'll have no choice but to use those Mortas connections. Become an ambassador. Talk for a living."

"My dad offered to make me the envoy to the Holy Whisper, after Twelfth Corps let me out of jail. I turned him down."

"Well that proves it. You really are a shithead."

"I proved that a long time ago." He raised his eyebrows at her, and they both finished the sentence together. "When I joined the Force!"

They both sagged against each other, chortling like fools but trying to hold it back. Jander put his arm around Erica's shoulders, and felt her hand grasping the fabric of his shirt as the mirth ran through them. Temples touching, bodies wracked with near-convulsions, they still couldn't hold it back.

From inside the dome, several of the closest Whisperers turned to look outside when they heard the sounds of raucous laughter.

"In the Human Defense Force, many of the combat units have a tradition." Jander looked across the somber faces. He stood at the back of the dome on a slightly raised platform, his audience backlit by the star-filled night sky. "When we lose somebody, we get together and say a few words about them. It's a way of celebrating their lives, and commemorating the impact they had on us."

He stopped to gauge the audience. So far the pacifists had shown no interest in hearing about his war experiences, or Varick's, and he wanted to make sure they weren't offended.

"I only knew Roan Gorman for a few days. His last days. We were marooned right here." Earlier chats with the colonists had indicated that they were fond of the alien whom they insisted on calling Amelia, and he now decided not to broach the topic of her betrayal. "He was an astronomer, a chartist in the fleet, and on the first night he stayed up and studied the stars. With no instruments at all, he determined where we were."

Several heads nodded, and he continued.

"We all suffered enormously during that trek. We had no food, no weapons, and in the beginning we had no water. We walked for miles and miles, and Gorman's feet blistered terribly but he didn't complain. When the snakes surprised us at that first stream, he pulled both me and Corporal Cranther out of the way. He did things like that time and again, even though it put him in danger. He was cheerful the entire time, and he never once deviated from his principles."

The words came more easily, and the memories warmed him. Mortas set his gaze on the back of the audience, and was rewarded with a smile when he found Varick.

"You already know that we infiltrated the Sim colony by mixing in with a column of their walking wounded. That group eventually hitched a ride with a convoy that was hauling captured HDF vehicles, and we rode on one of those all the way into the base. There was an accident, and Gorman suffered severe internal injuries. Despite that, he helped us move one of the wrecks out of the way so that I could create a diversion. We hoped it would cover us as we crossed the runway and stole an enemy shuttle.

"That diversion was a tank round that I fired into a Sim storage hangar. It exploded into a million pieces, and I believe that blast was what killed Gorman. I found him lying on the tarmac, and when we captured the shuttle he used his last strength to lock in the coordinates that took us to safety. He died shortly after that, reciting the prayer he had said over a dead Force soldier much earlier. We recited that prayer with him."

Jander's gaze had shifted to the floor, and he avoided eye contact when he looked up. He scanned the back of the throng, trying to locate Varick again, but didn't notice when he found her. His jaw tightened as he recognized the face of the alien, standing next to Erica. The Banshee had taken a step back, and was watching the Amelia-thing, but the creature was staring straight at Mortas. He imagined it was offended not to be mentioned, and decided he didn't care what the thing was feeling.

"I've soldiered with a lot of tough people in this war, but I have to say that the strongest individual I ever encountered was Roan Gorman. I'm a better man for having known him. I can't thank you all enough for locating Corporal Cranther, and for giving those two men a resting place side by side. Like me, Cranther didn't understand Gorman at first. Like me, he came to respect and admire him.

"I'm going to stop talking now, except to say that I've eulogized far too many young men. I'm tired of burying the Tel Cranthers and the Roan Gormans and all the others. I speak for a lot of the people fighting this war when I say I will not miss it when it ends."

He was rewarded with a great many smiles and friendly nods. Elder Paul started moving toward him, no doubt to offer thanks for the address, but Mortas couldn't pull his gaze from the back of the room. The alien made sure it had his attention, and then shut its blue eyes and bowed its head.

"That was very well said, Jan." The alien had waited until Mortas worked his way through the crowd. The Whisperers had been moved by his words, and several of them had asked him a few questions about Gorman and their ordeal. He'd kept checking on the thing's location, and Varick's, but neither one moved. Other Whisperers spoke to both of them, and his apprehension lessened when he saw the thing was never alone with Erica.

"It's not an easy story to tell, when I have to leave so much out." There was no heat to the words, even though his suspicions hadn't diminished. Mortas turned to Varick. "I do feel a lot better. I never got to say the words about either of them."

"It's important to do that." Erica's earlier frivolity had vanished. "You can't let go until you've properly said goodbye."

The Whisperers were drifting out of the room, obviously heading to their bunks, and so Jander motioned for the three of them to step outside. A chill had entered the air, but he walked them all the way out to the edge of the stone patio, trying not to limp. He looked back, making sure they were out of earshot.

"Okay. I'm sick of being at your beck and call, so I want to know exactly what you expect from all this."

"I've been completely open the entire time. I would have thought you'd have detailed instructions from your superiors. What do *you* expect?"

"We heard you chirp a little bird language, but you're offering to serve as translator for the biggest negotiation in human history. How do we know you can speak to the Sims, or that they even know you're here?"

The face of Amelia Trent took on a bemused expression that could have been mockery or respect. "That's very good. We're on the same wavelength after all."

"Meaning?" Erica asked flatly.

"I wasn't playing games with you, being gone like that. I had to contact the ship that brought me here, and they had to relay my findings."

"A Sim ship? Near here?"

"Near enough. It's a warship, but a small one. Your planetary satellites wouldn't detect it unless the commander wished otherwise. He's ready to come down here, as proof that I can deliver what I promised."

"You've thought this all the way through, haven't you?" Despite the accusation in the words, Mortas was already following the suggestion to its logical conclusion.

"You really are going to have to start trusting me, Jan." The Amelia-thing fixed him with an earnest expression that was hard to doubt. "Tomorrow, you're going to become the first humans to ever talk to the Sims."

CHAPTER 14

"I recruited the slave girl known as Emma, who was part of Horace Corlipso's household staff." On the screen, the orange-hued face of the Misty Man spoke in a monotone. "She resisted at first, and claimed she had always been treated well by the Corlipso family."

"Treated well." Reena snorted the words from behind her desk at Unity. "She was the latest of his sex slaves, and he abused them abominably."

"He's been drugged, and fed this story," Leeger, watching the tape, commented quietly.

"My immediate superior, Hugh Leeger, had kidnapped Emma's family during the wedding of Olech Mortas and Reena Corlipso. I told Emma that her family would be murdered if she didn't cooperate."

"I wonder why they're not showing that he's missing an arm," Reena mused.

"Probably concerned that it might look like he'd

been tortured. They cleaned up the orange pallor as best they could, but all the rebels I saw looked like that. The dirt in the mines gets into the skin."

"I know what happens in the mines, Hugh."

"I trained Emma in the use of a stone knife I provided, one that she could smuggle into the Corlipso household. She was supposed to assassinate Horace Corlipso in his private chambers while serving him his dinner. However, he invited her out onto the balcony when he was receiving the congratulations of the Celestian people on the selection of his sister as head of the Emergency Senate."

"Laying it on thick, aren't they? No one knows how Emma ended up on that balcony."

"I freely and openly confess my involvement in the murder of Horace Corlipso, and only offer one factor in mitigation. I was a paid operative of Reena Mortas, who ordered the assassination through Hugh Leeger. I am deeply sorry for the role I played in this brutal murder, and for all the suffering it has caused."

The scene cut to a park in Fortuna Aeternum that Reena recognized only from the surrounding buildings. The grass had all been trampled away, and none of the trees remained, but that made room for a set of gallows. The Misty Man stood on the platform, encased in a large canvas bag with straps that concealed his missing arm. Two Celestian military policemen stood behind him, and a voice boomed out of a loudspeaker.

"For the murder of our beloved leader Horace Corlipso, a crime to which you have willingly confessed, you have been sentenced to death." A third figure, draped all in black, stepped up and placed a noose around the Misty Man's neck. As the hood went in place, the voice continued. "The sentence is carried out now, in the name of the people of Celestia."

The executioner stepped out of the frame, and then the flooring swung away. The Misty Man dropped out of sight, the thick rope giving a single, solid jerk and then going still.

"I recognized that voice," Reena said, shutting off the screen. "Damon Asterlit. Your counterpart in my father's organization."

"I know who he is, but never heard him speak before. From what my people have learned, he's the head of security in Fortuna Aeternum—which basically makes him the military governor. I hear that gallows gets a lot of use."

"The Misty Man's confession's going to get a lot of use. How is the denial coming along?"

"It's been ready to go for some time. Heavy emphasis on his defection to the rebels, accusations of war crimes committed against civilians caught in the fighting . . . the usual lies."

"It won't do any good. In a very short time, I'm going to be asked to appear before the Senate committee investigating the rebellion." Reena shook her head. "Even more lies."

"It doesn't have to be. I strongly suggest that you reconsider recognizing the rebels."

"We've been over this. No amount of political maneuvering can change what's already happened. I made a call, and it went wrong. Now we're stuck with it."

"With respect, ma'am, it didn't *all* go wrong. The slaves have freed themselves."

"At the cost of thousands of lives—a tally that's still running—and the removal of Celestia from the war. How do you suggest I claim that?"

"We did something good here, despite our motives. You and the Chairman tolerated this crime, in the name of fighting the war, but neither of you liked it. Honestly, I think it was the biggest reason the Chairman undertook his last mission."

"And see where that got us."

"If this rebellion hadn't occurred, someone was going to have to address this sin at some future date, probably not until well after the war ended. But we can do that *right now*. You can turn the tables on the Alliance members who are pretending they didn't know that slavery was being practiced on Celestia. Some of them are the same people who've been putting the screws to you."

"That's enough, Hugh."

"The HDF units on Celestia would welcome a cease-fire, ma'am. They signed on to fight the Sims, not to prop up a dirty bunch of fat cats."

"That's *enough!*" Reena came to her feet, palms slapping the desktop. "You disobeyed my orders by going to Celestia. I put you in charge of the most important mission ever undertaken by humanity, and you used it to put yourself in the hands of my enemies.

"What if Asterlit had caught you? What if it was *you* making that confession?" She sat back down. "No one's going to believe the coerced testimony of a hired killer like the Misty Man. But the chief of security for the Chairwoman? You almost finished me right there, Hugh."

"I needed to see it for myself." Leeger stared at the carpet. "It's awful. The camps, the squalor, the hopelessness, the brutality. It's every lousy thing humans can do to each other, all in one place."

"That's why we have to end it as soon as possible. By restoring order."

"Restoring order is only going to end it for one side, ma'am."

"We do what we can." Reena's voice was wooden. "That's something Olech understood. It's impossible to do any more than that. And we're kidding ourselves when we try."

Though physically a passenger on the *Delphi*, Mira Teel was somewhere else entirely. Her body was asleep in her Transit Tube, but her mind was awake in a setting it easily recognized. Colors slowly swirled in her vision like clouds, and warmth surrounded her. Others dreamt of people and events in the Step, but the communications Mira Teel received were always impressions.

Just then the gently shifting panoply was a mix of light green, dull yellow, and rose. Soothing, comforting colors. So often this meant an important message, as if telling her to be open and aware. Messages came in many forms, from simple objects that appeared on the clouds to nothing more than a hint of an emotion. Although the former method was more straightforward, she'd come to believe the latter held greater significance.

Weightless and formless, she floated in the colors. As always, she felt the presence of intelligence, intent, and interest. Something was there with her in the variegated void, and it ardently wished to communicate. Sadly—and many times Mira believed she detected true sadness—it didn't know how, or she was simply not smart enough to understand.

But here, now, a throb of expectation pulsed in the mist. She focused her attention, studying the swirls and eddies as a paltry means of indicating that she was ready. The response was immediate, and she recognized the first of the objects to float into view. It was one of the stones from previous dreams, polished and sparkling and smoothly rotating. She'd found the riddle of the ornaments impossible to solve, but tried not to think of the frustrated hours she'd spent trying to unlock their meaning.

A second one appeared, and then a third, and her own excitement matched the vibration around her. In all of the other dreams, only one of the unexplained baubles had appeared at a time. Her eyeless, undirected vision drank in the sight as the last of the five skidded into line with the others. The rocks stopped revolving, as if calling for her attention.

The flowing colors behind the ornaments brightened in one spot, and then that grew until it was a ball of light. The sphere slid into the center of the row, and then the stones began to circle it. Some came close to touching it while others seemed almost to sail away before coming back into view. At times the ball of light effervesced bright, tiny bubbles that quickly vanished, while the rocks kept up their prearranged dance.

Mira's consciousness tried to scream her comprehension. The light was a star, and the rocks were planets orbiting it. It was no formation she recognized, and might not exist at all, but that was clearly the intent.

A wave of warmth lapped over her, and she awoke.

CHAPTER 15

The hill seemed to get bigger as Ayliss climbed. Tall, thin trees stuck up out of the hardened soil, their tufted tops swaying in a breeze she couldn't feel. The rest of the trainee squad was spread out to her left and right, also struggling up the incline, also loaded down. She sweated freely inside the badly fitting training armor, the overladen rucksack pushing down on her shoulders. If she arched her back at all, the shift in weight threatened to pull her over backward, but if she bent over too far, it tried to drive her face into the hillside.

The mock Scorpion rifle was constantly in the way, and she kept switching it from one hand to the other in order to grab the nearest tree. As for the bizarre saplings, they swung back and forth as soon as they were touched, offering no support except for a brief handhold. At one point in the ascent she'd leaned back against one of them, only to have it slip away and almost send her crashing back to the bottom.

Ayliss looked up, telling herself not to, but needing to see where the rising ground met the blue skyline. There it was again, not twenty yards ahead, but she tried to remember seeing that mirage twice before in the last thirty minutes. The training cadre had called this phenomenon a false crest, warning that it only appeared to be the summit. They would reach what they believed to be the highest point in the ascent, only to find that the ground continued to rise just beyond a short patch of level soil. Ever helpful, the NCOs had included this punishing escarpment in the march route to demonstrate the effect. Ayliss's thighs trembled with the effort of keeping her upright, and so she raised a boot and forced it upward.

She heard a low moan to her left, and already knew it was Legacy. They'd been walking for three hours, over varying terrain, and the short woman had struggled right from the start. That had been surprising, based on her performance on other rucksack excursions, and Ayliss had silently wondered if her squad mate was sick. Looking over, she saw that the gutty civilian's face and fatigues were completely soaked in sweat. She was about to say something encouraging when Bontenough called out.

"It's the top!" she rasped, just loud enough to be heard by the other four. Although she found Bontenough's constant advice annoying, Ayliss had been forced to admit the former corporal was right more often than not. Even more surprising, she was the only trainee whom the cadre had not yet given a nickname.

Immensely relieved, Ayliss sidestepped across the slope to get behind Legacy. Litely had the same idea on the other side, and together they shouldered the short woman and her ruck the last twenty yards. The top of the ridge was a flat expanse lined with more of the wispy trees, and all five of them collapsed in a circle.

"I'm sorry." Legacy spoke between huge breaths. "I just don't have it today. Feels like I'm carrying two of these things."

"It's all right." Bontenough was standing now, her load on the ground and a canteen in her hand. She poured some of the water down the back of Amery's neck. "But we're going to have to pick up speed on the downhill. We're behind on the time."

"What did I tell you?" Plodder blurted out, sitting with her back against her ruck and her Scorpion across her lap. "She's too short for the load we're carrying. If she'd done a hitch, maybe she'd have learned how to do this."

"Oh, *enough* of that I've-been-fighting-the-war-and-you-haven't bullshit!" Ayliss yelled. "You telling me you did a lot of ruck-humping in the military police?"

"More than you did, *Minister*," Plodder snarled, sliding her arms free and starting to rise. "And while we're at it, how about you stop acting like some kind of hero just because Sam took a few shots at you?"

Bontenough and Litely were already stepping between them, wearing the same expression of exhausted annoyance, when the anger on Elliott's face drained away. Ayliss's tired mind found this confusing for a moment, but then cleared. She exhaled loudly in embarrassment.

"So how many push-ups is that?" Elliott asked, looking away.

"You spouted off, she spouted off, then you came back again. Three stupids at ten push-ups apiece," Bontenough recited, and then spit on the dirt. "Let's do 'em."

It was an agreement they'd reached the night Yerton was dismissed. To end the infighting, the entire squad had agreed that they would all do ten push-ups for every barb passed in anger, regardless of who said it. Silently, regretfully, they all lay flat in a circle, facing each other. Their damp bodies bobbed up and down for thirty repetitions of the exercise, and then collapsed.

Bontenough moved over to Legacy's pack, and began unfastening the long straps that held its unwieldy load in place. Every one of the trainees carried the same assortment of oddly shaped weights, fiendishly designed to make it almost impossible to fit them inside the backpack so that they didn't shift around.

"Don't do that," Legacy protested. "You're not carrying my weight for me."

"Like you said, you haven't got it today. Tomorrow it could be one of us."

"In a pig's ass," Litely answered, but the accompanying laugh took the sting out of it. The cadre had finally nicknamed Litely "Lightfoot" because they'd decided she wasn't contributing up to her full potential. They'd accused her of holding out on the squad, but she'd replied that she was merely conserving energy. Ayliss believed Litely had been telling the truth, having observed her during their many training runs. Lightfoot had a strange, arm-hanging gait that was nonetheless graceful and effortless. Whereas the shorter Bontenough and Legacy bounced along with choppy, pounding steps and Plodder's long legs covered the ground with great strides, Litely looked like she could literally run all day.

Bontenough opened the rucksack flap, and selected one of the weights. This one was long and rectangular, with a handle cut into one end. Orange like the others, its poundage was stamped into its side. Ayliss watched Lightfoot and Plodder both grimace because Bontenough had selected the heaviest of the weights, the twenty pounder, and then realized she was frowning herself. One of them was going to have to add that to her load. Still, Ayliss managed to look directly at Bontenough instead of reflexively looking away.

"What is going on with *this*?" the short woman asked the air, raising the orange plate with difficulty. It was clearly marked with a two and a zero. "This thing is a *lot* more than twenty pounds."

Ayliss rose, taking the object with one hand. After so many marches, they were all familiar with the heft of the different items. It pulled her arm toward the dirt.

"You're right. What the fuck?"

Plodder and Lightfoot each gave it a try, and a marginally rejuvenated Legacy did the same. Expressions of mystification quickly changed to anger.

"Those *fuckers*. They changed out my twenty with this *anvil*."

"When did they do that? We moved out right after weigh-in."

"Naw, that's wrong. They got mad at Plodder for rucking up early."

"I can't believe this. They must have switched it out while we were in the thinking position." Lightfoot slapped Legacy on the shoulder. "The trainers sure must like you."

They exchanged a few more profanity-laced comments before noticing that Bontenough was undoing the straps on her pack. They watched as she began removing the familiar rectangle, three squares, two spheres, and a single orange pyramid from the bag.

"What are you waiting for? We have to figure out if they pulled this same trick on anybody else, and then we have to reconfigure the load across the squad."

Each of them started to imitate Bontenough, and Ayliss spoke without thinking. "This sucks. Here I thought I was getting the hang of this."

"Huh?" Legacy grunted with raised eyebrows. "You knew your pack was light?"

"No, that's not what I meant." Remorse changed to resentment. "And who says my load's light?"

"Let's not add any more stupids to the bill today, huh?" Plodder asked. As a codicil to their agreement, they'd decided that the punishment push-ups could be avoided if a warning stopped an argument before it got going. Ayliss and Legacy broke eye contact, and returned to the rucksacks.

Bontenough quickly devised a method for comparing the like-sized weights. The extra poundage added to Legacy's load had been subtracted equally across the other four rucksacks.

"They really put some thought into this. Nobody noticed, because the change was so small," Litely observed. "And they kept the squad's load exactly where it's supposed to be."

"We have five more miles." Bontenough took the heaviest weight and slid it into her ruck. "Everybody except Legacy carries the extra for one mile. Put it at the top, so we can change it out quickly."

"Who carries it for the last mile?" Plodder asked.

"I will," Bontenough answered. "Strict rotation. It comes back to me at the end."

"No." Legacy spoke, already tightening her rucksack straps. "I'll be all right by then. Strict rotation, like you said."

"You already carried it for five miles."

"Yeah." Legacy gave a huge grin. "Let's play with *their* heads for once. See if we can make them think I didn't notice."

"**S**o what did we learn during our little walk in the woods?" Sergeant Stempful addressed the trainees in the middle of a clearing. Several Force vehicles were parked around its edges, including an ambulance, with several enlisted men and women gathered near them. The training squad stood in a row, the sweat-soaked rucks and dummy weapons on the ground before them.

"Not to trust the training cadre, Sergeant!" Bontenough popped off. One of the squad's minor rebellions was to respond to questions as if they were new enlistees instead of Banshee candidates; the cadre had already indicated they disliked this.

"Good answer, but wrong." As always, Stempful spoke at a conversational level. "Here's why. First you trust your squad. Then you trust your platoon. After that, you trust your company. Outside of that, you trust *no one who isn't actually going with you*. So the notion of trusting your trainers is just plain silly."

Standing at attention, Ayliss kept her face rigid while pondering Stempful's advice. It was the first time the NCO had voiced any kind of opinion that wasn't in lockstep with Command.

"Private Legacy, what did you learn today?"

"I learned to speak up, Sergeant!"

"Excellent. You see what you did wrong." Stempful appeared impressed. "The team is only as strong as its weakest member. You are not individuals, dealing with your own injuries and issues. I know it's easy to get that idea, humping a heavy load over rough terrain, but that, too, is wrong.

"Banshees get injured. Banshees get wounded. And sometimes, believe it or not, your body simply doesn't have what it takes on a given day. When that happens, the team has to adjust. By keeping silent, Private Legacy slowed you down and almost injured herself. Out in the war, that could have doomed your mission. But Private Bontenough realized something was wrong, and the rest of you took action once you identified what it was. That was the object of this exercise, and even though you took too long recognizing the problem, you did fix it."

Ayliss tried to peer out of the sides of her eyes to see the others, and thought she detected the twitch of a smile in the corner of Elliott's mouth. Stempful called out to the enlisted people near the vehicles.

"Break out the chow!" The support personnel sprang into action. Some of them started setting up a pair of long tables, while others began to unload the insulated boxes that brought hot food to the field.

"Believe it or not, you passed a major test today.

You are still a *long* way from being Banshees. But you're getting there." Stempful glanced at the workers across the clearing, and lowered her voice. "Today you learned something vital. Take care of each other, ladies. Out there—" her prosthetic eye seemed to shine when she briefly looked up at the sky "—we are all we have."

"Rig. You're up." Litely's hand was on her shoulder. Ayliss blinked hard, her cheek against her grounded rucksack, surprised she'd been allowed to fall asleep. The trainees had enjoyed their meal, and then cleaned their gear while each one in turn had been called to the ambulance. Although medics had accompanied them during most of their training, Stempful had announced that, from now on, they would be receiving regular checkups with the support unit's PA.

The sun was warm, and the tufted trees surrounding the clearing had stopped moving. Ayliss found it delightful to walk without the load on her shoulders or the armor wrapped around her torso. The troops who had brought out the food were quietly chatting near the vehicles, waiting to be sent back, and Ayliss noted with a quiet joy that she didn't yearn to accompany them. A female medic stood by the ambulance's open back doors, and Ayliss spread her arms while she scanned her vital signs.

"Okay, go inside."

She went up the folding steps into the narrow bay, stopping short when she recognized the gray-haired PA. What had his name been? She'd heard it not long ago, but now it seemed to be on the other side of a vast chasm of time.

"Have a seat, Ayliss." Scalpo had traded his lab clothing for camouflage fatigues. He was studying a handheld, probably analyzing the results of the preliminary scan. "Seems you're none the worse for wear. You've dropped a few pounds, just like the others."

She looked around the compartment. So many questions she wanted to ask, about Blocker and Tin and Ewing, but the cadre's constant scrutiny and trickery made her hesitate. Scalpo looked up.

"Wondering why I'm here, right? Last time you saw me was on Larkin." He waited, but she didn't respond. "You can speak freely with me, Ayliss. About anything. I can't take care of your health any other way."

"What happened? Why *are* you here?"

"The Guests didn't care for the assistance I gave you. They paid me a visit, but that didn't go quite the way they planned." He reached for a stethoscope. "Take off your fatigue top."

Ayliss obeyed, stripping to her T-shirt while Scalpo continued. "Then some thoughtful individual took the bomb meant for Rittle and put it inside a ZQ cargo hold strong enough to contain the blast when it went off. It destroyed several hundred units of expensive equipment the Guests were about to ship out at an obscene profit. I'd already left by then, and when I caught up with Dom, he had everything arranged with Assignments."

"How is he? What's he doing?" The words tumbled out in a whisper. She felt again the oxygen-stealing punch when Tin had dropped her back on Larkin. Remembered the Banshee's accusation that Ayliss had precipitated a blood-soaked disaster when she'd ignored Blocker's commands. Accepted for the first time that Tin had been right.

"Deep breaths." Scalpo listened to her chest, front and back. "He's the new First Sergeant of the support company that handles Banshee Basic. The troops who brought your chow today are some of his. He had the PA slot waiting for me when I arrived."

"And Tin?"

"Shipped out. She's a sergeant now. With the way the war is going, they need all the experienced people they can get. Ewing's been attached to Banshee Basic HQ. He's already reconfigured their commo."

"How is he?"

Scalpo flashed a light in her eye. "Surprisingly well. That episode on Larkin had a bizarre effect on him. He's off his meds, if you know what I mean."

"But he's all right."

"Don't worry. Dom's got him in hand. Take off your boots and socks."

"And the fallout? Apart from what happened to you?"

"You mean your family. Don't worry about them. The upper crust have their own way of working things out." Ayliss pulled off her socks, realizing that she hadn't considered how Rittle's death could have affected Jan or Reena, and feeling more guilt.

Scalpo lifted her left foot, studying the small square bandages that shielded her quickly hardening blisters. "Put all that high-level nonsense out of your head. You've got a job to do, and a lot of room for improvement from what I hear. Your trainers refer to your squad as a bunch of frantic fuckups."

Ayliss pulled her foot away, slamming it down on the metal flooring. She brought a finger up in front of the other man's nose. "Don't you say a *word* about my squad."

Scalpo leaned back, smirking. "My, my. Blocker was worried you wouldn't gel with your new playmates. He'll be happy to hear that's not true."

"You're a bastard, Chief." Ayliss presented her other foot, and the PA went back to work. Her thoughts returned to Jan and Reena and, surprisingly, to Mira Teel. So many people impacted by her rashness, too far away to take any of it back. How many pushups for all that? Her brain attempted the calculation, and then found the solution. "Chief, there's something I need to fix. Do you think Dom can get a message to Mira Teel, the Step Worshiper?"

"I know who she is. The *Delphi* was temporarily

impounded when two of her passengers misbehaved themselves on Larkin." Ayliss waited. "Yes, I'm sure he can."

"I lied to her, about my experiences in the Step. She thinks my father's still alive, and that he tried to contact her. She dreamt about a set of polished rocks, basically jewelry, and I didn't tell her I'd had similar dreams. The stones were gifts from my father."

"Interesting." Chief lowered her foot. "Considering what the Steppers believe, and the way your dad disappeared."

"Yes. Dom will remember the stones." A wave of regret passed through her. "I wanted to get off of Mira's ship, so I lied to her. Please have Dom tell her about the stones, that I dreamt of them, what they mean . . . and that I'm sorry."

"I will."

"Tell Dom, too. And Ewing. I'm sorry." The torment of the past weeks pressed down on her, and she couldn't keep the words from coming out. "So sorry. So many people have had to pay for the things I've done."

"Ayliss." The voice was stern, and she looked up. "Stow that away. They don't blame you. Maybe somebody does, but not them."

Instead of comfort, the PA's words called up a face that she hadn't thought of since leaving the Delphi. Lee Selkirk, the last time she'd seen him alive. That strong, confident smile, promising he would fix things with the veterans on Quad Seven. It was the last time she'd seen him alive, and the mess he'd sought to clean up had been her fault. Ayliss let out a long, shaky breath.

Scalpo started putting his instruments away. "You know, the trainers are actually calling your squad a gang of *flailing* fuckups. But it's a compliment."

"What?" She barely got the word out. He turned away for a moment, allowing her to wipe away the tears.

"It's true. They only have two categories for the trainees, and your squad got the good one. If you're flailing away it means you're trying hard."

"What's the second category?"

"Flaccid fuckups. They're not really trying. They just kinda lay there."

Outside, the medic listened to the sound of the new Chief and the infamous trainee laughing.

"I never thought I'd see this place again, much less enter it willingly." The high-pitched whine of Dev Harlec's voice sounded from the center of Reena's office at Unity.

"I'm glad you dressed for the occasion." Reena raised her eyebrows from behind her desk. Harlec was clad in an expensive warm-up suit that hung off of his slight frame like a sack.

"I'm always cold, these days." The light flashed off of his thick glasses and bald head as he looked around.

"For God's sake, sit down. If we meant you harm, it would have happened already."

"But not on Broda." Harlec eased himself into a chair. "That's why Selkirk didn't kill me when he had the chance."

"He had good reason, but showed better judgment."

"He did have good reason. I planned to have him killed, and to turn Ayliss into such a pariah that she'd have to seek refuge on Broda with me." The researcher laughed without making a sound. "Now he's dead, and Ayliss is an exile in the war zone. Somehow my little scheme doesn't sound so bad anymore."

"Is that the important information you brought me?"

"No, just small talk." The glasses shifted around some more. "I'm a bit surprised to be talking to you without Leeger. Is he listening in?"

"No one's listening." Reena kept her face frozen. Leeger had disappeared shortly after their last argument, and no one had been able to locate him. "You can speak freely."

"All right. You might not know this, but Gerar Woomer and I were secretly in communication for years. Regardless of my status with the Mortas family."

Reena straightened in her chair. "I did not know that."

"That's good. There's a bit of a network out there, like-minded intellectuals trying to make sense of this ridiculous war. Gerar was part of that."

"Go on."

"Shortly after he killed himself, I received a heavily encrypted video from one of the network's couriers. It was from Gerar, and it was a confession. Horace Corlipso offered to find Gerar's grandson a safe place in the war, in exchange for a favor. His spokesman, that dilettante Kumar, made it clear that refusal would result in the young soldier having a nasty accident. Gerar felt he had no choice."

Reena's hands gripped the chair harder, but she said nothing. In her mind, Kumar was being lowered onto a sharp spike in the middle of an enormous fire.

"Gerar arranged for Olech to disappear during one of the legs of his trip."

"That's not what happened. The capsule disappeared on the first leg."

"Neither one happened, actually. He went on to explain that an impossibly small but incredibly powerful Threshold opened just as Olech's capsule was about to launch. I've seen the data; it's true. Your husband was pulled into a Threshold that is beyond the capability of man to produce. Gerar believed that the entities Olech was attempting to contact snatched him."

Thoughts of Kumar fled, and Reena's hands came together in her lap. A wild surge of hope pounded through her body, but she silenced it.

"Where is this recording?"

"I can have it delivered to you."

"For what? Name it."

"Nothing." Harlec removed the glasses, and pressed wrinkled fingers into his eyes. When he lowered them, they were damp. "Gerar was my friend, and he was a scientist. He didn't deserve this."

CHAPTER 16

"It's not too late to retract your invitation." Erica turned goggled eyes toward Jander as the mover bounced across the ground. "We can blame it on Command. We just tell Elder Paul that we wanted him along, but got countermanded."

"He deserves to be there. The alien revealed itself to him and his people first, and the Whisperers passed that information right to my stepmother." He felt warmed by the sun, and the memory of Paul's open joy at being asked to attend the first meeting with the Sims. Jander had waited until the Amelia-thing departed, headed off to wherever it was staying in the wasteland, before seeking out their host.

"Your stepmother's not going to be happy, when she finds out we brought a civilian along."

"Just building that rapport with our neighbors

that you keep mentioning. Did you see his reaction when I invited him?"

"He was really touched. This is a very big day for them, if it leads to a cease-fire. Heck, even if it doesn't. Chatting with the youngsters last night, I could feel their excitement. They were afraid they were going to get shut out of this, once Command got involved."

"Another good reason to bring Elder Paul along. Command can make us shut our mouths. They can't do that with the Whisper."

"You know more about politics than you let on, Jander Mortas."

"After what I saw on Verdur, I'm not taking any chances. There's too much interest across the governments, the corporations, and Command. They all want to use the alien as a translator, but not for the same reason. I'm not going to let any of them twist this the wrong way."

"I doubt they'd be able to do that with any secrecy now. Look."

Erica slowed the mover as they reached the perimeter sensors. Waiting outside the main dome was the entire population of Gorman Station, all of them kneeling except for Elder Paul. He was obviously addressing the congregation, but their arrival broke the group's concentration. Happy faces started craning their necks, and Mortas swore he saw the heavyset Nibbit give a small wave.

Elder Paul raised both hands in a lifting motion, and the colony members all stood. Varick drove toward them, and through the windshield they watched the group converge on their leader. A long line formed as each Whisperer hugged Elder Paul, but they didn't have to wait for it to end. Dru, Felicity, and Nibbit approached with several others, so Erica killed the engine and they dismounted.

"Just one question," Erica asked before the others were in earshot. "Do you realize that you're including them, at least partly, because you're jealous of the alien?"

"Yes, in a way. It's disturbing that they like her so much."

Felicity walked up to Mortas and embraced him, kissing his cheek and whispering, "God bless you, Jander. Good luck."

Nibbit was next, hugging him by the armor and then shaking his hand. "Thank you for taking Elder Paul along. We knew there might be some kind of negotiation right here, but we never expected the Force to include us."

"How could we not?" Mortas heard his father's diplomatic voice in the words, and mentally winced. "You were the ones who got this whole thing going."

Nibbit squeezed both of his upper arms, and moved over to Varick. Dru stepped up, the sun shining in his eyes and hope lighting his face. "I know you're a man of peace, Jander. Do your best today. End this holocaust."

"It's only the first meeting. I doubt we'll be ending anything today."

"Then begin something." He was replaced by a succession of colonists Mortas didn't know, and finally Elder Paul was there. The congregation moved back a few yards, hands raised in a form of benediction as the three emissaries climbed into the mover.

As they drove away, Jander looked in the mirror. The Whisperers were watching them disappear, their hands still in the air.

"I know I already said this, but it's important you understand that this meeting is a little dangerous." Jander sat sideways, fighting the brace while straining to look at Paul. "The Sims are going to be on edge, just like we are, and it wouldn't be the first time a meeting like this one ended badly."

"That just can't happen." Paul was beaming. "This is an extraordinary event in human history. We've been fighting the Sims since our very first encounter, unable to speak with them the entire time. Who knows if this whole horrible war could have been avoided, if we'd just been able to talk? And now we're going to have an actual discussion."

"That is the plan." Erica spoke from behind the wheel. "But Lieutenant Mortas and I have a job to do here as well. We have to verify that the alien is able to communicate with the Sims. We can't just let it lead us around by the nose."

"I understand, and as promised I won't interfere. I am pleased to see that your weapons are stowed away."

"We wouldn't even have brought them, but this is still an unexplored planet. The Sims insisted that we ground our drones and that the *Ajax* move out of range, so we can't be completely defenseless out here."

"You're not going to be carrying them when we meet? I'm very encouraged. That's not what I expected from two combat veterans."

"Two rifles won't make much difference if this goes south, Elder." Varick laughed. "Besides, if this whole thing is a trap, they went to an awful lot of trouble just to kill a lieutenant and a captain."

Jander continued. "The Sims won't be coming near us, out of fear of whatever it is about humans that kills them if they're exposed to us for too long. So we've brought along two speaker systems with microphones. It's loud, but radios or other electronic gear might tempt our translator to get cute. This way we'll hear what the alien is saying to the Sims, as well as what they're saying back."

"But you won't understand any of it."

"Right now, we don't need to. We need to know if the alien understands them." Jander settled back into his seat. "We'll also be recording every bit of it, so at the very least our linguists will be getting something they never had before—an exact translation of recorded Sim language. Sort of a Rosetta Stone."

"You know, I was pondering the way you've been referring to Amelia. It made me think of something quite interesting."

"What's that?"

"In the more than forty years of the war, I don't think humans ever called the Sims aliens. I'm not sure when we came up with the 'Sim' name, but I do know that Command referred to Amelia as an alien right from the start. Isn't that odd?"

"That we recognized the Sims resembled us physically, and that the shape-shifters are something completely beyond our understanding?" Jander asked.

"The Sims were the first intelligent life forms we encountered, but they're very different from us. Enough so that we would have been forgiven for calling them aliens."

"Is that what you found interesting?"

"No. I thought it was intriguing that we immediately acknowledged our similarity to a race that reacted to our presence with violence."

"I'm not sure I'm getting your point, Elder."

"No point, just a little advice. Don't get so caught up in your hostility toward Amelia that you miss the opportunity to meet some creatures that may just be our relatives."

The lone figure materialized in the distance as they approached the place where the meeting would be held. The location was in the middle of a miles-wide expanse, free of concealing ravines. Jander watched the dark dot slowly elongate, until it took on the greenish hue of Amelia Trent's flight suit. The alien's head was cocked to the side, which he took as a sign that it believed it was going to run this show. Mortas glowed inwardly in expectation of the surprise he'd concocted.

The thing was standing normally by the time they stopped and climbed out, walking toward Elder Paul with a broad smile.

"I'm so pleased to see you, Paul. I'd been told you wouldn't be allowed to come along." That was a lie, and it locked taunting eyes with Jander over Paul's shoulder. No doubt it was hoping for a scowl, but Mortas winked at it instead.

"I wouldn't miss this for anything. Are they here already? I mean, on the planet?"

"They have a small scout ship in orbit." The alien patted a Sim radio slung from its shoulder. "They just called to say their shuttle will be landing shortly."

"I see it." Varick pointed skyward, where a black speck was slowly moving toward them.

"Excellent." The alien turned to Mortas. "We should get ready."

Erica and Jander walked to the back of the mover and removed two large cases. Varick lowered hers to the orange dirt and opened it, revealing a speaker with a telescoping stand, a microphone, and several cables. Jander handed the other case to the alien.

"I'll set it up, but I can't carry it with my leg this way. Let's go."

"I don't mind, Jan." The alien took the handle, but then stopped when Mortas reached into the back of the mover again. "What are you doing?"

Mortas emerged with a covered box in his arms. "I'll tell you as we walk."

The shuttle was taking shape in the sky, its stubby wings visible as it did a lazy turn. The Amelia-thing strode across the flat, but Mortas didn't attempt to keep up. She reached a spot roughly fifty yards away from the mover, and set the case down. She'd already opened it and was extending the legs of the speaker stand when he caught up.

"So what's in the box?"

"Just a few harmless, everyday items from our shelter. We're going to give you a list once we get back to Erica and Paul, and you're going to describe those items for the Sims. They're going to take out each one as you ask for it."

"They aren't going to like that." Without being told how, the alien mounted the speaker on the tripod and stood it up. "They don't like anything human."

"Didn't stop 'em from taking our vehicles last time around—or did you forget that's how we got inside their compound?"

The Amelia-thing attached one of the cables to the speaker and ran it down the stand to the case. She then took out the microphone and hooked it up to a smaller cord. "My people had a very difficult time convincing them to even attempt this meeting. You're going to doom both sides to continuing this war, if you keep playing around like this."

"Sorry I diverted from the script. You'd better get used to that."

It finished connecting the microphone to the case, and flipped a switch. The microphone screeched with feedback, and then went still. The alien placed the microphone inside the case, and walked up to Mortas.

"I know you don't believe me, but my people are genuinely trying to end this conflict." The words were tight and hot. She pointed into the distance, where the Sim shuttle was coming in for a landing. "The Sims are trying, too. Otherwise they wouldn't be here. Now wouldn't it be a shame, if the first civil conversation between humans and Sims was ruined by a mere lieutenant who isn't half as clever as he thinks he is?"

"Tell me what you're really after. You just dropped the mask, so drop the games, too. *What do you want?*"

The shuttle taxied to a stop a hundred yards away. The alien lowered its chin, Amelia Trent's blue eyes regarding Mortas with distaste. For a moment he thought she was going to actually answer, but then the shuttle's rear hatch started sliding downward.

"I want what they want. Peace." It waved at the craft, and several figures appeared at the top of the short ramp. Despite his skepticism, Mortas couldn't deny his astonishment. A group of Sims stood watching him from one hundred yards away, with no weapons in sight. The war had predated his birth, and consumed his very existence. It had almost taken his life, and he'd seen it claim the lives of many others. All that time, all that toil, all that waste, and had he ever seen them without weapons in their hands?

The alien's voice was in his ear. "So what is it *you* want, Jander?"

One of the delegates came down the ramp, bareheaded and wearing a flight suit similar to the alien's. He appeared to be middle-aged, and an ugly scar ran diagonally across his face. He raised his hand and waved.

Without believing it was happening, Mortas waved back as if greeting an old friend.

"Use the microphone. Tell them the box is just a test so that the humans can make sure you can actually speak their language."

A trio of unarmed Sims, the one with the scar and two younger ones, stood waiting by the shuttle.

The alien raised the microphone, and the otherworldly chirps and trills boomed across the expanse. Though steeled for it, Mortas felt the enemy noises penetrating to his very core.

The one with the scar nodded, and the alien started warbling again. "I told them I don't know what's in the box."

The trio conferred, and then the leader signaled that Jander should move away.

"You're coming with me. They can inspect the box without your help. Tell them to look at the items, but not to remove them until you ask."

More birdsong danced in the air, and then they walked back to Varick and Elder Paul. Erica handed the alien the microphone, and Jander turned to see that the Sims were looking inside the box.

"So much for hating everything human." He didn't look at the Amelia-thing, instead taking out a folded list. "Tell them to let us know when they're ready."

Elder Paul couldn't seem to decide which image captivated him more, the humanoid creatures across the way or the alien speaking their tongue. His face had taken on an expression of near-rapture, and Mortas hoped he wouldn't upset the man with what he had planned. Tweets and chirps passed between the groups.

"They're ready." The alien's confidence had returned. "They think this is a little silly."

"Really?" Jander's voice hardened. "Tell them we would have chosen something more complex, but their technology is so lousy they wouldn't be able to keep up."

"What?" The alien lowered the mike, dumbfounded.

"You heard me. Say what I said, word for word, and don't try anything funny because I know how they're going to react to that."

"And how would you know something like that?"

"Easy." Jander saw the alarm on Varick's face, and raised a palm to reassure her. "That scar on their leader? He's like Erica and me. He's a fighter. You couldn't possibly guess his reaction, but I can. Now do it."

"I never should have asked for you."

"That's right. Get talking."

The microphone came up, and the song came out, but this time it was halting, as if the Amelia-thing was searching for the words. Jander shifted the focus on his goggles, zeroing in on the scar. The Sim leader was still relaxed, in expression and posture, but that changed once the sounds reached him.

"Incredible, how much they're like us," Varick murmured, now standing right next to Mortas, watching the reaction. The Sim's jaw had clenched, and his shoulders rose. When he answered, the chirps contained anger and resentment.

"What did he say?"

"He said that true warriors don't rely on technology. He also called you a stupid asshole, and said that anyone who talks like you do is probably a coward."

"Do they really call each other assholes?"

"Don't test them! They don't like it."

"Maybe they are human, after all. We don't like it either." Mortas studied the distant group, and then drew Cranther's knife from his armor. He held it over his head. "Tell them I've killed lots of Sims with this."

"You are trying to ruin this. On purpose."

"Tell them what I said, or we're leaving."

Frustrated warbles bounced off of the air, and all three Sims responded. The two subordinates called out with pugnacious trills, and their boss tucked the microphone under one arm while reaching behind him. Mortas almost told the others to get behind the mover, fearing the Sim was going for a hidden gun, but something in the way he'd juggled the mike told him to wait. Mortas squared his body, to show he wasn't afraid of whatever the leader produced. Despite the sensitive optics in his goggles, his eyesight blurred when the item came into view. The Sim raised it in the air, and Mortas saw it was a knife similar to his own.

"Infiltrator knife. He's one of those bastards," Varick whispered. The Sim spoke into the mike, but now his tone was low and controlled.

"He says his blade has tasted its share of human blood." The alien spoke in a monotone. "And you're still a cowardly asshole who has probably never seen combat."

"Tell him I've seen plenty of assholes in combat who didn't act like cowards." Jan tried not to show pleasure at his ploy's success. "And that I've always wondered if they were actually brave, or just stupid."

The alien gave him a measuring stare, and then transmitted the words. Jander stood motionless, keeping his face frozen, feeling the enemy eyes studying him. The scarred Sim pursed his lips when the message reached him, and then broke into a smile. Nodding in what appeared to be appreciation, he answered in a short series of chirps.

"He says he's often wondered the same thing."

Jander grinned as widely as he could. He raised his arm again, so that the knife pointed at the sky. He moved it back and forth in a short arc, making sure they saw it, and then lowered his arm until it was parallel with the ground. He released the blade, dropping it to the dirt, holding his empty hand out with fingers extended.

The Sim leader nodded again, repeating Jander's motion, and then dropped his own knife. He trilled across at them, and the alien turned to Jander.

"He says he's glad the humans sent a warrior to talk with him. He was afraid it would be some scientist."

"Tell him there are two warriors and a pacifist here, all of us sincerely interested in arranging a truce."

The chirping elicited more nods, and the Sims shut off the sound system while they huddled in conference. The alien did the same with its mike, and aimed slitted eyes at Jander.

"You never meant to have me describe the things in that box."

"No. I wanted to make sure they weren't just three more of whatever you are, pretending to be Sims. And I wanted to show them that they have more in common with the three humans here than they have with you."

"You know next to nothing about me."

"You're no soldier, that's for sure." Jander gave it another wink. "And they know that. Tell me something. Is the Sim term for scientist—you know, the kind of human they didn't want to meet—the same term they use for you and your race of researchers?"

"But how can you pursue a lifestyle that prohibits violence, even in self-defense? If we as a race had chosen that course, we would have been annihilated by the cousins."

The sun was low in the sky, and the air was finally cooling. Both delegations had taken seats on the ground hours earlier, and so had the alien. The conversation had flowed freely, and after a time Jander hardly noticed the lag as the words were translated. The revelations were breathtaking, but the one he found most intriguing was that the Sims referred to humanity as "the cousins".

"That is a genuine risk of pacifism." Elder Paul nodded toward the seated trio. Varick had taken over the discussion after Jander had broken the ice, and the Sims had responded to her as another veteran of the war. They'd found the views of the Holy Whisper disconcerting, and were now trying to work their way through the unfamiliar philosophy. "However, it is one we embrace. We will not commit acts of violence, even if it costs us our lives."

The Sims conferred, which was something they did frequently. Varick had already asked them about their command structure, and learned that as a people the Sims valued a consensus approach. They'd admitted that this didn't work well in emergencies or in a military hierarchy, but maintained that it was followed whenever time allowed.

"When the cousins came to eradicate our predecessors, we would have been doomed if we had denied our right to self-defense. Even if we espoused this non-violent philosophy—which we do not—it would not have accomplished anything to merely allow ourselves to be killed. It is utterly futile to stand on principle, if the end result is the extinction of the beings who held those principles dear."

"I understand your point. Believe me, we wrestle with this ourselves. However, our philosophy is not based on making an argument. It is based on our relationship to our fellow human beings. Non-violence is just one of the things we hold dear, and human beings who do not share our beliefs frequently attempt to divert us from them. We do not allow others to dictate what we do in this life—which is what we would be doing if we responded to violence with violence."

The scarred Sim looked skyward, considering the explanation as the alien chirped it. After a few moments he responded, and the Amelia-thing translated.

"I agree that it is very important to uphold your values in the face of opposition. You've given us much to consider. All of you have."

Jander sensed the meeting was drawing to a close, and awkwardly rose with his weight on his right leg. The injured limb had gone to sleep, stretched out in the brace, and he winced at the pins and needles sensation. Varick and the others stood up as well, and he saw the Sims doing the same.

"Please tell our visitors how much we've enjoyed the discussion, and how encouraging it is that we're able to meet like this."

"Talking all these hours, and you finally said 'please' to me," the alien hissed. "I suppose that's progress."

"Maybe."

The alien twittered the message, and one came back immediately.

"We are going to return to our ship, and transmit what we've learned. As an asshole I once met pointed out, our technology is not equal to yours. We will contact you again as soon as we have received instructions. It may be several days."

"Tell him we're not going anywhere."

The alien transmitted the words, and all three Sims waved. Mortas glanced at Varick, who was returning the farewell, and remembered a question he hadn't been able to ask.

"One more thing."

The chirping stopped the Sims, and the scarred one picked up the microphone again.

"Go ahead."

Earlier attempts to provide names had failed miserably, so the best they'd achieved was identification by rank.

"I already told you that the captain here is one of our elite commandos." The Sims apparently had no equivalent for the concept of the Banshee. "When they go into battle, they paint female biology on their armored suits. It's meant to point out that you are fighting a unit that is entirely female. We've long believed this was a source of irritation for your people, and yet today you spoke with the captain at length, with politeness and respect. What is your opinion of this armor-painting custom?"

The alien turned to Jander when the answer came back. "He's genuinely surprised. He wants to know if that really is the purpose of the markings on the fighting suits."

"It is," Varick responded, and the alien translated. "He says that females do serve in their combat units, but that their percentage in the overall Sim population is actually quite small. The records are not clear on this, but they believe that the crews of the original missions were mostly male. The replacement crews were artificially grown, and as there was no provision for raising children during the voyages, they believe every crew member had been sterilized."

"I'm certain that their troops react badly to the markings," Varick answered.

"They do, but not for the reason you suggest. They see the markings as mockery of their inability to reproduce. Flaunting the glands that feed an infant and the orifice from which it is born." The alien stopped, listening.

"They find this deeply offensive, because they suffered their mutations in the service of humanity, and humanity tried to eradicate them because of those changes. That's why they mutilate the genitalia of fallen male cousins." The alien paused, but the Sim was done talking. "He said the mutilations are a reminder that you wronged them."

Late that night, Varick dropped onto the couch next to Mortas. Elder Paul was back at Gorman Station, the alien had walked off into the barrens, and the shelter's perimeter scanners were all engaged. Jander had removed his fatigue top, but then an overpowering weariness had taken hold. He still wore the brace, his leg propped up on the small table in front of the couch, and had watched as Erica downloaded the recordings of the day's events.

"Readout says it's gonna take most of the night to

encode all that." Erica's voice was soft, her eyes on the console where a flickering light indicated the all-important encryption was in progress.

"They're gonna lose their minds when they see that. An actual translation of Sim speech."

"An actual *conversation* with the Sims." Varick gave a contented sigh. "Up until today, I figured this was going to be just one more of those crazy plans that never amounts to anything. But then that shuttle landed, and the next thing I knew, we were swapping war stories with the bad guys."

"Crazy is the word. The more we talked, the more I opened up to them. I kept flashing back to that column of walking wounded, how I had to keep reminding myself they were the enemy."

"I swear, if I was reading a transcript of some of the things that Sim commander said about combat, I'd think it came from one of us."

"He did have a couple of funny stories, didn't he?"

"It was nice to hear that they run into the same kind of absurd situations we do." Erica stretched, and Mortas heard her joints pop. "I think the alien felt a little left out."

"Me too. But it better get used to that, if it's going to serve as a translator." Mortas waved a finger at the blinking light. "And right there is its audition tape."

"You know that once we send that, our job here's gonna end."

"What?"

"No way they're going to leave this in the hands of

two junior officers." She slid closer and nudged him. "Especially when *somebody* started the negotiation with a bunch of insults."

"You said you liked that." He nudged her back, enjoying the closeness.

"I did. I do. You're a surprising guy, Jan. And you're too smart to be in the Force."

"You really think they'll take this away from us?"

"Absolutely. The bigwigs are going to move in now. We did what they asked, and proved that the alien can act as a go-between. The high-level negotiations will start next."

"That worries me. The alien's going to run circles around our diplomats."

"If it ends the war, who cares?"

"I suppose that's how to look at it." He let his head sag against hers, and she didn't pull away. "I'll be sorry to see this end. Not the war. I mean this, right here."

"There's still plenty of time." She sat up, and he felt disappointment. "Come on, let's get that brace off of you."

"Why?"

"Because it's going to get in the way." Varick leaned in, kissing him. He returned it eagerly, and pulled her into his arms.

The gray light was dull, but it still reflected off of the silver scar tissue on her cheek. Mortas stroked the old wound with the knuckles of two fingers, causing her to giggle. He'd kissed it several times, to show it made no difference to him, but the response had always been the same.

"Does it tickle?" he asked.

"No. There's a little sensation, but mostly it's numb."

"How did it happen?"

"Well that took you long enough."

"I thought it was impolite to ask."

"That's you—all manners and diplomacy." She shifted slightly, sending a twinge up his injured leg that he minded not at all. "I was a platoon leader, pretty new. Banshee platoons aren't the same size as regular Force units. We pack so much firepower, so much armor, and can move so fast that we don't need all those bodies. Besides, the suits are really expensive and they're hard to maintain. So it was me and fourteen other Banshees.

"Two Force divisions were going to assault the Sim colonies on Platinus. You ever heard of it?"

The name was familiar, and Mortas tried to dredge up the memory. His brain was edging toward sleep, and it fought him, but it seemed important and he finally found it.

"That is very strange. Cranther said he was on Platinus. He said the Sims had aerobots that looked like the local birds."

"They did."

"He said it took Command way too long to figure it out."

"He was right. But that was later. My platoon was one of several Banshee detachments, inserted two days before the invasion to scope things out. They shuttled us in far, *far* away from the colonies so we wouldn't pop up on their defense systems. We walked for a day and a half, and at nightfall we were looking at the target."

"Spacedrome?"

"Near enough. Satellite surveillance had been restricted, so we wouldn't tip Sam off. Command needed to know the exact coordinates of the fuel bunkers."

"They sent Banshees for that?"

"I know. Any competent groundpounder could have done that job. But you know Command; why do it the easy way? They wanted a force in place that could assault the fuel dumps if rockets couldn't be used."

"How could they *not* be used, if you had eyes-on?"

"Platinus has a funny core. Magnetic waves, supposedly strong enough to mess with the guidance systems. Anyway, that's what they told us. But hey, we're Banshees, right? This was just a good stretch of the legs, and then a little spotting for the ships in orbit. If they decided not to use the rockets, we could always go in and take care of it ourselves.

"So we scouted out this tall ridge overlooking the

settlement we were going to hit. There were a bunch of targets, each assigned to a Banshee platoon, spread out by hundreds of miles. Our ridge was this bizarre formation, like a row of big round hills shoved together."

Mortas raised his hand and fondled her right breast. "Big round hills, you say."

"Pay attention." She lightly slapped his hand. "Sam hadn't put anything up there, so it was still covered with trees and brush. Perfect concealment, so we spread out and watched the spacedrome all night. Didn't take long to spot the bunkers, and to lock in the coordinates."

"Sounds all right, so far."

"Yeah, that's what I thought." Her arms wrapped around his neck, pulling him close so he couldn't see her face. "But I wasn't taking anything for granted. I'd formed a plan if we had to go down there, how we were going to hit the place and run off, so we'd be gone before the bigger explosions started."

Despite the warmth of the shelter and their intertwined bodies, Mortas felt goose bumps rising on his skin. Too many memories of events that had seemed just fine that had suddenly gone badly wrong. He pressed his lips against her ear. "Go on."

"Turned out we didn't have to. The fleet performed a staggered Step, so that several cruisers just suddenly appeared in orbit. They had the targeting all worked out, and launched the rockets before Sam knew they were there." She shuddered.

"They missed? The magnetic field threw them off?"

"No, they were right on. I mean, they hit that place with a shit-ton of ordnance. We knew it was coming, so we were hugging the ground, and I felt the blast through my suit. The secondary explosions started up, but then they didn't stop. I was burrowing into the dirt, trying to figure out what was going on, when that ridge erupted.

"And I do mean erupted. That magnetic field stuff I mentioned? Platinus has a core that is incredibly large, all swirling magma, and very close to the surface where we were. The crust hid it from our sensors, but the rockets cracked that open. We were basically on top of a string of volcanoes."

"My God."

"More like the devil. Everything changed in a matter of minutes. The air filled with these falling boulders, all of them on fire, looked like a meteor shower. The ground was shaking and shifting so bad that even with the suits we just couldn't get any traction. The trees started collapsing all around us, and then they were on fire, too."

"What did you do?"

"What any good platoon leader does when everything goes to shit. I yelled, 'Follow me!' and ran like crazy. There's a locator on every suit, and there's a way for Banshee leaders to override their subordinates' navigation systems. Instead of getting the directions for the different legs of a march, they just know where the leader's suit is going. So I activated that.

"I ran back the way we'd come, because we'd passed this open plain and I figured that would get us away from the volcanoes. It did, but not soon enough. You should have seen it. It was literally hell. Everything was on fire. I swear the atmosphere was burning up all around us. A suit's got more than a hundred microcameras on its skin, all feeding together for a full-spectrum view, but all I could see was flame. I patched into all of the cameras on every suit in the platoon, and it was all the same. I couldn't see where to go, and that's when things got really nasty."

"Sounded nasty to me already."

"No. A suit's got temperature control like you wouldn't believe. Put us in space, in an ocean, in a desert, in a glacier, we're comfortable. It has to work that way. And it's supposed to work that way, even in a fire. But it didn't. I realized I was being cooked inside my armor, and my ladies were feeling the same thing. They were calm about it, damn good troops, but they were letting me know we needed to get clear of this but quick."

"You don't have to tell me the rest if you don't want to."

"But I do, don't you see? I reported it all later, every detail, while I was in the hospital, but I never just told the story, you know? It's not like the other stories. Maybe I would have talked it out with my platoon sergeant, but she was killed and her replacement was somebody completely new."

"I'm listening."

"Right about then my cameras started blinking out, some melting, some getting clogged with soot. Rocks were still bouncing off of me, and at one point I think a tree landed on me. Must have broken in half, because it dented the right side of my helmet and pressed it into my cheek.

"The armor was so hot that it burned my face. I was slapping at it as I ran, and it wasn't accomplishing anything, and it hurt so much, but then I heard the screams. It was just for a moment, because the ground had opened up behind us and the last two Banshees fell into it. One of them was my platoon sergeant, bringing up the rear, and I was yelling to them and then their voices just cut off and I was turning, I was going to go back, you don't leave anyone behind, but then we went right off of a cliff."

Jander squeezed her tight, but she seemed not to notice.

"Later on they couldn't tell how far we dropped, because the cliff actually collapsed under us, but falling off of that thing probably saved us. I thought I'd been killed when I hit the deck, but the impact cleared enough of the junk off of my cameras that I saw a path out through the fire. I'd lost two more of my people in the fall, but I pushed the others ahead of me and we managed to get away.

"The burns on my face were pretty bad, so I'm lucky that it didn't affect my vision and that this scar is all that's left. They said they could repair that, too, but I'd have to leave the war zone. I said no, and you should have seen the way they looked at me. How do you explain something like that to someone who hasn't experienced it? How do you make them understand?"

Jander pressed his lips to the deadened flesh, quieting her. "You just did."

CHAPTER 17

Jogging along with the squad, Ayliss was enjoying her newly issued PT uniform. The black outfits reminded her of the Banshees she'd known on Quad Seven, and served as another indication of the trainees' progress in Banshee Basic. Ayliss allowed her bare arms to rub against the smooth, skin-hugging fabric and remembered running with Lola and the others.

The run route was familiar by then, a rough trail that zigzagged up and down through a forest not far from their barracks. The tufted trees rose up all around them, and Ayliss knew exactly where they were on the course. Bontenough was in the lead, as always, followed by Amery, Litely, Ayliss, and then Elliott. Though ordered roughly by height, the group was moving along at a fast clip, and Ayliss had to concentrate on her footing.

"Look at us." Litely broke the sounds of footfalls and panting. "Running on our own, just like real Banshees. I bet we get to start working with the suits pretty soon."

"Working is right," Elliott called. "Before you even get inside a trainer model, they make you go through the whole maintenance course. That way, if anything goes wrong, you know how to fix it."

"Where'd you hear that?" Ayliss asked, hopping upward around a familiar series of roots that waited to trip the unwary.

"Mess hall, the other day. Sat near some of the support types, they said they'd be seeing us soon."

"Now I *know* we're getting somewhere." Amery laughed. "You got to speak to someone who wasn't cadre or a medic."

They were laughing when Bontenough, arriving at the crest of the latest ridge, stopped in place. The path was wide at the top, and all five of them came together to view the sight that had stopped the short woman.

"What do you make of that?" Bontenough asked.

Rain and time had caved in much of the ridge's face on that side, making this part of the route particularly treacherous. Untold footfalls had hammered out a pair of meandering trails that hugged the landslide's edges, but the center was a sheer drop-off. The running path resumed on the other side, but that wasn't what had their attention.

Clustered at the foot of the small cliff were four

landscaping robots, trying to find a way up. Independent wheels twisted and spun while their rectangular bodies rose, fell, and gave off a frustrated whining. A range of tools adorned the jittering bodies, saws and rakes on telescoping limbs, mowing blades on raised undercarriages, all surrounding a silver hemisphere set in the center. That part was actually a complete sphere, capable of flying, designed for trimming limbs and vegetation too high for the arms.

"Got the wrong coordinates today, is all," Elliott responded. "They're probably supposed to be mowing some bigwig's lawn right now. Somebody's gonna be in a lot of trouble before the day is out."

"Hold it." Bontenough stopped Elliott just as she was about to start down. "These things aren't stupid. They know their surroundings. You ever seen them out here? Out anywhere wild like this? Something's wrong."

"Cadre?" Amery whispered. "Messing with us again?"

The mere suggestion galvanized the squad. The five women turned to form a ring, and then the ring silently shifted backward, putting the crest between them and the robots. Bodies lowered to a kneeling position while eyes searched all around them, observing the machines, the trail in front and behind, the rise and fall of the ground to either side, the trees and the underbrush.

The complaining engines were now joined by deeper voices, the cutting tools coming to life with throaty growls. Bontenough was closest to the crest. "I don't know what they're doing. They've extended some of the arms, and they're cutting branches off the nearest trees, but that's not going to get them anywhere."

"Noise suppression," Litely offered in a tense voice. "They're masking something else."

"We need to scoot," Ayliss called above the steadily rising sounds. "And not back the way we came."

"Wait," Elliott barked. "Listen. Somebody's coming up the trail."

The trainees sprinted into the brush and threw themselves down, facing the path. Though eager to see what was approaching, Ayliss tapped Amery and they both reoriented themselves to cover the ground facing away from the trail.

"Get ready to run," Bontenough hissed. "Stay together, stay in the woods."

The footfalls rose above the machine sounds just before Sergeant Nestor came jogging around the bend. She was dressed in the Banshee PT uniform, but with torso armor as well. It was a common sight, veterans training to run under a load, and the squad collectively exhaled. Bontenough stood just before Nestor passed them.

"What's the ruckus all about?" Sergeant Nestor asked, breathing heavily and looking up the slope.

"We're not sure, Sergeant. There are four landscaper 'bots down there, bunched up. They were trying to climb the hill when we got here, and right after that they fired up the saws." Bontenough rattled off the report. "We, uh, thought it might be a test of some kind."

"Not that I know of." Nestor drew a handheld from a pouch on the body armor, walking toward the summit. The saws really started to roar, forcing her to shout. "Banshee Control, this is Nestor, out on the running trail. I've encountered—"

One of the flying spheres burst over the crest, its approach hidden by the racket, and then Nestor's head disappeared in a spray of red. The metallic ball swept past her, scoring the trunk of a nearby tree without touching it. Bark flew, and the aerobot tilted madly in the air.

"Leaf line!" shouted Amery, and Ayliss realized that Nestor had been killed by a yard of filament whipping so fast that it couldn't be seen. The NCO's headless body stood there for a long, frozen second before dropping to the dirt. Ayliss was staring at it when a hand gripped her arm, pulling her up.

"That grove there!" Litely was shouting over the noise of the engines, one hand on Ayliss and the other on Amery. Elliott and Bontenough were already racing off through the woods, headed downhill for a cluster of trees with thicker trunks than the others.

Litely's grip disappeared, and Ayliss turned, fearing that the trainee had been chopped down. Instead, she saw the dark-skinned woman go past her and accelerated to keep up just before tripping over a loose rock. Her vision abruptly turned into a kaleidoscope of dirt, sky, and thin trees, and then she slammed into something hard. Ayliss's ears filled with the muted sound of the engines on the other side of the ridge, and a high-pitched whine that seemed to be everywhere.

Kicking herself into a squatting position, Ayliss looked up in time to see the flying ball swooping straight for her. It zipped through the vertical obstacles with terrifying speed, as if focused completely on her destruction. Knowing what the invisible line could do, she dived to one side in a painful forward roll that luckily ended with her standing up. The sphere had been moving too fast to correct itself, and it bounced off of the tree that had arrested her tumble moments before. Bark fragments exploded into the air, but the scything line bit deep and got stuck. One instant the ball was rebounding from the collision, and the next it was whipping around the narrow trunk with a rapidly heightening scream.

She was already running downhill when it exploded behind her. Fragments zipped past Ayliss, clipping leaves that she didn't take the time to notice. The larger trees shielding the others were barely the width of a human thigh, but they were several times stouter than the rest of the surrounding forest. Reaching the squad, she threw herself down inside the protective ring. Dirt and humus blew up around her, but she was already searching for other 'bots.

"What the *fuck*?" Elliott hollered, crouching

like the others. "Did you see what that thing did to Nestor?"

"This isn't a test!" Amery yelled back, her head turning and twisting.

"No shit," Bontenough growled. "We have to get out of here."

"Uh-uh," Litely answered. "The aerobots can't hurt us here. We hang tight, wait for help."

"Help? Who knows we're in trouble?"

"Sergeant Nestor started calling it in." Litely stopped, thinking. "Damn. We should have grabbed the radio."

"Is it still up there? Did you see where it fell?"

"Are you nuts, Bontenough?" Elliott's voice had dropped almost to normal, and she put a restraining hand on the shorter woman. "You go up there, you'll end up like Nestor."

"Quiet down," Amery ordered, and they all went silent. The throbbing machines from the opposite side of the slope continued their growling, and for an instant they didn't hear it. Then a new sound rose above the background noise. The whining of another flying sphere, perhaps more than one.

"Rocks! Grab rocks! And fallen branches!"

The forest floor was littered with loose stones of different sizes, and the trainees scrambled out from the protecting limbs to get them. Eyes up the hill, heads swiveling, shoulders ducking, grabbing up the ancient projectiles and tossing them back into the grove. Elliott ran over to the only tree with a branch low enough, leaping in the air to grab hold of the limb. It gave a brief crack, but then she was suspended there, her running shoes dangling a yard from the ground.

Without a word, Ayliss and Litely scampered over and jumped, grabbing Elliott about the waist and shoulders. The big woman gave a slight yelp when their combined weight pulled down on her arms, but then the limb let go. It dumped them in a heap just as Bontenough yelled above the mounting whine.

"Here they come! Get back here!"

Taking an extra second to look back, Ayliss wished she hadn't. High in the air, but just below the tufted tops of the trees, three more of the spheres homed in on them. The 'bots passed close enough to the trunks that the leaf-trimming lines would have slapped into them, so the deadly filaments hadn't been deployed yet. An insanely inappropriate image came to her mind as she ran back to the grove, a luxury resort she'd visited as a child while on a family vacation. She and Jan had been enchanted by the flying cultivators, watching them trim an interlocking series of hedges into fantastic animal shapes. Elliott grabbed her when she reached the grove, bringing her to a stop, and Ayliss realized where the memory had come from.

"What other tools do they have?" she shouted as the machines began their descent. "Leaf lines, clippers, saws—what else?"

"Nothing that can get through these." Bontenough slapped the nearest trunk, and went back to sorting the rocks. She'd created five separate piles, so they wouldn't bump into each other while reaching for ammunition. Amery and Litely already had stones ready to throw, and Elliott held the long branch diagonally across her body while bouncing on her toes. Ayliss scooped up two of the rocks, and then the spheres were on them.

"Come on! Come on!" Elliott screamed, and the globes appeared to respond. They dived close to the ground, bunching up, and the target was too good to resist. A volley of rocks flew at them, but they separated at the last moment and came at the grove from three sides. Rising and falling, reversing direction with blinding speed, the spheres abruptly charged in as if on command.

Ayliss dropped to a knee, grabbing another rock, and heard a loud metallic clang. Amery hooted with joy before heaving another stone at a sphere that hung in the air, shivering as if stunned. A flat arm sticking out of its side seemed to be pulling it off balance until Ayliss recognized it as a pruning chainsaw, and then heard the roar when its blade turned on. Amery's second missile struck the damaged 'bot, and the machine toppled to the ground. It hopped crazily, the saw spewing dirt all around, and Ayliss hurled her rock straight at it. The mechanism gave off a loud burp, and lay still.

A high-pitched buzz drilled into Ayliss's left ear, and she swung around to look into a set of gnashing clipper blades only a yard away from her face. She hurled herself to the ground, and was trying to roll away when a rock hit her in the chest. Several more rained down as the others found the new target, the stones clanging against the metal. The sphere wobbled as if punch-drunk, and then shot straight up and out of sight.

A stuttering, slapping sound brought Ayliss's eyes back around to see Elliott repeatedly jabbing the branch at the last aerobot. The limb never reached the dancing ball, but the bizarre sound erupted with every lunge. Ayliss saw that the 'bot had deployed its deadly filament, and was chopping segments off of the branch. Elliott's makeshift lance was rapidly turning into little more than a club, but a salvo of rocks flew over her head to strike the sphere. It gave off an agonized screech before zigzagging away, but its propulsion system had been damaged and it wasn't nearly as fast as before.

Ayliss managed to throw a rock along with the others, smashing the 'bot and sending it bouncing past them down the slope.

A sudden silence embraced the woods, and the five soldiers dropped to their knees in a group, chests heaving, mouths hanging open, and then gripped by the swell of victory. Crazy expressions of triumph and amazement moved across their dirt-streaked faces, and their hands reached out for the nearest shoulder.

"Holy shit, that was close."

"No it wasn't. We kicked ass."

"Height of technology, and we killed 'em with *rocks!*"

"Seriously, now." Amery gave off an insane giggle. "What did we do to piss them off?"

Already swinging back into defensive posture, turning to watch the ground and the air, the trainees joined in her laughter. Bontenough cut it off.

"Four of them, right? There were four of them?"

"Yes. Yes! Four."

"Then what am I hearing?"

Joyful looks changed to puzzlement. The distant engine sounds had died, leaving a fragile silence. A gentle wind brushed the trees far above them, the swishing of the tufts making it difficult to hear anything else, but then it came on. Loud. The whining of so many aerobots that it sounded like a swarm of angry bees.

The spheres crested the ridge and raced straight for them this time, one right behind the other. In the moment before they struck, Ayliss thought there were at least a dozen of them. An instant later, her vision disappeared in a curtain of silver that blasted straight through the widest space in the grove. Her arms came up, and then a tidal wave bowled her over.

Ayliss went over backward, feeling the soft flesh of another falling body before crashing into the bole of one the trees. She landed on her back in the dirt, feeling the rush of air as the first spheres sailed straight through. Her running shoes came up, kicking madly, and she felt hard contact. Something slapped her left foot out of the way, but she kicked again with the right. Completely missing, the flying leg rolled Ayliss onto her stomach.

A scream cut the air as she scrambled around the tree, terrified to be outside the protective ring but knowing there was no choice. Seeing Bontenough curled up in pain, a splash of blood on the trunk next to her. Elliott and Litely both fighting over a silver beach ball, their bodies twisting and tugging while the 'bot tried to shake free. Its clippers deployed, snapping at the air while the two soldiers strained to jam the tool into the bark. Amery shouting madly as she charged forward, skidding down under the ball and putting her shoulder into it. The clippers snapping off, and the three women bashing the device against the tree.

A cloud of brown mist exploded all around them, and the escaping aerobot shot up into the treetops. Plodder, Lightfoot, and Legacy transformed into frenetic dancers, hands rubbing at eyes and clutching throats while they coughed and shrieked.

Insecticide. The one tool they'd forgotten. Ayliss was already scrambling to her feet, too far away, seeing another one of the hated machines coming, the three women standing, blinded, right in the path of its saw. Knowing she'd be too late, Ayliss charged forward, legs pistoning with every fiber of muscle and throwing dirt as her running shoes refused to gain traction. The blade howled, and then disappeared when the sphere began to spin in anticipation of impact.

Ayliss left her feet in a frantic dive, shocked to reach them and expecting to feel the metal teeth at any second, but then all four of them slammed into the ground. The noxious aroma of the insecticide rose up all around her, but she was looking for the sphere. The 'bot bounced off of the grove, but now they were all outside its shielding circle, rolling, twisting, looking up to see nothing but the whirling silver balls.

A series of flat explosions sounded, and the orbs were being flung around like tethered balloons in a high wind. More sparks, and then the rattling gunfire was joined by a chain of metallic pings that reminded Ayliss of hail on a metal roof. The spheres were swept away, some of them exploding while others simply fell, and then Ayliss was looking up at the trees and the sky between arms that were crossed over her face.

More gunfire up the hill, women and men shouting for them to stay down, and then another roar of machinery, this time vehicular. Two MPs slewed by on motorcycles and continued down the slope. Then armed figures were running past them, Banshees and a mix of others, taking up positions in a protective circle.

An instant later Stempful was in their midst, again telling them to stay down. Torso armor with no helmet, Scorpion at the ready, she knelt over their prostrate bodies. A drop of water landed on Ayliss's upturned face, and she frowned in confusion. Looking for Bontenough, she saw Chief Scalpo skid to a halt in front of the fallen trainee. A med pack slid from his shoulder as he holstered a large handgun, but Bontenough was already starting to sit up. Her hand pressed to her cheek, blood streaming red between her fingers, Bontenough mumbled that she was all right. Ayliss's muscles all relaxed at the same time, a delicious sensation of release, and her shoulders sagged into the dirt.

Looking up, she saw that Stempful's hair hung in damp tendrils and that shampoo suds were running down her neck. Under the armor she wore a pink bathrobe, and her feet were bare.

"You know who was behind this." Blocker stood at the top of the crest with Ayliss. Bunched at the bottom of the landslide was a smoking pile of shot-up landscaping robots, being examined by the MPs. "The Guests needed it to look like an accident."

"They didn't seem any more interested in me than in the others," she answered. "And they killed Sergeant Nestor."

"Supports the cover story. Defective software, crossed signals because of all the waves beaming all over this base. If they just went after you, it would have been too obvious."

"Even if they'd killed us all, Reena would know what really happened." Ayliss turned affectionate eyes up at Blocker. "You would, too. So why would ZQ take a chance like that?"

"They're a hard bunch to figure. One moment it's

all about profits, the next it's about saving face. The truth is, they don't fear the Mortas family the way they used to."

"They're gonna learn how, all over again."

"Maybe. But it won't be you teaching them. Or me."

"Speak for yourself." Ayliss looked back down the hill, to where the investigators were interviewing the rest of the squad. Plodder, Lightfoot, and Legacy were doing much better, having had their eyes flushed out and receiving injections to counter the insecticide. Ayliss absently kicked the toe of her left running shoe on the ground, trying to shake out the loose dirt. The slap she'd felt from the aerobot had been its whipping leaf line, and it had neatly sliced the sole in half.

"It's already decided." Blocker started down the incline, and Ayliss went with him, emitting a squeaking noise every time her left foot hit the ground. "Normally a squad stays here for the full basic training cycle, but the war's not going well. Your group has been doing okay, so you'll complete your training with a Banshee company assigned to the fleet. It'll be much harder for the Guests to do anything stupid if you're on a warship in the zone, surrounded by Banshee veterans."

Ayliss studied the damage as they moved, amazed by the marks on the trees. Precise cuts stood next to ugly gouges, and she pointed at the dead 'bot still wrapped around the tree trunk. It had been shot several times, just to be sure. "That one's mine. Came right at me."

Chief Scalpo had spray-sutured Bontenough's forehead where the leaf line had cut her, and the three-inch wound was now hidden under a bandage. Ayliss hugged her briefly, and then introduced Blocker.

"This is an old friend of mine. Two full tours in the war zone, and a couple of scrapes I got in on, too. His name's Dom Blocker, and he's running our maintenance support." She stopped, alarmed. "Hey, are you staying here when we ship out?"

Blocker shook hands with Bontenough, ignoring the question. "I'm Sergeant Blocker. That's a nice ding you got there."

"Finally got my nickname. Sergeant Wolcott wanted to call me Bullseye because of this." She pointed at the wound. "But Sergeant Stempful changed it."

"What is it?"

"Bullhead." She radiated pride, and Ayliss embraced her again.

"It fits."

Bontenough spoke to Blocker. "So what was this about us shipping out?"

"Just a slight acceleration of the timeline. You've handled all the stress test nonsense they can throw at you, so you'll all be going to an active Banshee outfit to complete your training."

"All of us?" Bontenough appeared confused. "I thought they split Basic squads up when they assigned them to units."

"Not if I have anything to say about that." A cheerful voice came from above, and Ayliss turned to see Tin standing at the crest in fatigues. The Banshee bounced down the slope without once looking down, stopping next to Blocker. "You see, there's a Banshee company out there that needs to be rebuilt. Hard service, lots of vacancies. I happen to know the new skipper, so I sold her a package deal.

"Your whole squad's going there, along with some maintenance personnel headed up by Sergeant Blocker." Tin's lips parted when she looked at him. "We're even bringing along this squirrely guy named Ewing, supposed to be some kind of commo genius."

"Excuse me, but who are you?" Bontenough asked.

"No need to apologize, Bullhead. From what I hear, you'll be one of my team leaders in just a few months." She looked directly at Ayliss. "I'm Sergeant Tin, and I'll be your squad leader in the war."

In a darkened room at Unity Plaza, Reena Mortas hung in space. She was only three legs into the daily replay of Olech's aborted Step voyage, but she'd been halted in the middle of nowhere for several minutes. The cosmos spread out all around her, and yet she saw none of it. Gerar Woomer's taped confession played in her mind instead, blowing on the glowing ember of hope that her husband was somewhere out there, still alive.

"Excuse me, Madame Chairwoman, but Minister Kumar is insisting on an audience." One of the technicians spoke to her out of the void. "He says you're avoiding him. He's outside the chamber, and refusing to leave. Should I have him escorted out of the tower?"

"No. Let him in. And then secure the room's communications." The lights came up, and the chair known as Olech Mortas's throne descended. When she reached the empty floor, Kumar was standing there dressed in a gray suit.

"Nice to see you changed out of your adviser outfit." Reena spoke without rising. "Is there some significance to that?"

"You could say so." Kumar's sureness had returned, reminding her of why she so disliked him. "I've moved on. I'm working with a certain big corporation now."

"Zone Quest. Why am I not surprised?"

"If I were you, I'd go easy on the sarcasm. You're in deep trouble, and you don't even know it." Reena didn't respond, causing Kumar to smile. "That's better.

"Your man Leeger has been sighted on Celestia. No, don't bother telling me he's still here, or on a mission of some kind. The rumors about his disappearance have been flying all over the complex, so I alerted Celestian Command to be on the lookout. Apparently your chief of security has gone over to the rebels—just like his former subordinate, who confessed to Horace's murder."

"I assume you came here with an offer."

"A generous one, considering you murdered your own father and plunged your native planet into chaos. Lucky for you, the Celestian delegation to the Emergency Senate was here on Earth when your idiotic plot blew up on you. It's surprising how malleable they've become, now that they're homeless paupers."

"Malleable enough to forget about what happened to Horace?"

"Let's just say that my new sponsors have promised to help them rebuild their wealth in return for voting in a certain fashion."

"Would this fashion leave me in power?"

"You're going to have to earn it. There are some mineral-rich planets in the war zone that your dead husband gave to the Veterans Auxiliary. You're going to reverse his decision."

"That's going to be very unpopular."

Kumar walked up close. "More unpopular than the revelation that you caused all the suffering on Celestia, as well as the resulting reverses in the war?"

"No, I suppose not."

"Then we're in agreement?"

"I'm going to have to give it some thought."

"Take all the time you need. You have until I leave this room." Kumar's eyes ranged over the bare gray walls and the towering ceiling. "They say that only Olech and you were allowed to use this contraption."

Reena vacated the heavy seat. "Please. Be my guest."

"Olech's throne." The tall man settled into the cushions. He rested his hands on the wide, block-like arms, and tilted his chin upward. "How do I make it work?"

"It has several pre-programmed trips." Reena stepped around to his right, and pressed a button. "You'll like this one."

The chair ascended atop its telescoping pole, and the room darkened. A tiny white dot appeared, rapidly expanding until Kumar was looking down at the Earth from orbit.

"This is amazing!" he called out. "I had no idea it was so realistic. What an effect!"

"Just wait. It gets much better," Reena called from somewhere below.

The glowing orb of the Earth dropped away, and Kumar hooted as the projections shot him through space. Past Mars, through the ghostly asteroid belt, and then he was moving so fast that he barely registered the gas giants before leaving the galaxy. Darkness descended again, but not for long. Another white dot came to life, growing as it approached.

"What am I seeing?" the scientist shouted. "I don't recognize this."

"You will."

The looming planet slowed, and then resolved into a craggy, flesh-colored mass. No oceans or lakes were in evidence, and Kumar was leaning forward when the orb opened its eyes. He gave off a low moan.

"My name is Gerar Woomer, and I wish to make

a complete confession." The planet coalesced into the dead physicist's face, consuming Kumar's field of vision. "I was coerced into attempting to murder Olech Mortas, Chairman of the Emergency Senate, by my colleague Timothy Kumar. Kumar was speaking for Horace Corlipso, who offered to protect my grandson while he served in the war zone. He also threatened to murder my grandson if I didn't comply."

"No. No. This isn't happening!" Kumar yelled.

"I personally charted the multi-Threshold voyage Chairman Mortas was about to undertake, and also arranged to have his capsule destroyed in the middle of that voyage. When the Chairman disappeared, Timothy Kumar congratulated me on his murder."

The gigantic face went silent, blankly staring at him as another light approached from below. Kumar's legs came up against his chest, and he wrapped his arms around them while mumbling unintelligibly. The view beneath him was the expanse of a star, a seething sea of fire waiting to consume him.

"What do you think, Timothy?" Reena called out from the center of the fireball. "Quite a show, right?"

"This proves nothing! He's *dead*. You have no evidence."

"Aren't you forgetting who my father was? What he was like? How do you think Horace would have responded to something like this?" Reena's words echoed all around him. "When I walk out of here, Nathaniel Ulbridge is coming in. He's going to take something with him when he leaves and, unlike my father, I'm going to give you the choice of what that is. Your confession . . . or your life."

"That won't stop anything! You're *finished*! Zone Quest owns enough votes to have you tossed out of power, no matter what happens to me!"

"Gerar had more to say, you know. About that tiny, super-powerful Threshold that took my husband's capsule. So it really doesn't matter if I stay in power, although it would be easier if I did. You can help me do that, by influencing your new friends. You're a slippery little thing, so it'll be easy for you."

Reena's words got softer as she walked away.

"But I don't really care what you do. You see, the love of my life is alive. Out there. Somewhere." Shuddering in the darkness, Kumar heard the door open far below. "And I'm going to find him."

CHAPTER 18

Jander's leg throbbed lightly when he awoke, alone in Varick's quarters. The door was open, and he could see her at the console in the main room. Despite the mild aching of his wound, every one of his muscles was completely relaxed. He made no effort to rise, enjoying her scent on the bedclothes and watching her type.

Remembering the unsent report brought the unpleasant reality that their time was drawing to a close. Prodded by that, he slowly sat up and carefully swung his legs to the floor. The muscles in his left thigh protested when he put weight on them, and he stopped in the doorway to let the sinews stretch out.

"I don't care how much you tempt me, I'm not going back in there until the report's done." Varick kept typing. Her hair was mussed and she'd donned the same T-shirt from the night before, but the console hid the rest of her.

"I'm not posing; it's my leg. You've set my recovery back a week."

"More like a month, hero." Erica looked across at him, tilting her head. "Another night like that, and you'll never walk again."

"I'm going to take that as a dare."

"More like a promise." Varick kissed the air in his direction, and went back to the keyboard. "Put your brace on. We've been invited to a service at Gorman Station."

"That was fast. How did they find out?"

Varick frowned, and then gave him a dubious look. "You really are a self-centered idiot, you know that?"

"Here I thought the Whisper was into free expression of affection, and it turns out they're prudes. We'll go along with the ceremony, and of course the honeymoon, but it shouldn't be too hard to get it nullified."

Erica threw a pen at him, careful not to come close. "It's a thanksgiving service, to commemorate the first conversation with the Sims. The alien's invited, too."

Jander limped into his room and pulled on a set of running shorts. He strapped on the stiffer of the two braces, and hobbled to the console. When he rested his hands on Erica's shoulders, she pulled them down so he was holding her.

"I've added my observations to the report," she murmured. "It's ready to go."

"Let's negotiate a deal of our own." He nuzzled her scalp. "Tell them they can have the report and the tapes, and take over the talks, if they just leave us here."

A contented moan was her only answer, and the two of them hung there for some time.

"You know, with my leg the way it is I won't be rejoining the Orphans for a while. I'll probably be heading back to Earth to brief my stepmother in person."

"No." The hands held onto his arms, but the word was firm. "I cut my own deal, coming out here, and I'm headed back where I belong. With the Banshees."

"It was just a thought." He kissed her. "And who knows? Maybe I'm wrong about the alien, and the war might actually be about to end."

"I don't think you're wrong. I want to believe otherwise, but I just can't shake the feeling that we're missing something here." She gave off a slight shiver. "That's why I need to go back with the troops."

"I know how excited everyone is feeling. I share your hope that a day might be approaching, possibly in the near future, when this horrendous bloodletting will cease." Elder Paul was concluding the service. Though invited to the front of the congregation, Jander and Erica were seated almost outside. The venue was the same hall where the reception had taken place, and the back wall had been raised again. The alien had joined them at the last minute, sitting quietly through the brief ceremony.

"The sad truth of human history is that peace overtures sometimes do not lead to peace. I urge you all to hope, and to pray, and to believe, but also to prepare yourselves for possible disappointment. The meeting I witnessed was an extraordinary event, one I'll never forget, and our dear friends Amelia, Erica, and Jander performed as true diplomats, as genuine peacemakers."

The seated assemblage turned as one, stood, and broke into applause. Brightly colored sashes hung across their work clothes, which Dru had explained was a sign of Whisper celebration. The three honorees also stood, nodding and smiling with a fair amount of embarrassment. Jan caught Erica's eye and winked at her, earning a cautionary glare that quickly changed to mirth. The congregation turned its attention back to the rostrum, where Elder Paul was pulling a robe over his outfit. It was blindingly white, and he raised his arms in benediction.

"Let us all remain optimistic that the seed planted yesterday will bear the fruit of a lasting peace. Now we will process to the fields where we have sown the seeds of a different crop, to bless those seedlings and ask our creator to guide our hands and our minds as we learn how to grow sustenance on this new world."

The Whisperers moved outside while the trio of diplomats stood out of the way. Jan and Erica had been greeted with warm hugs when they'd arrived, the jubilant colonists having learned the details of the meeting from Elder Paul. They now received friendly waves and passing murmurs of thanks, while the nearest Whisperers embraced the Amelia-thing before joining the others. Elder Paul approached, accompanied by a small retinue carrying water buckets sprouting the wooden handles of some kind of tool. When they were close enough, Jander saw that the implements were cylindrical brushes with densely packed hairs.

"We sprinkle ceremonial water over the fields as part of this blessing, and it's customary to invite our guests to participate." Elder Paul's face shone with a serene light, and Jander found himself slightly envious. "If your leg isn't up to it, I certainly understand."

The infantryman inside him almost blurted out a stubborn insistence on participating, but a more compelling thought took its place. "Thank you for noticing, Paul. The leg's been acting up a little. Erica, would you represent us?"

"Of course." Varick's eyes slid past him. "Amelia, would you like to come with me?"

"Actually, I was hoping to have a few words with our translator." Jan spoke to the alien, and then to Elder Paul. "I hope you don't mind."

"Mind?" The holy man placed a hand on his shoulder, and squeezed. "Talk is good, Jan. We'll leave you to it."

The colonists had arranged themselves in a happy column, with much discussion and laughter, and Varick went to its head with the others. They moved off at a slow walk, headed for the fields behind the station, singing a hymn that Mortas didn't recognize. Despite the heat, every one of the colonists displayed a joyous activity. Open hands reached for the sky, uplifted arms swayed back and forth, and here and there he saw individual Whisperers dancing.

His imagination conjured up different parades, the long-denied end of the ceaseless war, the troops coming home for the last time, the races no longer striving to kill each other.

"So what nasty accusation did you bring with you today?" The Amelia-thing interrupted his thoughts, but the peaceful imaginings remained. Was it possible? Could it end?

"No accusations. Let's walk, shall we? All that sitting's made me stiff."

The sun was almost at its zenith, and the warmth was pleasant. The notes from the singers rode the light breeze, a soothing background as they crossed the dirt toward the water.

"No armor today," the alien offered, pointing a thumb at his midsection.

"We left it in the mover, with the weapons. We didn't think it was appropriate, given the nature of the ceremony." He glanced at the tail end of the column. "They're pretty happy about all this. Hope it's not misplaced."

"The Sims were pleasantly surprised yesterday. Their commander was impressed by all three of you."

"Despite the rocky start."

"I'll give you that one. You really scared me, but you knew what you were doing."

Though slowed by the brace, Mortas saw that they were getting close to the river. The anti-snake fencing rose up against the sky to their left, reminding him of the waterborne predators.

"Your people have been around the Sims for a long time. Do you think they'll approve the cease-fire?"

"The delegation came away believing that you, Erica, and Elder Paul are sincere. Their commander is a decorated veteran of many years' service, and highly influential with the Sim command structure. I'm optimistic."

"What about the things that created them? They put in a lot of work, right at the start, to make sure the Sims can't even speak to us. They must be monitoring the war, and how their creations are behaving. What might they do to stop this if they get wind of it, or to start the fighting up again if the cease-fire takes place?"

The alien stopped, regarding him with approval. "You continue to surprise me, Jan. No matter how this works out, you should use that family name to get a better job. One where you can make a real impact. You figured it out."

"I haven't figured anything out for a long time."

"Nonsense. You answered your own question, about what's in it for me and my people." The Amelia-thing started walking again, toward the riverbank fifty yards away. "I told you, we're researchers. We have a driving need to understand the things we encounter. Do you have any idea how maddening it is to see all the evidence that a titanic force is present in the galaxy, and yet we can't even *find* it?"

"We've been faced with the same question for quite some time. Our answer was to ignore it."

"My people don't have that ability. Everything we've learned about the Sims suggests they were fashioned by something else. That thing, those *things*, whatever they are, severed their connection with the Sims by planting the mythology in their heads that they're a mutated form of human. We expect that a cease-fire will force the Sims' creators to reveal themselves in some way." The alien's left hand came up, grasping the air in a shaky fist. "Just proving they exist will be a momentous achievement, but who knows? Perhaps this will allow us to finally study them. Maybe even *contact* them."

"They might not like that." The singing had vanished in the distance, and Jan was sure he heard the rushing of the water. He slowed down.

"You mean humanity might not like that."

"It crossed my mind. The first version of you was allied with the Sims, working against us. And these creators have a lot more to offer than the Sims."

"I understand your concerns. But just remember the Sims' creators have intentionally and completely eluded us. I don't think they're interested in my people—or humanity—beyond keeping us away."

"Is that why they made the Sims? We got the Step, and then came too close?"

"It fits." The alien stopped, facing him. Mortas waited several seconds, but the expected question never came. He felt his heart thudding a little harder, and then went ahead.

"One thing's been bothering me. You keep telling us about your obsession with understanding everything you encounter. Yet you haven't asked me a single thing about the most advanced technology mankind ever developed."

The blue eyes flashed, and then dimmed. "All right. Give me your extensive knowledge of the Step, Platoon Leader."

"Mockery's not going to be good enough." Mortas felt the adrenaline rising, along with the belief that he'd finally struck a nerve. The excitement came with a heavy undertone of dread. The colonists were nowhere in sight, the brace and his wound made him vulnerable, and he was alone with the thing. The slight weight of Cranther's boot knife pressed against his calf, and he found it comforting enough to press on. "I'm the son of the highest official in our government. I would have expected a researcher entity like you to ask me about the Step before now. Even if you thought I knew nothing."

"You do know nothing. All of you. You're unconscious in the Step. Passengers, the crews, even the *captains* of Step-capable ships don't know how it works. They might as well be monkeys, punching buttons before climbing into the Transit Tubes." The alien shook its head. "Your technology pales to insignificance when compared to the real prize here. We *have* to learn about what's making the Sims."

Jander's handheld vibrated in a fatigue pocket, an emergency sequence from the *Ajax*. He looked back at the settlement, disturbed to see how far away it was. No one was in sight, but he thought he heard bits of sound that might be more singing. Somewhere out there, Varick's handheld would be receiving an identical signal.

"I need to look at this," Mortas said, annoyed at being forced to drop the line of questioning. He limped away a few paces, the handheld shaking with increasing urgency.

The broken rhythm he'd taken for a hymn rose a bit, and he now recognized it as the sound of an approaching engine. Jander searched the empty sky, and then his attention was jerked back to the handheld. The warning vibration had run its course without answer, and so the machine spoke in a loud, robotic voice.

"Emergency. Emergency. Emergency. Unidentified craft converging on your location. Air and ground vehicles. Hostile intent. Find cover. Find cover. Find cover."

Movement pulled his eyes toward the settlement, where he saw a lone figure sprinting around the side of the buildings. Varick was waving at him, and he was raising his hand to indicate he'd received the message when a sledgehammer blow struck the side of his face. He was hurled to the dirt, the handheld flying away, the horizon spinning as the engine noise grew.

Hands, titanically strong, grabbed the front of his shirt and hauled him to his feet. Still stunned, he shook like a stringless puppet when the gripping talons yanked him forward. His vision cleared, and he was looking deep into blue eyes that glowed with malice. He'd seen that look once before, when the original alien had been burning up on Glory Main.

"Took them long enough to make a move, didn't it?" the Amelia-thing shouted, the voice booming with fury and triumph. "So many of you greedy, grubby humans trying to get hold of one of my people, and look how long I had to wait here.

"I was *really* hoping to meet your Reena, and all those other half-bright egomaniacs you let run your lives. But getting kidnapped works just as well."

Mortas raised a feeble hand, the muscles refusing to curl into a fist, but he swung anyway. The alien didn't even dodge the slap, instead twisting him around so that he was looking at the colony. It hugged him tight, forcing him to watch as three black dots appeared in the sky. "Who do you think they are, Jan? Zone Quest? The Tratians? Doesn't matter. They'll show me what my people need to know."

Varick was racing toward them, still hundreds of yards away, shouting something, but the words were completely drowned out by the noise of straining machines. The three dots resolved into drone gunships, hurtling downward, but they were still too far away to be making all that racket. A sash-covered mob appeared far behind Varick, also running. At their head was a figure in white.

"No. No. No!" He grunted, and then shrieked, his body finally responding as he clawed at the iron bands wrapped around him.

"Look at it! Look at it, Jan!" the thing hissed in his ear. "We can always count on human brutality. I'm thinking they need a diversion for the *Ajax*, so they can grab me and then get away."

He drove his right elbow back, punching it hard into the alien's solar plexus. Blue flashes shot across his eyes just before the pain lanced through him. It was like hitting a boulder, but forgotten as the drones came into range and he saw the gusts from the first rockets. Mortas kicked back madly, feeling like he'd fractured his right heel when it connected.

"Oh, stop it. You saw me get *impaled* at the spacedrome, and it didn't hurt me at all. Look! Watch!"

The first rocket struck the back of the crowd, exploding in fire and smoke and dirt and flying bodies. Mortas was thrashing and shouting, but the thing clasped him to it as the next missile slammed into the settlement. One of the domes seemed to expand, and then collapsed in upon itself before disappearing in an ugly brown cloud. The third rocket landed just in front of the fleeing colonists, the concussion throwing the front rank back into the others before raising a wall of dust.

"I'm afraid I'm going to have to leave you now, Jan. My kidnappers are here." His feet were no longer on the ground, and he swung in the air like a rag doll when the thing made him look in the opposite direction. A row of bubbles seemed to be rushing toward them, just above the ground, and then he realized they were military-grade scooters. Fast, light, perfect for screening missions and prisoner snatches. The alien whipped his body around again, raising him up at arm's length so that he was staring down at the hate-filled face.

"It's the Step," he snarled. "That's what you wanted."

"Congratulations, Jan! You *did* figure it out! You thwarted us by accident last time, hiding that you were Olech Mortas's son, but now you know the truth. And that you lost anyway."

Jander bent his right knee, his hand scrabbling at his pant leg, trying to get at the knife. More explosions boomed behind him, and the hum of the scooters rose.

"That's why I asked for you personally." It pulled him closer, almost nose-to-nose. "Even if the talks succeeded, even if you decided to trust me again, understand this. You were *never* getting off this planet alive."

His hand found the handle of the dagger, but the safety strap fought him. His left hand reached for the Amelia-thing's face, trying to distract it.

"Do you know why? *Because you got my predecessor killed.*"

The safety strap let go with a pop just as the alien raised him fully over its head. One hand on his shirtfront and the other on his belt, it twisted its torso and hurled him like a javelin. Impossibly high, impossibly fast.

Straight for the river.

The brace sent him somersaulting through the air, his straightened leg whipping his body over and then over again. Visions of a bright sky, then sand, then the smoke rising from the settlement, then the sky, then the river. Hurtling along, arms flailing at nothing, knowing the thing had made sure he wouldn't land inside the safety of the swimming area. Crossing the distance with incredible speed, unable to do anything about it, the evil water rushing up.

His oscillations slowed just enough for him to see a cluster of color, a dozen or so Whisperers still running in his direction, and then he was descending. A scream of mortal terror welling up, the arc directing him for the very center of the water, finally getting his right leg tucked against the brace and wrapping his arms around his face.

He hit the water like a dart, feet first, moving so fast that one moment he was cutting the surface and the next he was striking the bottom. The pain jolted through both legs, the wound from the wolf bite blazing hot while the rest of him registered the startling cold. The current grabbed him, spinning him around as his arms stretched and pulled and tried to reach the air. He could see it, high above the dark depths, but the unseen forces shoving and tugging him sent him back down. He'd barely inhaled half a breath before impact, and his chest ached.

Stroking hard, both arms going up and then away, kicking with the one good leg, horrified that the brace was pulling him down. Unable to make out anything in the darkness, startled when his boot struck bottom again, pushing off but he'd landed on a pile of rocks and they shifted at the wrong moment, ruining his launch. Sediment burned his eyes while the torrent propelled him downstream, but then his head broke through for just an instant, his mouth stretching open to its limit before the current got him again and yanked him back down.

Still fighting, feeling the weight of his sodden fatigues taking him away from air, seeing the light receding, and then he bounced off of something solid. Something metal. The deflection spun him around, just long enough to see an angled section of fencing buried in the riverbank. The swirling water pushed him away from it, but not before he remembered what it was. One of the anti-snake obstacles, to keep them from building up a head of steam.

The swimming area! He'd landed upstream, and was being swept toward the fence. If he reached it, there was a slim chance of climbing up before the snakes got him. A frigid hand pressed against the back of his head, somersaulting him, driving him lower, a chilling reminder that he might drown before he reached the obstacle at all.

Now summoning everything he had left, tearing at the cold liquid that enclosed him, kicking madly, and there was the light again, if he could break into it just once more, his lungs were crying out for it, he might be able to see the fence.

The braced leg, trailing behind him, slammed into two large boulders and wedged tight.

Abruptly anchored, Mortas was shoved forward at the waist while the rushing water continued to buffet him. The pressure jammed the brace even deeper into the space between the rocks, and he thrashed around in a desperate effort to break free. He could see the stones, huge, unmoving, and the current fought him as he tried to set his right boot against one of them for leverage. His hands slipped along the smooth material when he reached to tug the leg loose, water rushing up his nose, his chest threatening to explode, and then a dark form flew up over the rocks and into him.

He had no air left for screaming, but he tried anyway as the phantom's enormous jaws closed on his chest. It was the size of a man, and moving so fast that it yanked off his pinioned boot and sent both of them tumbling away from the rocks. Helpless in the grip, numbly surprised to feel no pain yet, he twisted in its grasp until his cheek was pressed right up against the face of Erica Varick.

The Banshee's eyes were enormous, and she was shouting something that he couldn't hear, bubbles spewing from her mouth, but it all ended when they slammed into the fence. The impact tore them apart, and Mortas found himself spread-eagled sideways against the rigid mesh, pinned by the flow. The water and the sediment turned his eyes into slits, but even so he knew he saw movement.

The first snake missed them completely, charging forward with such abandon that the torrent carried it straight into the barrier. The entire wall reverberated, shaking Mortas free, and then he was rolling upward and trying to find a handhold, fueled by the terror of knowing he was in the water with the monsters. The spaces between the links were too small for all four fingers, so he jammed three of them in and reached up with three more.

A hand latched onto his shoulder, yanking him skyward, his head finally breaking the surface but no time to savor the oxygen even as he gulped it down. The toe of his boot couldn't find a purchase, and his left leg hung as if paralyzed. His fingers drove into the holes, one after another, his arm muscles pulling him up, and then the weight was increasing because he was leaving the water. The entire wall shook again, no doubt from another snake running into it, and he remembered how the evil things would lunge up on land a short distance to snag their prey. The next ones would leap for his back, tearing him from the puny handholds, back into the water.

"Climb! Climb!" Varick was hollering, almost in his ear, and he looked up to see she still had him by the shoulder. Her left arm was stretched far above her, but she couldn't move while pulling him. In his mind he saw one of the snakes snatching her from the wall.

"Let go! Get over the top!" His throat was full of sand, the words coming out as choking rasp, but she wouldn't do it. The fence rose another ten yards above them, and even though Mortas knew it was impossible he forced his tiring arms to drag him higher. The water on the other side was empty, so inviting, so safe, and he knew they'd never reach it.

The river erupted behind them, water spraying them both, Varick yelling instructions at someone while he remembered Elder Paul speaking of antisnake devices. More explosions, more spray, from concussion grenades being hurled into the water. A moment later the holes in the mesh in front of him turned a brilliant green, then the sash shifted to show a human face. A flabby cheek pressed against the barrier, arms outstretched, grasping the links and straining, and he recognized Nibbit. Other figures crushed in against the fence as if trying to reinforce it from the other side.

Struggling higher, reaching a point where Erica

had to let go, seeing her clamber up a couple more handholds and reaching down again.

"Keep going! I'm all right!" he yelled, and then another sash was in front of him and he understood what they were doing. The colonists were building a human wall on the other side, right to the top so that they could assist the two soldiers.

"Come on, Jan!" a woman's voice grunted, and he was looking through the barrier at Felicity, hugging the fence and wincing as more Whisperers used her as a ladder.

He almost answered her, but that was when the snake shot up from the river and latched onto his leg. The teeth bit into the brace, and for a moment he was somewhere else, nighttime, in the middle of a hurricane of fire, being knocked to the ground by a giant wolf. The snake's jaws caught on the brace somehow, and its full weight yanked him down, pulling his hands from the fence.

The pain in his injured leg only registered slightly, causing him to dumbly wonder just why all these monsters wanted to bite him in the same spot, quickly replaced by the question of why he wasn't back in the river already. Mortas looked up to find Varick there, both hands gripping his fatigue shirt, hanging upside down because the Whisperers had reached the top and held her by her boots.

The snake thrashed in the air, now desperate to let go because it couldn't breathe, threatening to break the chain of damp hands and sodden fabric keeping him aloft. Erica lunged downward with one arm, then the other, locking her hands behind his back and pulling him up so that their heads were touching.

"Not letting go," she growled in pain. "Not losing you."

Taking hold of the fence again, he weakly kicked the thing to no effect, as its tubular body whipped back and forth. The brace slid down, digging into the flesh at his ankle, and another salvo of stun grenades sent geysers of water into the air.

"Room! Give me room!" He heard Dru's voice, and saw the bodies shift around below him on the other side. A slim pole came through, and a fiery vibration convulsed the muscles in Jander's trapped leg. The snake went crazy just then, getting the full voltage of the shock-stave, and its agonies tore it loose. It fell back into the water, and then Mortas was ascending without effort. Hands grabbed his neck, his shirt, his arms, his belt, hauling him and Erica up and over, and then the entire human pyramid collapsed backward into the swimming area.

Mortas was in the water for only a few seconds before a multitude of hands took hold of his wet clothing and carried him out. His eyes rebelled against the sunlight, closing over the stinging sediment, so he couldn't tell who was doing what anymore. An authoritative voice, too young to be Varick's, was calmly directing the removal of his brace. The straps were released, and only then did he feel the excruciating pain in his ankle.

"It's all right, Jan. All that weight pulled your brace half-off." A body dropped to its knees next to him, bumping into someone holding his hand. Fingers pried his eyelids open and rinsed them with clean water.

"Where's my handheld?" he sputtered. "I have to call the *Ajax*."

"I'm on it, Jan." Erica spoke from nearby. "They shot down the drones, and they've got emergency teams shuttling down."

"How bad is it? The casualties?"

A hand pressed against his cheek, and he looked up at a colonist he didn't know. Her black hair stuck to her face and neck, but he recognized the voice of the medic when she quietly gave him the news.

"It's not your fault, Jander. You're here on a mission of peace."

He struggled free of the people trying to help him, and sat up with difficulty. "How many?"

"Our people are tending to them now. There are three dead and eight wounded." Dark eyes spoke to him without blinking. "Elder Paul has crossed over."

The group around him had already diminished, but one of them returned to slide an arm around his shoulders. "Do not grieve, Jander. Erica was telling us all to hug the dirt, but Elder Paul knew you couldn't run on that leg. He yelled for us to save you, and then we were all running. We saw what Amelia did to you, before the scooters caught her."

Varick joined in, pulling him close to whisper in his ear. "They wouldn't listen to me. I told them to stay put, to let me get you. We'd both be dead if they had."

He reached up a hand to grasp her arm, pain shooting through a thousand tiny cuts on his fingers. A dull throb of betrayal woke up inside him, but he had to know if the thing had evaded their precautions. "What's the *Ajax* say about the alien?"

"Everything's under control."

Hours later, with the fires at Gorman Station extinguished and the casualties evacuated, Mortas unfastened an intricate harness holding him to a seat inside one of the *Ajax*'s shuttles. Varick was already up, standing in front of him, waiting to help. Dried sand encrusted her hair and fatigues, and her hands mirrored the spidery latticework of cuts on Mortas's fingers.

"This can wait, Lieutenant." Captain Everest, commander of the *Ajax*, spoke through the bud in his ear. "They're not going anywhere, and my med teams tell me you're awfully banged up."

"It won't take long, Captain." Mortas reached for Varick, who grasped his wrists and pulled him up onto his right leg. A new brace covered his entire left leg, including the foot this time. He winced when he put weight on it, but then nodded at Erica.

"Not sure what you hope to accomplish. They're all asleep," Everest continued.

"I guarantee you, that *thing* is not asleep."

"My people checked out every inch of that boat. Every reading says they're all in stasis."

"Then this will take even less time than I expected."

"I'm not comfortable, letting you and Varick on there alone."

"With all due respect, Captain, I'm in command of everything that involves the alien." Erica slid his left arm up over her shoulder, and they began to walk. "Are we in agreement?"

"As much as I've ever agreed with an order I thought was foolish."

"Sounds like you and I have had the same experience in this war. I'll let you know what we determine. Mortas out."

One of the shuttle's two pilots, its only other passengers, activated the side hatch without a word. Varick and Mortas passed into a short umbilical, a passageway connecting the shuttle with the craft that had tried to whisk the alien away from Roanum.

"They said this boat was built for snatch missions like this one," Erica commented, her right arm around his waist. Sand cascaded off of them as they moved. "Super-fast, just big enough for a set of Transit Tubes, headed to rendezvous with a Step-capable ship. The crew and the alien were probably inside the tubes before they left Roanum."

The hatch leading into the special craft was open, and a low red light bathed its interior. They turned left as soon as they were aboard, to face a double row of the coffin-like Transit Tubes. There were ten of them, stretching away in the shadows.

"Talk about irony. The device that almost killed me at Glory Main was what kept them from getting away." Mortas reached out for the nearest coffin, and Varick released him. "I can still feel it, how it took over the controls of the shuttle we stole from the Sims, and sent us flying straight for the surface."

"I bet the Twelfth Corps commander wasn't happy when your father made him give up his toy. Considering Twelfth Corps developed it."

"I guess that's what you do with your spare time, when you're a great big general who isn't interested in fighting the war." Jander placed his palms on the electronic coffins to either side, finding he could walk using them as supports. "You develop a next-generation defense, and then the father of the guy you tried to kill with the thing steals it from you."

"Jan."

He turned in place, seeing Varick's concern. "It's all right. I have to do this."

"The last alien took over your mind when it was trapped in a sterilization tube. What do you think this one's gonna do?"

"That's what I'm counting on." He heard the words as if someone else was speaking them. "We have to know the truth."

"It's lied to us the whole way. It's smarter than we are. You won't get the truth. You might get more than you bargained for."

"That's why we brought the stunner." He pointed at the box-like pistol strapped to her thigh. "Don't be afraid to use it."

"Keep your mike on. Get this done." Varick lowered her voice. "And then come back to me, Jander Mortas."

"You got a deal." Turning on his right leg, he started down the aisle. His arms trembled as he propelled himself, lurching side to side on his lacerated palms. He'd refused the offered painkillers, and his leg felt like it was going to drop off. As he slid along each box, Mortas looked through the viewing pane in search of the borrowed face of Amelia Trent. Each time he was disappointed, seeing only the still features of total strangers.

The kidnappers hadn't been identified yet, and the vessel they'd meant to join up with had emergency-Stepped itself to safety when they'd been caught. Just as Leeger had planned, the closest satellites the *Ajax* had emplaced around Roanum had moved into position to intercept the kidnapper's craft when it left the planet's atmosphere. The ship-hijacking system confiscated from the Glory Corps had been vastly improved in the intervening months, and it had directed the escape boat's systems to take up an orbit.

Jander's bizarre locomotion, coupled with the close-up viewing of each tube's occupant, brought back a memory from Glory Main. When the alien, the first Amelia Trent impostor, had blasted its own consciousness into his mind. Showing him its memories to explain the whole twisted plot that had begun with his capture while sedated in a tube very similar to these. The thing's viewpoint had been from above, as if it were a floating vapor, cruising over rows of Transit Tubes and a gaggle of Sim technicians.

It had descended to look into one of the carriers, and he'd seen his own face.

The last coffin on the right was different from the others, and so he wasn't surprised to see the reddish-brown hair and attractive features that had once belonged to a Human Defense Force psychoanalyst named Amelia Trent. She'd died screaming in agony while the original alien had burrowed right into her mind. Mortas had seen that, too.

The journey down the aisle had tired him out, so Jander pulled himself up onto the Transit Tube's lid. He sat there, catching his breath and studying the motionless face, unable to tell if the alien was actually unconscious. Looking back at Varick, he gave her a thumbs-up before leaning over the viewing window. He engaged the intercom.

"I know you're awake."

It didn't move, but Jander just waited. After several long seconds, the blue eyes appeared and the shapeshifter smiled in amusement. "You look like shit. You should see yourself."

Mortas lightly rapped on the lid. "Maybe you should see what I'm seeing."

"I knew the trip was taking too long. How did you catch up to them?"

"You barely left the planet. Remember that secret device on Glory Main, the one that took control of our shuttle and almost crashed us? My father's people took that away from the Glory Corps and improved it."

"You knew someone would try and steal me."

"As did you."

"But I forgot how hard it is to kill you."

"No harder than anybody else. Varick and the Whisperers got me out of the drink. She jumped in with me, in with the snakes. You can use that as evidence for that bullshit story about being impressed by us humans."

"But we're not."

"That's good. Finally the truth. The game's over, so no more lies. Who are you? What are you?"

The blue eyes twinkled, and the thing laughed. "The game's not over. Not yet. You made a mistake, capturing me alive. If you'd blown me up with these fools, you'd be in the clear. But you're exactly where you were this morning. You're about to watch your superiors take me out of your hands. You kill me now, you'll be right back in a jail cell. If you're lucky."

Mortas sat up, stretching a muscle in his back that had started to complain. Another memory, from the sterilization tubes on Glory Main, after the first alien had been incinerated.

"I don't have to tell anyone we took you alive. Did you notice anything about your coffin here? Different from the others. Heavily secured, and positioned over a special hatch. Your kidnappers weren't too comfortable with their new cargo, it seems. They were ready to jettison you, and the control panel's right here." Mortas looked around, as if bored. "You'd burn up in Roanum's atmosphere, trapped inside this thing."

The smile melted away. "You have no reason to do that."

"No reason?" he shouted, bringing his face close to the window. "Everything about you is a lie. It always was. You were after the Step the first time, and you're after it now. You threw me into that river, knowing what lives there, and you say I have no *reason*?"

The blue eyes narrowed, filled with hatred. "You're just a lieutenant. You don't get to make a decision like this one."

"You see, that's where you're dead wrong. Out in the field, I make all sorts of very big decisions. Life-and-death decisions. And sometimes little, low-level people like me have to save our bosses from their own bad judgment." Mortas slid himself onto the flooring, gritting his teeth when the weight settled on his leg. "And there is no way, in hell, that I'm going to let you anywhere near the half-bright egomaniacs we've got running this war."

He limped around the coffin, to inspect an illuminated panel set into the bulkhead. Its large letters prescribed the sequence for lowering the alien's Transit Tube through the decking, sealing the hatch over it, and then dumping it into space. After making sure he understood it, Mortas went back to the window.

"Last chance. Tell me what you are, or I'm throwing you in the furnace."

The alien's facial muscles tightened involuntarily, its hands reaching out to press on the unyielding walls of the container. Its eyes seemed to bounce around, and it shuddered all over before regaining control.

"Told you. We're researchers. We want to understand the Step. This can still work, for everyone."

"Aw bullshit. Enjoy the ride." He stumped toward the panel.

"Wait! *Wait!*"

Mortas took his time coming back. Separated only by the window, the two creatures glared at each other.

"There are thousands more just like me." The voice was flat and cold, and Jander swayed on his feet when he saw that the alien's mouth was tightly shut.

Its words rebounded inside his brain, calling up the faces of the anonymous soldiers, miners, technicians, pilots, and support personnel he'd seen in the war zone. Unknown, unidentified, unremarked, passing by in an instant and never seen again. Hundreds of thousands of them in the war zone, working here and flying there, and thousands of shape-shifters ready to assume their identities. Only one needed to get through.

The blue eyes burned with loathing, but the lips curled into a knowing sneer.

"We just need to find one greedy human who can explain the Step to us, and then a Sim armada will descend on your so-called settled planets. You can't stop that from happening, Lieutenant Jander Mortas. Your race is doomed."

His vision swam, the alien's pronouncements echoing down the chambers of his mind. Reaching out, he covered the window with a flat hand. The low lighting seemed to converge on him, but he managed to shove himself away from the tube.

The voice followed him as he tottered to the panel and began activating buttons in accordance with the instructions.

"Isn't that ironic, Jan? Isn't it delicious? The same greed and selfishness that you despise in your superiors is the very thing that will remove your species from existence. Look around you. Someone paid these fools to bring one of us to them, and sooner or later one of us will get through. No more tricks, no more schemes. All we have to do is get their attention."

Varick was beside him, eyes wide in alarm. "Are you hearing that, Jan? It's inside my head. It's *laughing*."

"I know." He pointed at the panel. "It's ready to go. When I push that bottom button, this evil thing will get roasted. I'll say you didn't know I was going to do it."

He was reaching out when Erica stopped his hand. Lips pursed, head shaking. "The hell you will."

Varick pressed the final button, and the red lighting started to strobe. Taking his arm over her shoulder, she moved them both away from the hatch in the floor. The Transit Tube descended through the opening, and a mechanical voice announced that the container would be jettisoned in ten seconds.

The decking closed over the coffin, but the laughter continued even after the ship lurched and the alien was launched into the waiting inferno.

CHAPTER 19

In the middle of an empty plain on Celestia, Hugh Leeger sat on a rock. He had no weapon, only the most essential clothing, and a small bag containing one meal and a bottle of water. A tiny transmitter sat next to him, sending out the recall code for a man who had been executed in the planet's largest city. He'd been sitting there for hours.

A small herd of the hogs the Misty Man had requested trotted across his field of vision, and then a figure on two legs appeared where the animals had passed. It seemed to be far away, but as it got closer Leeger saw it was a child. Wearing only a ratty pair of shorts and handmade sandals, the boy carried a rifle that was old enough to be a museum piece. The image of the martyred slave girl Emma had been etched into the weapon's stock.

When his visitor arrived, Leeger saw that his skin was a dark orange and that his curly hair was as well. The child stopped, waiting, and so Leeger tossed the transmitter at his feet. Not wanting to risk damage to the rifle, the boy picked up a rock and smashed the device to bits. Then he shouldered the rifle and sat down next to him.

"I'm Hugh Leeger. What happened to Emma was my fault."

"Emma made a choice. She chose to die free."

"I'd like to die free."

"Then you will." The child stood up and took his hand. "Come on."

In a Transit Tube on a troop transport inside the Step, Ayliss Mortas dreamt. Somehow she sensed the others asleep in the tubes around her: Blocker, Ewing, Scalpo, Tin, Bullhead, Lightfoot, Legacy, and Plodder. Despite the uncertainty of her future, their presence made her feel comforted and protected.

The dream took shape, and she was no longer afraid to face the approaching figure. She stood atop the plateau that held the ruined Zone Quest complex on Quad Seven, and the smoke from McRaney's wrecked ship drifted all around her.

The silhouette was familiar, and she knew its movements by heart. Its dark clothing blended with the smoke, but when it emerged she saw the bullet holes in the fabric. She hadn't been able to force herself to look at them when the man had been lying dead before her.

"Lee."

"Hello, dear." The handsome features bore no reproach. "I wish you could have seen me go over that last fence. Maybe ten guys in the whole galaxy could have cleared that thing. And only one of them could have done it with so many holes in him."

"I'm sorry, Lee. I used you. In so many ways." She began to sob, but Selkirk made no move to comfort her. "I've been so selfish, so hateful. I was surrounded by people like you, good people looking out for me, caring for me, loving me, and I gave them nothing in return."

Selkirk stepped in close, and kissed her once on the forehead. His hands rested on her shoulders, and they brushed her arms as he turned away. He was disappearing into the smoke when she heard his final words.

"You may just make it after all, Ayliss Mortas."

Asleep inside the tube, her lips moved as she spoke to a ship without a single conscious passenger.

"I'm Rig. They call me Rig."

In one of the most secure rooms in all of Unity Plaza, Reena Mortas sat looking at the walls. She'd once spent entire days there, after Olech had revealed its existence to her. She knew every one of the gold-colored panels that covered the room's vertical spaces, having studied them thoroughly. Simplistic diagrams, some of them featuring stick figures, they detailed the complex process for building and operating the technological marvel known as the Step.

Olech had disappeared trying to contact the anonymous entities that had sent these instructions to mankind, and now his son had destroyed mankind's only chance at communicating with the Sims. Reena had read Jander and Erica's report several times, and yet she still couldn't quite believe it. Two junior officers in a war that had lasted decades had taken it upon themselves to guarantee the conflict would continue—all because they believed the alien envoy had been some kind of Trojan horse intended to gain the secret of the Step.

She darkened the handheld that contained the report, no longer willing to acknowledge its presence or its finality. The Misty Man's confession was gaining traction across the alliance, and a powerful Emergency Senate committee had already requested a conference with her. Leeger's desertion to Celestia had been confirmed, but she found it strange that his likely capture and confession held no fear. The destruction of the shape-shifter was the final nail in the coffin of the Mortas family's management of the war, and the son of Olech Mortas had wielded the hammer.

"All this time I figured Ayliss would be the one to bring us down." Reena stood, stretching muscles that felt strangely relaxed. The hovering doom had finally descended, and it wasn't half as bad as she'd feared.

There was a certain level of comfort in knowing the game was finally over, that she would be removed from office under the cover of a politically satisfactory lie such as reasons of health. The propagandists would probably suggest she needed to concentrate on the well-being of her husband's two orphaned children, both of them off fighting the war.

But that wasn't accurate anymore. Jander was headed back to Earth at her command, accompanied by Varick, and Reena intended to question them both herself. The recordings of the alien communicating with the Sims had been given to a super-secret team that had been trying to translate the birdsong for years, and they'd expressed great optimism. Perhaps something could be salvaged from that, and so Jander and Varick would be needed to provide context and explanation.

And after that, who knew? The news of the alien's existence had obviously leaked, and soon there would be even more questions about how the son of Olech Mortas had encountered the shape-shifting alien not once, but twice. Perhaps a quiet retirement didn't await her after all.

The handheld lit up, signaling that Leeger's replacement needed to speak to her. She activated the entrance locks, and Nathaniel Ulbridge strode across the shadowy floor.

"Apologies for interrupting you, Madame Chairwoman."

"Good news?" Reena almost laughed.

"Possibly, ma'am." The sentence hung in the air, forcing her to remember that Ulbridge lacked Leeger's sense of humor.

"What is it?"

"Our operatives inside Zone Quest have alerted us about a major shake-up. Several senior managers have been demoted, all of them from Victory Provisions."

"So it's true. Victory Pro is part of ZQ."

"We've suspected that association for some time now."

"So what's causing the problem?"

"I've confirmed the report through our sources on Celestia, and through Celestian Command. Apparently someone fed a counterfeit order into Victory Provisions's communications stream. It told them to transport twenty thousand feral hogs from Dalat, and to release them in ten different remote locations on Celestia. The justification in the order was that the hogs would provide a food source for cutoff Human Defense Force units, and possibly for long-range patrols."

Despite herself, Reena giggled. "Only Victory Pro would believe something that stupid."

"I didn't initially understand the significance of this development, Madame Chairwoman. However,

I have since learned that this breed of hog is wildly prolific and incredibly destructive." He paused. "I'm sure you know more about them, being from Celestia yourself."

"Nathaniel, I want you to be more direct when we talk."

"Ma'am?"

"You're my security chief and my spymaster now. That uniquely positions you to give me advice. I need your intuition along with your information, so you're going to have to learn to speak freely."

"I'll work on that, ma'am."

"This pig delivery is going to change everything. In a short time, the troops there will be spending more time killing these animals than fighting the rebels. They'll have to switch over to defense, just to keep the infrastructure intact." Reena looked up at the panels, not seeing them. Instead, she imagined the smirk Olech wore every time he was contemplating a risky political stratagem. "You know Hugh did this, right?"

"That was my assumption. I've accessed his communications logs. He conducted extensive research on these creatures shortly before . . . disappearing."

"You can say it. He's joined the rebels." Reena nodded slightly. "When I meet with the senators, I'm going to tell them that Hugh plotted the assassination of Horace Corlipso without my knowledge. He believed Horace had somehow arranged for my husband's disappearance, and wanted revenge. The

Misty Man's confession pointed to him, and his defection proves his guilt."

Reena turned a bland expression toward the man who had been Leeger's adjutant, certain that he knew the real story.

"Yes, ma'am. I should have noticed that his behavior was changing."

"He blamed himself for Olech."

"It started much earlier than that. When Jander went missing in the war zone. Hugh killed the interrogator who tortured him on Glory Main, with his bare hands. It was quick, but still uncharacteristic. And that side trip to find the Misty Man was practically suicide." He squared his shoulders. "Are you planning to release Timothy Kumar's confession to the Senate? It would support the story."

"Not right now. He's more valuable as a plant with our opponents. You did a fine job, turning him."

"You'd already broken him."

"Was there anything else?"

"Mira Teel is waiting outside. She requested to speak to you alone, in a secure location. I'll send her in."

"Stay. You're my eyes and ears now. You need to know everything." Reena unlocked the entrance, and Mira walked in at a fast clip.

Reena was about to explain Ulbridge's presence when the words died in her throat. Mira was dressed in a simple flight suit, and her face shone with optimism. The old woman strode right up and took her hands.

"Reena, I am certain that Olech is alive."

"How? How do you know?" Fragments of questions tumbled off her tongue, but Reena quickly composed herself.

"I've experienced several dreams in the past few days, all of them featuring a series of small, polished stones. The dreams all had the feel of a communication with the entities, but I didn't understand what the stones represented."

"They were gifts. Mementos he brought back for Ayliss when she was a child, because he was traveling so much."

"Yes!" Mira almost shouted. "I only just learned that. Ayliss saw them in her dreams as well, but she didn't tell me because she wanted to leave the ship."

"So how does this indicate Olech is alive?"

"Each dream added another stone, and the last one showed me what it represented. It arranged them in a certain order, and then they all started revolving around a glowing light. To orbit."

"They represent planets? A star system?" Ulbridge asked.

"That's exactly what it is." Mira turned back to Reena. "I had my people search the known systems for an arrangement like the one I was seeing, and we found it. Far, *far* away. Unexplored, but mapped out. A perfect match."

Reena wrapped her arms around the Step Worshiper, and Mira returned the embrace. "And you think this was Olech?"

"It has to be. If it was a communication from the entities, why bother with the stones at all? And look at the recipients. No one else has reported anything like this—except Ayliss." Mira beamed. "I believe we know where he is."

They hugged again, but Reena was already looking at Ulbridge. The security man raised open hands, fingertips almost touching, while tilting his head slightly. Cold reality struck her, along with the darker explanation.

"Mira, Olech didn't undertake this voyage just to send us a rescue message."

"What else could it be? We have to get ships out there right now!"

"We'll investigate it right away, but from a distance." Reena turned to Ulbridge. "With careful planning. And great care not to be detected."

Mira's happiness slid away, and her hands dropped to her sides. "I never considered that. Do you really think that's what it is?"

"It's exactly what Olech would have sent us. Exactly what he would have asked for." Reena's eyes sought the panels high above. "The place where the Sims are made."

ACKNOWLEDGMENTS

First I'd like to thank my editor, Nick Amphlett, for his efforts and insights on the earlier drafts of *CHOP Line*. His advice helped to connect this, the second-to-last book in the Sim War series, with the earlier novels while nicely setting up the final book. Additionally, I want to extend special thanks to the Harper Voyager artists who designed the book's cover. I've been very pleased with the artwork for this entire series, and can only say they keep getting better and better.

I also want to thank my West Point classmates Michael McGurk, Meg Roosma, Duane O'Laughlin, and Ginni Guiton for reading *CHOP Line* as it progressed to its final form. Their comments and observations, based so strongly in their military service and life experiences, greatly improved this book.

ABOUT THE AUTHOR

HENRY V. O'NEIL is the pen name used by award-winning mystery novelist Vincent H. O'Neil for his science-fiction work. A graduate of West Point, he served in the U.S. Army Infantry with the Tenth Mountain Division at Fort Drum, New York and the First Battalion (Airborne) of the 508th Infantry in Panama. He has also worked as a risk manager, a marketing copywriter, and an apprentice librarian.

In 2005, he won the St. Martin's Press Malice Domestic Award with his debut mystery novel *Murder in Exile*. That was followed by three more books in the Exile series: *Reduced Circumstances*, *Exile Trust*, and *Contest of Wills*. He has also written the theater-themed mystery novel *Death Troupe* and two books in a horror series entitled *Interlands* and *Denizens*. His website is www.vincenthoneil.com.

Discover great authors, exclusive offers, and more at hc.com.